SHOW ME THE STARS

BELINDA BENNA

vinci
BOOKS

Vinci Books

vinci-books.com

Published by Vinci Books Ltd in 2026

1

Copyright © Belinda Benna 2026

The author has asserted their moral right to be identified as the author of this work in accordance with the Copyright, Designs and Patents Act 1988.
This work is a work of fiction. Names, characters, places and incidents are the product of the author's imagination or are used fictitiously. Any resemblance to actual persons, living or dead, places and incidents is entirely coincidental.
All rights reserved. No part of this publication may be copied, reproduced, distributed, stored in any retrieval system, or transmitted in any form or by any means, including photocopying, recording, or other electronic or mechanical methods, nor used as a source for any form of machine learning including AI datasets, without the prior written permission of the publisher.
The publisher and the author have made every effort to obtain permissions for any third party material used in this book and to comply with copyright law. Any queries in this respect should be brought to the attention of the publisher and any omissions will be corrected in future editions.
A CIP catalogue record for this book is available from the British Library.
Paperback ISBN: 9781036733834
The EU GPSR authorised representative is Logos Europe, 9 rue Nicolas Poussion, 17000 La Rochelle, France contact@logoseurope.eu

By Belinda Benna

Marie & Lukas

Promise Me

Show Me the Stars

Halifax Harbor Hospital

A Glimmer of Hope

A Twist of Fate

Miracle Glow

Love and Other Dreams

The Dreams We Share

The Sky We Seek

The Colors We Desire

The Dance We Remember

The Stars We Chase

Chapter One

Yes, our weekly planner has a TV night together scheduled for this evening, and we were actually going to watch Star Wars. We've made ourselves comfortable on the sofa, popcorn and drinks are ready. But even before the movie starts, my thoughts drift away. To the place where, after five long months of searching, they've finally found their new home.

Accompanied by the epic film music, I go through everything once more. It's a bit as if I had a checklist in my head that's magically pulling me in.

My camera is clearly outdated. I've already taken many good pictures with it over the last few days, and for the time being I'll keep using it. Still, I should look for a DSLR. Maybe I can find a used one at a good price, and also the lenses to go with it. Only, which are the right ones? I need a specialist shop, someone has to advise me. Also about software for editing the pictures. So I grab my phone and type the words "camera shop" and "Vienna" into the browser's search function. It shows me five stores in the old town at once.

"Tell me, what are you actually doing?" Lukas's voice reaches my ear so faintly it's as if he were sitting in another room.

I tap on the first homepage that comes up. The shop is on Getreidemarkt, right next to the Kunsthistorisches Museum. Strange that I've never noticed it before.

Lukas jiggles my leg. "Mhm," I mumble absentmindedly and look at the next store. It's only a few streets further on. How convenient.

"Hello? Earth to Marie, please wake up."

Something moves at the edge of my vision. My gaze jerks in that direction and I see that Lukas is giving me very clear hand signals. He's also eyeing me with raised eyebrows.

He looks unbelievably cute when he's this confused.

"Nothing." I give him a beaming smile. At the same time, it's almost unbearable not to continue my research. Now that I finally know where my path is leading me, there's only one thing I want.

To get started.

With every passing day I feel more of a new kind of energy. And sometimes everything about me feels light. As if I could fly. The world turns colorful and I know very well that these colors shine just for me.

Happiness finds me. More and more often, and more and more intensely.

"That doesn't really look like it, Miss Red-in-the-Face." There's a mixture of curiosity and love in his expression.

Should I tell him? No, I'll stick to the original plan. It's better to present him with my new future once I've got everything together. So he can see that it's been thought through responsibly. Exactly the way he likes it. It's a compulsion I can't resist, so I turn back to my phone and tap on the next link. "I'm just surfing around on the internet a bit," I murmur with a grin, then I start reading the text.

This might be the right business for me. I save the address and look at the opening hours. Tomorrow I'll go and check it out, and already the anticipation overwhelms me. It feels as if, after a long dry spell, it's finally raining again. It's liberating.

All at once I feel Lukas's hand on my forearm. I look up and see his questioning face.

"We said we'd tell each other everything," he reminds me, his voice warm.

We did. And we do. Always. Just not in this one thing.

Hesitantly, I pull up the corners of my mouth. "It's supposed to be a surprise. But I need a few more days for that."

He snuggles up to me and strokes my hot cheek. "And what if I can't wait?"

Whenever he looks at me like that, everything inside me turns soft. I love this man more than I could ever put into words.

Maybe my hesitation is unfounded. Because if he loves me just as much as I love him—and he does—there's nothing I should have to worry about.

Expectantly, he raises his eyebrows. "Come on."

I should do it. Here and now I should tell him about my dream. About what photography means to me. And about this passion that I know for sure will never let me go again.

About my *later*.

I'm going to work toward earning my money as a travel photographer. I want to capture the whole world in pictures and bring my impressions home to share them with others.

In my imagination, I'm already running my hand over the glossy cover of my very first photo book, and I know exactly what will be on the cover image.

Colorful cloths, red deserts, golden bangles.

India.

For a moment I pause and gather all my courage. I lock my gaze on him.

He gives me a trusting nod. "Come on," he repeats impatiently.

I don't know how he'll react, but there's one thing I know for sure: our entire future depends on this. Even so, I don't want to put it off any longer.

Now or never, I think to myself in silence as I clear my throat at length. Then, my heart galloping, I start to speak.

"I take photographs," I announce bluntly, full of pride and with all my conviction.

There's no change to be seen in his face. "Application photos?" he asks, without moving even an inch.

"No, not for applications. I photograph nature. Interesting faces, everyday scenes, basically everything that catches my eye."

In the next few seconds I can practically see the information seeping into his consciousness. Instead of being happy for me, his expression darkens. "What for?" he wants to know, with a mocking undertone.

There it is again, that expression that tells me without a single word that I'm crazy. Marie Berger, a case for the head doctor who's supposed to drive out unwelcome daydreams.

This can't be happening. Please, no.

Why the hell can't he drop the role of the dutiful adult for just one single moment? If he did, he wouldn't have to ask anything else. And I wouldn't have to tell him anything more. He'd understand right away, and it could be the beginning of something completely new.

I know my goal, I can feel exactly where it's driving me. If he would give me the chance to show him how amazing it is, then he would come with me. But he doesn't. Not yet.

"What for?" I repeat his question and try to put a loving tone in my voice. "Because photography is my passion and I want it to become my profession." His skeptical look scares me, so I hurry on. "Lukas, I finally found what I was looking for. When I take pictures, I'm just happy, you know?"

"You already have a profession." His words are full of panic, his hands keep moving restlessly over his thighs.

I quickly shake my head. "But it's wrong for me. Try to understand, I'm not a secretary, I'm a photographer."

My joy seems to bounce off his stony façade. Is not a single one of my words getting through to him? He suddenly jumps up, as if he can't bear the situation any longer.

I hold my breath.

What happens next can destroy everything. Or make it whole again.

"Are you completely out of your mind?" he asks, sounding as if I had just announced that from now on I intend to live a polygamous life.

His words drill painfully through my eardrums, my shoulders grow heavy.

No, no, no. This wasn't how it was supposed to go.

"I'm not crazy at all. There's nothing wrong with me. I think you're the one who's crazy here!" An accusatory tone had slipped into my voice all on its own. What else could I even do? Beating tolerance into him is the last option. This situation is almost unbearable. Nervously, I grab one of the lilac cushions and knead it in my hands.

"Oh no, don't you dare try that on me. This is about you. And about the fact that you want to throw your whole life away. For some nonsense that only exists in your imagination." He practically spits out the words, as if they were disgusting slime that had built up in his throat and now finally wants out. "And about the fact that you're throwing our life away."

I stare at him in disbelief. That's what he thinks? That I'm throwing our life away? Which life does he even mean? The one in which we'd recently done nothing but function? "I'm doing what?"

A strained groan leaves his mouth. "Don't you notice it? For months you've been sending me on a roller coaster ride that just makes me want to puke all the time. Marie is depressed, Marie is overjoyed, Marie is cuddly, Marie is distant. And where, my dear Marie, where is Lukas, huh?" Now he's pacing up and down the living room like a lunatic.

No, this won't do. "Where is Lukas? He's where only reason lives, right?" Gesturing wildly, I throw my arms up. How can he accuse me of something like that? He, who in the past few months hasn't made a single effort to really understand me. He, who has constantly nipped my attempts to tell him about happiness in the bud.

"I'm the one who has to keep everything running while you pretend you're looking for a job, but in truth you just lean back and keep chasing pointless fantasies!" With his index finger pressed against his chest, he blinks at me in anger.

"They're not pointless fantasies, why don't you get that? I was unhappy in my old life, and I'm finally able to breathe again." I'm yelling at least as loudly as he is. Everything has to come out until there's nothing left.

He stops abruptly and folds his arms across his chest. There he stands, right in the middle of our colorful living room, as motionless as a statue. "I really can't listen to this esoteric crap anymore." His voice is clear and firm, just like his expression.

"But I'm not going to stop just because you don't like it. I have a right to live my *later*," I whisper in a choked voice. Instantly, hot tears carve their way down my cheeks. They're back again, bringing with them that sadness I thought I'd already left behind.

Everything is going wrong. Again.

Unimpressed, Lukas looks me over and starts moving again. Even more agitated than before, he paces up and down in front of the coffee table.

"And what about my wants? Have you ever thought about that? For so long I've been understanding about you and this insane crisis. I've held back, given you all the freedom you wanted. Again and again I tried to motivate you, and again and again you slapped me in the face." His arms drop to his sides, dragging his shoulders down with them. All at once he looks tired, and drained. Despair and hopelessness suddenly appear in his eyes. "My mother was right. She really was right," he murmurs softly.

I wished I could go over to him and wrap my arms around him, rest my head on his chest and feel his heart-beat. Then he could pull me close and we would both know again that one of us can't exist without the other. Still, I don't do it. Because I'm at least as frustrated as he is and probably twice as helpless.

Is no one capable of stopping what's happening here right now?

"I wanted to save you. I wanted to save us," Lukas whispers in a trembling voice, "but in between all your daydreaming, did you think of me even once?"

It would be easier if he looked at me accusingly. And yet there's only disappointment in his eyes. No hatred and no reproach.

"So no. Fine, then just answer one more question for me: What is this relationship even worth anymore?"

Paralyzed, I crouch on the sofa, unable to think clearly and not knowing what to say. "Is there really nothing left of us? Of the two people who, in the middle of a meadow of flowers behind the Gloriette, dreamed of conquering the world together?" I finally manage to say. Where has our love gone, the blind understanding and the feeling of togetherness? Helplessly, I look at him through the vale of tears in my eyes, but he turns away with a stony expression on his face, as if he didn't care about any of it.

"Go find yourself another idiot you can take advantage of. We're done."

His words pierce my whole body like a thousand stab wounds. I should fight back, but I can't. Because what this overthinking man wants to hear from me will never cross my lips. Helplessly, I watch him leave the living room. I listen as he rushes down the hallway at top speed, and a few seconds later he slams the door with such force that the walls shake.

Now everything is quiet. I don't move and I don't breathe. Because I need all my strength to understand what has just happened here.

What if our relationship really isn't worth anything anymore? What if this realization is the only thing we still share?

Is it really over between us?

"Over, over, over," it echoes in my head like an echo breaking against the abysses deep inside me. And very slowly I begin to understand that my "later" might just have dissolved into thin air once again.

Chapter Two

I nod to her. So she knows that the two of us can still be who we were. When this game is over. Here and now. "Come on."

As if she had to summon all her strength, she holds her breath for a moment. "I take photographs." Defiance is written all over her face, as if she wanted to prove something to herself.

Still, I feel relief rising inside me. "Application photos?" I ask hopefully.

Her conspicuously strained groan is a warning to me. "No, no applications. I photograph nature. Interesting faces, everyday scenes. Basically anything that catches my eye."

Excuse me? What is she talking about? "What for?" Maybe my question sounds mocking. But I don't have the energy to hide my frayed nerves from her.

She doesn't answer. Instead she looks at me so accusingly, as if I'd said something wrong. She has no right to do that. I'm still allowed to ask where this is suddenly coming from. And what she wants to do with it. In truth I'm the one who could be looking at her reproachfully.

"What for?" she repeats my question, and I can clearly hear that she'd like nothing better than to fling the word back at me. At least she holds herself back; maybe all of this still means something to her after all. "Because I like taking photos and I want to make it my job."

As much as I'd like to, I'm not going to react to that. Because I don't understand what that's supposed to mean. Photography as a job? You can't earn any money with that. Do you really want to go on being the one who keeps everything running while she loses herself even more? I immediately hear my mother's voice asking. But that isn't even necessary, because by now I know myself what's wrong and what's right.

For the sake of peace I ignore this idiotic behavior and instead reach for her hands. In contrast to her expression, they're soft and warm. Marie doesn't meet me halfway but pushes her lower lip forward. Just a little, but it's enough for me to know that right now she's simply annoyed with me. As stiff as a shop-window mannequin, she sits on the dark gray mottled woven-fabric sofa, directly in front of the oversized picture of the two of us. In this photo we're smiling at each other. It looks as if we don't even notice that there's someone else there pressing the shutter.

That's who we used to be. Marie and Lukas. Forever. How on earth did we both forget who we are? I'm sure she knows just as well as I do that we can't go on like this.

"Lukas, I've finally found what I was looking for. When I take pictures, I'm just happy, you know?" Marie doesn't just sound like a crazy person, she looks at me that way too.

No. That can't be true. I let go of her hands and draw

back. Panic flares up inside me, unstoppable, but I still have to clear this up. "You already have a job."

Her vehement shake of the head can't mean anything good. "But it's wrong for me. Don't you see, I'm not a secretary, I'm a photographer." Suddenly there's this sparkle in her eyes. I know it, even if I can barely remember it anymore.

That's exactly how she used to look at me. Back then.

In that moment one thing suddenly becomes clear to me: the woman sitting in front of me on the sofa is no longer the Marie I fell so madly in love with back then. She has turned away from me. I can't make her happy anymore, and she probably can't make me happy either.

Everything around me froze, the cold tearing my hopes away with it. And with them the vision of our shared future. All that was left was my incomprehension, mixed with the anger that had been seething inside me for so long and now finally had to come out. I jumped up, because the days when I met her on my knees were over as of now. "Tell me, have you completely lost it?" I sounded agitated and stern, but that was exactly how it needed to be.

"I haven't lost it at all. There's nothing wrong with me. I'd say you're the one who's lost it here!" The shrill tone in her voice shot through my whole body. Agitated, she grabbed a cushion and squeezed it with all her strength.

There was no reason to talk to me like that. Absolutely none.

I was supposed to be the crazy one, when just a year ago I had been the best man in the world for her? I hadn't changed one bit since then. On the contrary, more than ever I had tried to be there for her. To support her when she needed someone to lean on, and to show understanding when she drifted off to places I couldn't follow.

My God, what an idiot I had been to stick by her for so long!

"Oh no, don't you dare try that with me. This is about you. And about how you want to throw your whole life away. For some nonsense that exists only in your imagination." I couldn't help it, the words had to come out. They had been lying in my stomach for so long, sitting on my throat and blocking my mind. Why I had held them back all this time was a mystery even to me. It hadn't done any good. "And about how you're throwing our life away," I added, with all the fury I carried inside me.

She stared at me as if she didn't recognize me anymore. At least for once she was feeling in her own body what it was like when you no longer knew who the other person really was.

"I'm doing what?" Her hands kept digging into the cushion. I heard her fingernails scraping over the fabric.

How could she pretend she didn't know what I was talking about? "Don't you notice it? For months you've been sending me on a roller coaster that just makes me want to puke the whole time. Marie is depressed, Marie is over the moon, Marie is cuddly, Marie is distant. And where, my dear Marie, where is Lukas, huh?" The words left my mouth louder and more forcefully with every sentence. I couldn't stand still any longer, so I paced tensely up and down in front of the coffee table. My head felt as if it were about to explode.

With her eyebrows drawn together, she watched my every step. "Where is Lukas? He's where only reason lives, right?" Now she was also flailing wildly with her arms in the air.

I stop moving abruptly and point my index finger at myself. "I'm the one who has to keep everything running while you pretend you're looking for a job, when in truth you just lean back and keep chasing stupid pipe dreams!"

Of course, there it is again, that defiant expression on her face. As if she were a little girl who isn't getting what she wants. "Those aren't stupid pipe dreams, why don't you get that? I was unhappy in my old life and I can finally breathe again." She yells so loudly I'd still hear her standing next to a plane taking off.

All at once it feels as if the living room walls are closing in on me. They're coming closer and closer. They're taking the air from my lungs and the clarity from my thoughts. I have to get away from her, away from this apartment. Away from this life. Marie will never get that the world doesn't revolve around her alone.

"I really can't listen to this esoteric crap anymore." Strangely enough, my voice is completely clear and so steady it's as if none of this could touch me.

As if she had to hold on to herself, she pulls her legs up to her chest and wraps her arms around them. "But I'm not going to stop just because you don't like it. I have a right to live my *later*," she whispers in a choked voice. To make matters worse, tears are running down her now horribly pale cheeks.

How can she? Why is she acting as if she were the victim here, when in truth I'm the one who's in the process of losing everything?

"And what about my wants? Have you ever thought about those? For so long I've been understanding about you and this absurd crisis. I've held back, given you every freedom. Again and again I tried to motivate you, and again and again you slapped me in the face." If she doesn't get it this way either, I don't know how else I'm supposed to explain it to her. "My mother was right. She really was right," I mutter, even though I hadn't wanted to say the words out loud. But it's the truth, surging so violently through my whole body right now that I can't fight it.

If she would just once stop thinking only about herself, we'd still have a chance. The two of us, Marie and Lukas, forever. That was all we ever wanted, nothing else.

All I need is one small step from her. Just once she should come over to me. Stop my pacing through the living room, put her arms around my shoulders and smile at me. Apologize and admit that she's lost her way.

Still, she does nothing.

She stays where she is. On that damn sofa between the damn purple cushions and the damn soft blanket. That's where she sits with her damn honey-blond hair, looking at me out of her damn dark brown eyes as if she'd run out of damn feelings for me.

"I wanted to save you. I wanted to save us," I say in a choked voice, because a part of me can't believe that this can't be stopped anymore. "But between all your daydreams, did you think of me even once?"

She doesn't answer. Her eyes are empty, her shoulders slump forward. She looks like a lost chick that has just been cast out of its warm nest. But that's exactly why I can't let myself go soft.

I stop at the living-room window, my gaze drifting outside. Behind the pane of glass, the day is just coming to an end, while in here something entirely different is ending. Without turning back to her, I go on speaking. "So no. Fine, then just answer me one last question: What is this relationship even worth anymore?"

That was it, the all-decisive question. And now that it's out, I can barely stay upright. We've arrived at the place we never wanted to be.

Forever. That was our goal. And what did it turn into? A never again.

I whirl around to face her. Over on the sofa, Marie is rocking herself back and forth. No matter how hard I try to read anything in her face, I can't. When did I stop knowing what she's thinking and feeling what she feels?

All I can make out is her empty gaze and the trembling of her lips. She doesn't reach out her hand to me and she doesn't come toward me. "Is there really nothing left of us? Of the two people who, in the middle of a meadow of flowers behind the Gloriette, dreamed of conquering the world together?" she asks in a choked voice.

She'll never stop resisting growing up. But that's reality, whether she likes it or not. I can't stand it any longer. And there's no strength left in me to keep believing in us. "Go find some other idiot you can use. We're done." The words leave my mouth wearily.

I give up.

She can go wherever she wants. I'm not going to go with her anymore.

I'd love to say, "If I leave this apartment now, I'll never come back," but I don't have the energy for that anymore.

I look at her one last time, but still there's no reaction from her. So I start walking. Away from Marie's madness. Away from the pain and the disappointment. Out of the apartment. Out of this relationship that hasn't been one for far longer than either of us would ever admit.

Chapter Three

He's gone. The apartment is quiet. My head, on the other hand, is full of questions.

What if our relationship really isn't worth anything anymore? What if this realization is the only thing we still share?

Is it really over between us?

Rigid with horror, I sink back into the sofa cushion that suddenly smells only of Lukas.

Did he just tell me that everything I dream of is nonsense? Did he turn around and just run off as if he had nothing more to say to me?

Of course he did.

When he can't be the perfectionist who knows exactly what to do, he runs away. Right now he's probably wandering through the streets of Vienna, breathing in the exhaust-laden night air and looking for a solution to something that in truth isn't a problem at all. I can see him in front of me, with that petrified expression he gets whenever he has to think. The more time passes, the calmer his breathing becomes, the tension eases, and he starts to understand how idiotically he behaved. He just has to, there's no other way.

I have to move too, because I can't stand just sitting here doing nothing until he comes back. So I push myself up from the sofa and march into the kitchen. There's a stack of dishes waiting to be loaded into the dishwasher, and the trash really needs to be taken out as well.

That will distract me. That way I can keep the awful feeling in my stomach somewhat in check and stop these terrible doubts from spreading any further inside me. I can't let them get the upper hand. Because I'm afraid of what that would do to me.

At top speed, plates and cutlery go into the dishwasher, I scrub pots and wipe the light wooden countertop with a damp cloth. Anyone who could see me would think I was a lunatic who believes her life depends on getting this kitchen clean.

But I don't care. I'll do anything not to think about Lukas and our fight. Still, I can't forget him. And even less his disregard for my dream. My gaze darts quickly around the room. Next to the fridge there's a half-empty glass. I grab it, yank open the dishwasher, and cram it in with trembling fingers.

Too hard.

With a clinking sound it shatters into thousands of tiny fragments. Everything is covered in shards, the whole dishwasher and the floor all around it too.

How fitting.

I need all my strength, but I still refuse to let it get me down. The broken glass doesn't mean anything at all. I was just clumsy, that's all.

I throw myself into the work, frantic. I have to clear up the mess. Make everything clean again.

Not twenty minutes later, it happens. The kitchen is perfectly tidied up. I'm hot, my breathing is heavy.

Slowly, a sense of calm returns, I look at my work and all of a sudden I'm just sad. Because what my eyes see is such a stark contrast to the state I'm in inside that I feel like a foreign body. Out here everything is in its place, but inside me there's so much chaos, as if a burglar had turned every last corner upside down beyond repair.

I mustn't think like that. I breathe in deeply and out again in a shaky sigh. Then I reach for my phone. If I don't talk to someone about what happened right now, I'll go crazy.

I dial Alex's number. Luckily my best friend picks up right away, and even faster she notices what's going on with me.

"You two had a fight," she says, sounding not at all surprised.

"He totally freaked out!" The moment the words leave my mouth, my nose starts to clog up. The pressure in my head keeps building. There's a war going on up there. How could Lukas be so ignorant? He trampled all over my dream. Why?

"Is it possible that, once again, you ambushed him just a tiny little bit?" she asks carefully.

Leaning against the kitchen counter, I let our argument run through my mind again like a movie. "No," I decide then. I couldn't have told him any more gently.

On the other end of the line I hear Alex breathing. She's thinking, and it's already taking too long. "Oh, you know what he's like." There's a soothing note in her voice. In the background I hear bangles clinking; she's definitely making that typically dismissive little hand gesture of hers. "Give him a bit of time to calm down."

"He just needs to straighten out his worldview," I add thoughtfully. That's just how he is. Lukas, the rational guy, who has to calculate every tiny detail and write it down on lists before he knows what he's supposed to think.

"This isn't the first time he's behaved like this." She sounds convinced. Thank God.

Of course Alex is right about that. And the fact that she's saying exactly what I already thought myself gives me a sense of security. Even though I'm barely capable of forming a clear thought, there's at least one thing I can see clearly in front of me.

Lukas will come back and we'll sort this out calmly. That's how it was before, and that's how it'll be this time too. Because who are we if we don't have each other anymore? We're Lukas and Marie. Forever. And nothing else.

Just like always, he'll be back with me in a few hours. We'll hold each other in our arms, kiss tenderly and then, then we'll talk.

Openly and honestly.

The two of us will say what we're thinking, and he'll understand how much photography means to me. It'll become clear to him that it isn't a pointless dream but a real goal. Our difficulties will come to an end. And what happened in the last few months will be behind us once and for all.

Chapter Four

I ran all the way here, to this dark brown apartment door. Because in all of Vienna there's only this one place I can flee to in a situation like this. To Anna.

Breathless, I press my index finger onto the doorbell. Not two seconds later she opens the door for me, wearing an oversized baseball shirt. She nods silently, and I'm sure she can see what's going on with me. She immediately pulls me into her arms so tightly, as if she wished for nothing more than to take some of my pain away. I bury my head in her dark brown hair and savor the feeling of having someone in Anna who gives me support. She's been by my side my whole life; I can always rely on her.

Far too quickly, Anna lets go of me. "Come in, darling," she says, an encouraging smile on her face. "You can stay as long as you like."

Her gaze, so understanding and warm, is exactly the right medicine for my wounds. "Thanks." I can't get anything else out, and then it happens. The moment I step into her apartment, I'm overwhelmed by emotions. Anger, grief, and despair sweep me away. I let it happen; I don't have to hide anything from my best friend.

For hours she just sits next to me on the sofa, handing me one tissue after another and soothingly stroking my back. The whole time I feel as if I don't belong here. Even though there are no curtains on the living-room windows and no plants anywhere, this room feels too cheerful. I, on the other hand, am like a dark stain. Sometime between my arrival and now I stopped counting how many bottles of beer I've had. I only know that my head now feels pleasantly numb.

Anna doesn't push me, she'd never do that. But now I feel ready to talk about it. I take one last deep breath, then I speak the crushing truth out loud.

"It's over. Done. Forever." I strain to find more words. But the letters just swirl through my head like wisps of fog, incoherent and gray. My tongue is heavy. "I did it. It just couldn't go on like that anymore. It didn't make any sense anyway."

Anna looks at me uncertainly out of her light-blue eyes. "I was already afraid it wouldn't work out much longer between you two." She sounds awkward, as if she's afraid of hurting me even more.

Exhausted, I let my shoulders slump forward. "In truth, it had already been coming for a while. Like an idiot, I hoped our problems would just vanish into thin air while Marie kept getting more and more lost in her crazy dream world."

In disbelief I shake my head. How could I have been so stupid? There were more than enough signs, countless small and big moments that should have been a warning to me. Not least the conversation with my mother. She knew it; I should have listened to her right away. Dreams have no place in the real world. Everybody knows that, only Marie will never get it.

Anna is at my side immediately. She takes my face in both hands and stops my movements. "It's understandable that you tried to hold on to your love. Every relationship goes through rough patches, and sometimes you do make it out of them again."

"What makes you so sure about that?" Maybe I sound defiant, but it's true. She can't know that; after all, she hardly has any experience with relationships. In the end she might just be parroting something she read in a women's magazine.

Anna lowers her gaze. "I just know." She's almost whispering, as if the thought hurts her. "I've seen that happen plenty of times." Even as she's saying the words, she starts fiddling with the hem of her pant leg. Suddenly she looks small. And helpless, the way she's sitting next to me on the worn-out sofa and, thanks to her wiry body, almost disappears between the cushions.

Did I just put my foot in it with her? "You okay?" I ask carefully, because she's the one person I really can't and don't want to lose as well.

"Oh, sure." Anna quickly shakes her head and jumps up from the sofa. "So, where do things go from here?" she asks, marching over to the kitchenette, where she grabs another bottle of beer from the fridge.

"I have no idea." It feels a bit like I'm standing in front of a blurred picture. Until recently, my future was so clear; now there's only a wild mix of colors, streaked with gray and black. I let out a heavy sigh; I'm probably too drunk to see anything at all anymore. "There's surely a lot we'll have to sort out, but I think I'd rather not see her for a while." Just saying it feels awful. In the last five years we were never apart for more than a week, and even then we talked on the phone. Marie was pretty much always with me, even if it was only her voice and her warm laughter. Can I really live without her?

Anna presses the beer bottle into my hand. "You're afraid you'll be weak?" she asks sympathetically, taking a sip of her lemon water before dropping back onto the sofa.

I barely hear the creaking I usually find so funny. Even the couch isn't what it used to be anymore, I think to myself, as if that were somehow important.

Absentmindedly, I wipe the tiny drops of water from the cool glass surface. "Maybe. I just don't want to see her." It's better this way. Probably.

"You don't have to. You can stay here with me for now, obviously." She gives me a furtive grin.

Anna's face blurs before my eyes. "Including talk therapy?"

"Including talk therapy," she confirms with an almost contagiously cheerful smile.

It's a start. At least. I'll stay here with Anna. Even if her place is tiny, the couch will be okay for a few nights.

And then? How is it supposed to go on after that?

A new apartment? A new life?

Dark as thunderclouds, thoughts drift through my head, because in this moment, despite my drunkenness, I sense that in one blow nothing is certain anymore. Of the former cornerstones of my future, only boulders, rubble, and ashes are left.

So I don't have to keep thinking about it, I drain my beer in one go and let myself fall back into the sofa cushions. Only now do I notice how drained I feel. And tired. My eyelids grow very heavy, everything in my head is spinning. I give in to the pressure and want only one thing: to sleep.

No matter what nightmare haunts me tonight, nothing can be as bad as what happened today. So I dive into the weightless darkness and hope it will catch me.

"Hey, darling!" I hear someone whisper in the distance.

The world around me vibrates.

Is that an earthquake? With my upper arm as the epicenter?

"It's late, we should go to bed."

I blink. For a moment I don't know where I am. "Why…? What…?" I stammer and rub my eyes. It's dark, only a narrow strip of light falls through the door in the opposite wall. This is Anna's home.

And I'm here because I don't have one anymore myself.

"Everything's okay, you just nodded off for a moment." Anna is smiling, I think. Her ponytail is gone, the dark mane frames her face. She tucks a strand behind her ear, then continues in a barely audible voice. "Come on, up you get, I'll make up the couch for you. You can go right back to sleep."

My gaze wanders downward. Sure enough, she's holding a blanket, a pillow, and sheets in her hands. This moment is becoming more and more real, but my head is spinning. I try to form a clear thought, but I don't even come close.

"Why are you whispering?" I ask, confused. It's quite possible I'm looking her up and down as if I were a little crazy.

She grins. "No idea, you're already awake anyway. Well, almost, judging by the way you look." She brushes my hair off my forehead so she can look me in the eyes more easily.

Suddenly Anna's expression turns strangely soft. Her hand stays on my face, her thumb moves across my cheek.

Is this real, or are my foggy senses playing tricks on me?

In disbelief, I reach for her fingers. They're really there. And they're touching me in a way they never have before.

I have no idea what's happening here. Are these my hands that suddenly guide her fingers to my mouth, and are these my lips that are just now touching the tip of her index finger?

They are. With gentle, tender kisses I cover every millimeter of her skin.

Why am I doing this? Is it the way her eyes sparkle? The twitch of her lips or the empathetic expression with which she looks at me? Is it because it feels good to matter to someone, or only because the slanting hallway light makes Anna's silhouette glow magically?

How many bottles of beer have I actually drunk?

Out of the corner of my eye I see the pillow, sheet, and blanket slip from the crook of Anna's arm to the floor. She comes closer. And closer still. She doesn't take her eyes off me for a second. And I don't stop kissing her palms.

Why? I don't know. There is a warmth in her gaze, a sense of home. Her body shows through beneath the long T-shirt. There are curves where there used to be none, and I feel a desire I've never had before.

I want her to be very close to me. I want to finally feel a sense of familiarity and safety again. After months of fighting, I just want to let go and know that someone will catch me.

I can't fight this longing, because it has been building up inside me for far too long. It takes command. And my body lets it happen. As if on its own, my hand lifts and rests on the outside of her toned thighs. It strokes them, wanders farther up, and slips under her T-shirt.

To her hips. Across her stomach.

Anna exhales audibly.

As if in a trance, I feel my way to her back. Then I pull her closer to me. She yields immediately, straddles my thighs, and looks at me in confusion. No one understands what's happening right now. Not her, and even less so me.

All my foggy head knows is that it must not stop. That her affection is too beautiful to push away, and that I want more.

She comes closer. Her breath brushes hot against my cheek. Millimeter by millimeter I close the distance between us until we're so close that even the last question in my head falls silent.

I don't want to wait any longer, and I definitely don't want to think about it. So I do it. I press my lips to hers. It shouldn't be more than a small, innocent kiss, but it feels completely different.

My gaze jerks in confusion to Anna's eyes, and in them I see absolutely everything.

She wants me.

At once she kisses me again. Wilder this time and full of passion. What she does to me feels so liberating that even the last spark of my reason burns out in the darkness of this night. I lose myself in Anna's nearness and forget the whole rest of this damned world.

Chapter Five

I don't know where I am. Only that it's loud. And surreal. The trees have pink leaves, the horizon is distorted. Over there is Lukas, far away on the other side of the street that, just a second ago, wasn't even here. He waves at me, his expression exhausted. Several lanes of traffic are suddenly between us, countless cars, motorcycles, and trucks roaring past right in front of my nose.

The smell of exhaust hangs in the stuffy, murky air. I have to cough, I can't stop. My coughing grows stronger and stronger, something forces its way up through my windpipe. With all my strength I heave it up until it lies blood-red in my hand. A muscle, weakly pulsing, close to death.

My own heart.

Panic rises in me. I have to save it so it can keep beating. If it died, that would be my end.

Desperately I try to resuscitate it, but it just gets smaller and smaller. A tiny puddle of blood in my palm is all that's left. I want to scream, but not a single sound leaves my throat.

Horrified, I search for Lukas with my eyes. He's still there, far away, over there on the opposite side of the street. All at once he's holding the heart I just lost in his hand.

Out of nowhere, his exhaustion turns into anger. He hurls my heart onto the street. The tires of a truck crush it beyond recognition.

"Stop!" I shout at the top of my lungs.

Then I tear my eyes open.

What's going on? Where am I?

It's bright. I want to lift my hand, to shield myself from the light, but it doesn't work. My arm is lying next to me as if it didn't belong to me. As if it had just died along with my heart.

I blink with difficulty. Specks of dust dance above me; otherwise I can't see anything. But I can feel that I'm not in my bed. The floor beneath me is fluffy and hard at the same time.

I try to push myself up, but collapse again. At least my senses are finally doing what they're supposed to. My ears tell me I'm alone. My eyes that I'm crouching on the floor in the living room in front of the dark gray sofa. In the midst of crumpled tissues that lie next to me like bright white dots on the cream-colored high-pile rug. Shouldn't there also be rows of empty wine bottles somewhere? Why else does my head feel as if it were balancing the whole world all by itself?

Suddenly it all comes back to me.

In my memory, an image of Lukas appears. He looks at me as if he had run out of feelings for me. Then there's only his back, growing smaller and smaller before my mind's eye.

He didn't come back all night. I waited until long after midnight. In vain.

I look around, find my phone, and reach out my hand for it.

The screen is black. Neither a message nor a call is displayed. It's 6:04 AM. That's all my phone tells me.

So Lukas hasn't been in touch.

Should I write to him? Would I even be able to find words that would reach him?

No. He can't understand me anymore. This blockage inside him is too strong, his fear too great of losing a kind of control that, in truth, only keeps him imprisoned.

Indecisively, I turn the phone in my hand. We've known each other for five years now, and it has never been any different. It's hard for him to adjust to something new. I'll wait until he gets in touch.

And if it doesn't happen?

Hesitating, I stare at the black screen, finally switch the device on, and open a new message.

"Why don't you understand me?" I type after thinking for a long time, only to delete the text again right away. "Where are you? Come back, let's talk." No, I can't send that either. "Give me a chance. I'll show you the stars," I write next, but that feels just as wrong.

I delete the words, and in an instant the message in front of my eyes is as empty as my head. There's only room for memory. For a time when the two of us could still feel each other.

"Forever," he swore to me in the light of the setting sun, surrounded by flowers and full of passion. "I want to be wherever you are." Those were his exact words.

He can't have forgotten that!

If Lukas swallowed his pride, his common sense would no longer dictate to him what it takes to have a good life.

But he needs time for that, this time maybe even more than usual, and I at least want to give him today.

That's still eighteen hours. I can't stay lying in the middle of the living room that long, so I push myself up and gather the tissues from the floor. When Lukas comes back, I want this place to look tidy. I open the windows, let the warm August air in, and straighten the sofa cushions.

Then I start up my laptop. I want to keep looking for ways to learn more about photography. But even though I find a great blog with tips on technical equipment and image-editing programs, I can't concentrate. To top it all off, there's an email from the employment office in my inbox.

Once again I have to go to a job interview, this time with a lawyer on the other side of the city. I print out the confirmation form without giving it any more thought, because my mind keeps circling only around Lukas and what happened yesterday.

Compulsively, I check my phone again. It stays silent.

Lukas has nothing to say to me.

Not yet.

Chapter Six

So here I am. In a strange bed. And I know I'm not dreaming. On the contrary, I'm wide awake. Even so, I can hardly grasp what happened tonight.

Once more I turn my head to the side. There, under my right hand, between the light blue checked sheets, she's lying curled up like a puppy. Her breathing is shallow, her brown curls tumble wildly across her face. Now and then her eyelids twitch as if she were dreaming. She's smiling blissfully.

Oh my God. Anna.

I clap a hand over my face and rub my eyes. For a moment everything around me is blurry, then the image sharpens again.

Anna is still here.

And so am I.

The woman who had been my best friend for years is lying next to me right now, naked, and suddenly she looks different. As if the light of the morning sun, peeking through the gaps in the blinds, were changing everything.

The way her lips curl and the warm skin of her body nestles against me, she suddenly no longer seems like the boyish athlete she still was last night.

Damn. What's happening here?

Carefully, I slide my arm from her hip and roll to the side. I crawl out of the bed as quietly as I can. I feel a bit like a criminal and, who knows, maybe I actually am one.

Did I cheat on Marie?

And Anna? What did I do to her?

I can't think about that right now. All I know is that I have to get out of here. And I have to do it before the naked woman in the bed wakes up and maybe starts asking me questions I don't have any answers to.

So I sneak away on tiptoe, even though the laminate floor doesn't make a sound anyway. With a nasty feeling of guilt in my stomach and a head that can't think anymore.

"Hey, darling," I suddenly hear Anna murmur.

For a moment I freeze and press my lips together. Then I slowly turn around. I try to smile, but I don't know if I manage it.

"Good morning." My words sound like a question. Nervously, my fingers wander through my hair.

As if she doesn't notice my confusion, Anna stretches her arm out toward me. "You weren't about to leave already, were you?"

And now she's doing it again. She looks at me from under her half-closed lids with that magical gaze that tells me she would do absolutely anything for me. That she won't let me down and will always be there for me. A warm feeling spreads through my chest, and there's nothing I can do about it. She's like a harbor, and I'm like a shipwrecked sailor who's wanted only one thing for months: to be safe.

Still, I shouldn't go over to her, so I lift my shoulders in an apologetic shrug. "I have to go." Her expression darkens, and instinctively I take a step toward her. "But that has nothing to do with wanting to, believe me."

That was a lie. Or was it? I don't know, my brain is refusing to work. And my feelings are so tangled that I couldn't sort them out even if I tried my hardest. Not now. Not here. And not when Anna is looking at me the way she is right now.

"Work?" She pulls her hand back under the blanket and turns onto her side.

Inside, I breathe a sigh of relief, as if I'd just been in danger and was now safe again. "Go back to sleep."

Anna's eyelids flutter for a moment, then they close. "Mhm," she murmurs, and buries her head in the pillow, a wide smile on her lips.

I could run. Still, I'm standing in the doorway, my gaze fixed on her delicate features. Right where the curled strand of her hair touches her neck is where I kissed her last night. A hundred times, maybe even more.

My memory is hazy, but there's one thing I still know. It was as if the two of us had been far away. In a place where there is no right and no wrong. I quickly shake the thoughts from my head. Because it was stupid to let myself go like that in the heat of the moment. That's my best friend, for fuck's sake, and no one knows what that night has done to our friendship.

Even though I have no idea what's best, I'm sure of one thing: I have to ignore the queasy feeling in my stomach and the weight on my chest. I turn around abruptly and leave the bedroom.

Even before I jump in the shower, my hand automatically reaches for my phone. I don't know whether I want a sign of life from Marie or whether I'm afraid of it. With a strange mix of hope and unease, I turn the phone so I can see the screen.

There's nothing. My chest tightens, and while I go through my morning routine, it stays clenched the whole time. It doesn't matter where I am. Whether I'm standing in the packed tram, walking along the sidewalk, or starting up my computer at work. With every minute that passes without a word from Marie, the tightness in my chest grows more intense.

Yes, I was the one who left the apartment full of disappointment yesterday. But she was the one who left our relationship—no, our life.

"Rough night?" My coworker Bernd is suddenly standing next to me, as if a magician had just pulled him out of his hat. He's holding a green folder in his hands.

Mechanically, I shake my head. "Doesn't matter," I mutter absentmindedly and try to focus on the documents. "What've you got there?"

I wish I could hear what Bernd is saying, but it's impossible. The sheet he's just opened is full of numbers, yet it's as if I can only see certain ones. Right at the top, the 6—that would have been our next anniversary. Over there on the left, a 30, the day of Marie's birthday. And, worst of all, at the bottom of the page, under the total line, it says 1509. That's the day we were out in the flower meadow and admitted to each other for the first time that we were in love.

My heart no longer cramped; it gave up.

It wants to go to her, wants to know how she's doing and talk things through with her. My gaze jerks to my phone of its own accord, but it's still silent. Marie is surely waiting for a sign of life from me. But this time I won't make the first move, I can't. Not after what happened.

She has to fix it herself; after all, she's the one who screwed it up.

And what about me? Didn't I screw it up just as badly with my insane stunt last night?

An overwhelming sense of guilt crashes over me. How could I have cheated on Marie? Even if, soberly considered, we were already separated, it was wrong. What on earth was I thinking? I feel like I'm about to sink; my head turns dull and heavy.

"So what do you think? Is this okay like that?" Bernd's voice reaches my ear as if from far away. He nudges me in the upper arm, or at least I think he does. "Come on, help me out. The junior boss already has it in for me anyway."

I clear my throat. "Um…" What did he want to know again?

Confused, I look up at him. His forehead is furrowed, there's a questioning expression in his eyes. "The credit note for the complaint," he says, as if that explained anything.

My gaze wanders back to the paper. I have no idea what he's talking about. Still, I nod—what else am I supposed to do? "Sure, do it like that," I confirm absentmindedly.

Fortunately, Bernd is satisfied with my answer. Together with the green folder, he disappears from my field of vision, and I resolve to focus on the screen. I should do my job. Prioritize work orders, send out purchase orders, and check delivery notes. But no matter how hard I try to distract myself with that, it doesn't work.

All my attention is on my phone. My heart keeps cramping up. The rest of me is waiting. I feel a bit like I'm standing still while everything around me keeps moving merrily on. Like in a documentary where the sun races over the horizon and clouds form and dissolve in the sky every second, while the tree in the foreground remains frozen in place.

I'm that tree. Hard and unable to move. There's only one thing that can pull me out of this paralysis.

There. Finally.

The phone vibrates, the display lights up. My hand shoots out for it.

The message is from Anna. "Hey, darling. Already hard at work?"

I wish I didn't feel it, but a heaviness still comes over me. I'm disappointed. I don't want to be; it's not fair to Anna. "Sure," I type quickly, just so this feeling will go away again.

Her answer comes right away. "Are we seeing each other today?" Strange how ordinary her words sound. As if last night hadn't completely turned our friendship upside down.

I hesitate. Because in my world nothing is the way it used to be. Over the past few months Marie has gradually slipped away from our relationship without thinking about what that's doing to me. And Anna? She hasn't just stayed with me like she has my whole life, she suddenly also seems closer to me than ever before.

A new message appears on my phone. "We could go for a drink. Or I could cook something nice."

The truth is, there's no reason not to meet her. But the thought of being alone with her makes me nervous. "Joe's?" I type, and hit send.

"I'll be there at eight!"

I've barely read the message when a queasy feeling spreads in the pit of my stomach. Because I know perfectly well what's going to happen tonight at 8:00 PM at Joe's.

The two of us are going to face what happened last night. And that even though I still don't know what to make of it or how things are supposed to go on from here.

Only one thing I can say for sure. I feel like I cheated on Marie. And with that I've dealt our relationship the decisive death blow.

Chapter Seven

The chickens' clucking sounds cheerful. Bright sunlight streams through the long skylight in the henhouse and illuminates the dance of the dust motes. Next to me, Grandma pulls on her work gloves. She's trying to spread good cheer with her warm expression.

None of that gets through to me.

Gloomily, I turn to the work and carefully take the last egg from the straw nest. I do my best to distract myself. Still, I can't forget that I fled all the way here to my grandma's house because I couldn't stand the waiting any longer. With every hour, the uncertainty torments me a little more.

What if Lukas is serious?

What if he really can't understand me?

What if he doesn't want to love me anymore just because I'm taking new paths?

"He'll get in touch with me. I know he will." It's supposed to sound like a statement. As if I were absolutely convinced of what I'm saying. But even I can hear the uncertainty in my voice.

So far, Grandma has listened to me in silence. I've told her absolutely everything while we took care of the chickens together. Now she's filling the drinkers with fresh water and looks a bit as if she doesn't know what to say.

"That's how it is, isn't it?" For a moment, a quiet panic rises in me. If even she doesn't believe in us anymore, how am I supposed to?

Grandma turns to me and tucks a strand of her blond hair back into her now-loose braid. "Of course," she says, with a smile on her face that immediately calms me down.

She sees it the same way I do. Everything will be all right again. "How much longer will it take?" I ask, reaching for a chicken and carefully lifting it off the nest to collect the still-warm eggs underneath.

"Distance can sometimes work wonders. Still, there's one thing you shouldn't forget: life is far too short to be needlessly offended with each other. With every day you don't make up, you lose 24 hours of your life. And for what?" I knew that thoughtful, sad look in Grandma's blue eyes all too well. Her thoughts were with Grandpa. And with everything they had missed out on in their time together because he had died far too early a few months ago. Because of vanity. And because they thought they had to do things that only turned out to be unnecessary when it was already too late.

Even though she was already doing better by now, in moments like this she threatened to lose herself in her grief all over again. She sank into her own darkness, and I knew what that darkness did to her. It was a pull you could hardly escape.

It was time to change the subject. For both our sakes. "Don't worry. I'm never going to let my happiness go again now that I've finally found it." A tentative smile spread across my lips, and I even saw it catch on with Grandma.

She nodded in satisfaction and lifted the empty feed bowl up from the floor of the stall. "When are you going to show me the first pictures?"

"Very soon. I just need to get this software I use to edit the photos." The thought of my passion couldn't push away the sadness about what had happened between Lukas and me last night. But at least I felt a little better. I pushed myself up from my crouch and set the basket with the collected eggs on the board next to the wooden stable door. "Of course I still need the right subjects and have to experiment a lot. I definitely have a lot to learn."

"That sounds like a good plan." She nodded at me appreciatively, then reached for the feed sack and opened it. The chickens registered the sound immediately and gathered around us, clucking excitedly. The countless laugh lines at the corners of Grandma's eyes drew upward.

It was nice to see Grandma like this after all the difficult weeks. Still, this joy was overshadowed. Because she, too, wouldn't let me forget that Lukas didn't want to understand my dream. Seeing me happy should make him just as happy. But it didn't. On the contrary, he preferred to see me dressed up as a prim secretary, unhappy day after day.

Why? How could my happiness mean so little to him?

Thoughtfully, I shook my head. There had to be a way to make him understand what he couldn't grasp from words alone. Once we had finally talked things through, I would involve him more, show him my pictures, or take him along on photo tours. I wouldn't just tell him about happiness anymore; I'd make sure he could see it. Because once he recognized my joy, he simply had to be on my side. Or didn't he?

Suddenly Grandma was very close to me and laid her hand on my shoulder. "You two will get through this, I'm sure of it," she said soothingly.

She seems confident, and I have no reason not to believe her. "Definitely." I give her an open smile.

"That's exactly what I wanted to hear." Smiling in satisfaction, Grandma turns away from me, lets the grain mix for the chickens trickle into the feeding trough, and sets it down on the ground. The animals appear at once and, pressed close together, peck up the kernels.

I look around; in here, we're done with the work. "Is there anything left to do outside in the free-range enclosure?"

Grandma's gaze wanders to her wristwatch. "I'll take care of that later," she murmurs, grabs the egg basket, and turns to go. "I have to make sure I get to Ludwig on time."

Ludwig? She's never mentioned that name before. She hasn't met a new man, has she? "Who's Ludwig?" I ask curiously, following her into the wildly overgrown garden. "An admirer?"

"You could say that." I notice very clearly that Grandma is smiling furtively. "He admires me beyond measure."

Her strange behavior makes me suspicious. She's teasing me; it can't be anything else. "How did you meet him?" I ask, intrigued.

She stops and turns to me. "Through a notice at the supermarket." The corners of her mouth twitch, her eyes shine. Standing there amid tall grasses and wild rosebushes, she would make a perfect photo subject.

I don't want to let myself get distracted by that thought, though. My photo ideas will have to wait; something is seriously fishy here. I raise my eyebrows, signaling that I want her to tell me more.

"'Daytime babysitter wanted,' that's what it said on a little note." She grins at me in amusement, probably because she can see the relief on my face right now. "I knew right away that something like that could be perfect for me. I've been meeting with little Ludwig ever since. Today we're already having our third date," she says and gives me a conspiratorial wink.

The cheerfulness in her face overwhelms me. Looking after the boy is good for her, I can clearly see that. But it's not just that. Step by step, she's building a new life for herself, one that makes her happy despite losing Grandpa. "That's great, I'm happy for you two." I can't help pulling her into a tight hug.

"In the end, everything will be all right," she whispers to me in that moment, and I know it's the truth. For Lukas and me, too.

To be sure, I repeat the words until I set off on my way home. Over and over again, as if they were my new mantra, I focus my thoughts on that sentence.

When I get home, no one is there. That's not a bad thing, I tell myself; after all, it's only three in the afternoon, and Lukas is surely still at work. It could be hours before he comes home and we talk about everything. Before I show him what makes me so happy and we start a new life together.

A life in which there's no such thing as "later" anymore.

Just as I'm hurrying into the bathroom, I hear a key being carefully inserted into the lock of the apartment door. The cylinder turns.

That has to be Lukas. He finished work much earlier than usual to make up with me.

In a flash, anticipation spreads through me. Like a warm sensation, it travels from my stomach straight through my whole body. With trembling fingers, I smooth my hair, tug my T-shirt into place, and check it for stains. There aren't any, but it's wrinkled and, thanks to my trip to Grandma's, it smells like a chicken coop.

It's not ideal, but I can't change it now, because I already hear the soft squeak of the door. Next come footsteps in the hallway. He moves so carefully, as if the floor weren't laminate but a thin sheet of ice.

Now he sets the key ring down on the dresser next to the coat rack, then everything goes quiet.

He hesitates, not sure if he should keep going. Maybe he's even wondering whether he wants to see me at all and whether he's ready to talk to me.

I can't make this decision for him. He has to come to me, that much is clear. So I wait in the hallway until he turns the corner. My ears pick up every sound. There are deep breaths and hands brushing over fabric. A hesitant step. And another. Instinctively, I hold my breath. Any second now he'll appear in my field of vision.

A split second later my features freeze. And with them the rest of my body.

That's not Lukas. It's Anna.

"Um… hi, Marie." Self-consciously, she checks her high ponytail. She looks like she jogged here. The functional sports outfit clings to her wiry body, her forehead is shiny, and her cheeks are glowing like furnaces.

I wish I could confront her about breaking in here without permission, but I can't. All I can do is stare at her with my eyes wide open. I probably look like I've lost my mind, but that doesn't matter. Because the fact that she's here is not a good sign.

"Sorry for barging in like this..." She shrugs awkwardly and shifts her weight from one leg to the other.

Lukas sent her.

A wave of disappointment floods my body. As if it would change anything, I fold my arms across my chest. "What do you want?" I ask tonelessly.

Either she doesn't notice my defensive posture, or she doesn't care. As if we were friends, she takes another step toward me and looks into my eyes, full of sympathy. "Come here," she says softly, puts her arms around my rigid body, and presses all her heat against me.

I let it happen, even though I don't know why.

"I'm so incredibly sorry. You two, that was something really special," she whispers in my ear.

She speaks in the past tense. As if it really were over. Done. Finished forever. On top of that, she strokes my back in a gesture of understanding.

What the hell is this supposed to be?

We just had a fight. That's nothing you couldn't clear up with a bit of good will and an honest conversation!

With all my strength I hold back the tears that still rise up in me unstoppably. I tear myself away from her with a jerk. We barely know each other; breaking down and crying on her shoulder would clearly be wrong. "Why are you here?" I sound weak, even weaker than I suddenly feel.

Hesitantly she looks at me, then she lifts her arms in apology. "I just wanted to pick up a few things. Clothes, toothbrush... you know."

Instantly a stabbing pain shoots through my whole body, no less powerful than a bolt of lightning. Is this really true? He's sending his best friend to move out of our shared apartment?

He means it. He can't love me anymore.

I swallow. Once, then again. But what's now crawling up my throat can't be suppressed that way. I'd rather puke the words out. "Take whatever you want, but hurry up," I hear myself say instead, my voice sounding flat.

She nods and presses her lips together. As if this were hard for her. As if she had any idea what hard even is.

Before she can keep looking at me like that, I make room for her and signal with a tired wave of my hand that she should finally get started. At least she understands that. She immediately squeezes past me and disappears into the cherry-red doorframe of the bedroom. I hear her open the wardrobe while I desperately search for a place where I can feel safe.

The kitchen. She won't want to take anything from there. I quickly head that way, and just a few seconds later I close the kitchen door behind me. Leaning my back against the blue-painted wood, I sink to the floor.

I may not see her here, but I still hear everything.

My ears recognize every sound; they know which drawer she opens and what she takes out. Clothes hangers clatter together, zippers are pulled shut, bundles of socks fall to the floor.

Then she marches into the bathroom. She's definitely packing cologne, deodorant, and shower gel in there. She pulls the toothbrush out of the glass with a scraping sound. All at once it goes quiet. I picture her sinking down onto the edge of the bathtub to look around. She wants to know if she has everything. So she doesn't have to come back. And neither does he.

This just can't be real.

"Forever," I suddenly hear Lukas's teenage voice in my head, as if the universe wanted to punish me even more.

It can't be over. We belong together. One of us can't exist without the other. Never!

Shouldn't tears be flowing now? Shouldn't they be pouring down my cheeks like little waterfalls, dripping from my chin and vanishing silently into the hem of my T-shirt? Shouldn't my world be collapsing in on itself at this very moment, going up in rubble and ashes and darkening the sky above me?

Maybe. Absolutely. And yet something completely different happens. I stop existing, as if my mind were leaving my body to retreat to a place where it doesn't have to endure any of what's happening here right now.

My mind hardly registers how Anna marches over to the coat rack to pack up shoes and jackets. It only notices in passing that she comes back and stops on the other side of the kitchen door.

"Marie?" She sounds unsure. As if she herself were overwhelmed by the situation.

I don't answer, because I don't know what good it would do.

To make matters worse, she now knocks as well.

What does she want?

With an effort I push myself up and open the door. For just a brief moment she looks at me with pity, then her gaze wanders to my right hand. To where I'm wearing my engagement ring.

No. Never.

"Sorry," she says, furrowing her brow.

This is what Lukas wants?

Impossible. Out of the question.

It takes less than a second for everything inside me to harden. My muscles go completely rigid, my expression freezes. "You're definitely not getting that."

"Sorry," she repeats, as if she couldn't think of anything better to say. She can spare herself that pitying shrug, because that doesn't change anything either.

Yesterday Lukas accused me of being a fucking egoist who never thinks about him or his needs. This time he'll get what he's asking of me. "His wish is my command." I sound bitter, because for me it's the only way to deal with it.

Mechanical as a doll, I twist the ring off my finger without taking my eyes off Anna for even a moment. I don't look at it, don't want to see its sunny yellow gleam. Because there's one thing I know for sure: doing that would be my downfall.

Instead, I grit my teeth and place the ring in Anna's hand.

I see only in a blur how the person opposite me lowers her lids in guilty shame. She might be saying something, something nice maybe, or maybe not.

I'm like in a trance, and that's a good thing. She turns her back on me and disappears from my field of vision. All I can still hear are her footsteps, growing fainter. The apartment door is opened, the rolling suitcase is pulled over the threshold. I wait for the click; that's my signal.

There it is.

The door slams shut. Anna is gone. And with her the things Lukas needs so he doesn't have to come back to me.

Chapter Eight

With a long, drawn-out yawn I walk into Joe's. I have to get used to the dim light first, but at least I can already see that there are only a few guests here today. A group of teenagers is playing darts, two women are whispering together at the corner table in the back. It doesn't take long before I spot Anna. She's sitting on a barstool, swinging her legs. Her lower lip is almost disappearing into her mouth as she picks at the loose ends of her bracelet.

She looks nervous, and she's not alone in feeling that way.

I take a deep breath, but it doesn't help. What's waiting for me now is uncharted territory. For both of us. And I still don't know what I want to say to her or how.

Anna lifts her head and gives me a restrained smile. This woman is my best friend; hardly anyone knows me as well as she does. There's no reason not to talk openly with her about what happened last night.

"Hi, darling. I was starting to think you weren't

coming." She winks at me and springs up from her stool. Her face comes closer to mine; instinctively I turn my head to the side so that her lips only touch my cheek.

When we pull apart, she doesn't look at me. She surely didn't expect me to kiss her hello, did she? Or did she?

"Work was really busy, you know how it is." I try to sound as relaxed as possible, probably just to get rid of my own tension. Awkwardly, I pull a barstool toward me and sit down.

Anna follows my lead, and a distance opens up between us that I'm not sure I like. "Yeah, sure, I know how it is."

Before I can say anything else, Joe is standing in front of us. As always, he's dressed entirely in black, a relaxed smile on his lips. "One large beer. And one lemon water?"

For a moment Anna grins furtively. "Not today."

The surprise is plain to see on Joe's face. Confused, he runs his hand over his bald head and down along his slightly graying stubble. "Got something to celebrate?"

Do we? I don't think so. Apparently Anna doesn't either, because once again she looks away. "I'll have a whiskey sour," she says instead of answering his question.

Joe's bushy eyebrows wander upward. In his face I can see his head searching for solutions to this riddle. I'd like that too, at least as much as he does. Alcohol is taboo in Anna's athlete's life. She hasn't had a drink in years, so why does she want to today?

She's tense. She needs something to calm her down. Yes, that must be it. But what does that mean?

A queasy feeling spreads in my stomach while Joe's eyes wander incessantly back and forth between Anna and me. "Very interesting," he murmurs, turning his attention to me. "What can I get you?"

Can he see it? Have Anna and I changed?

I quickly shake these confused thoughts out of my head. They don't belong here; everything is fine. What happened yesterday was meaningless, I had a weak moment and Anna wanted to comfort me. "The same, please," I answer, stubbornly trying not to let the nasty feeling of betrayal rise up inside me.

Because that's what really happened yesterday. I betrayed my relationship with Marie and our friendship. That night might have changed everything.

"Coming right up." With a smirk, Joe turns away and walks to the other end of the bar to get the glasses for our cocktails.

Anna and I are alone again. Neither of us says anything.

This unpleasant mood charges the air between us with a kind of tension I've never felt around her before. I should say something. But what? Can I just dive right in and ask her what the hell that was tonight?

I search for words, for sentences with beginnings and endings, but for the life of me I can't think how to bring it up. On top of that, I hardly dare even look at Anna. Not even when Joe sets the cocktails down in front of us on the dark-stained bar counter. Without a word he withdraws as discreetly as if he could sense exactly that something is going on here tonight.

Anna lifts her glass. "Cheers," she says, and drains the whiskey sour in one go. Then she takes a deep breath. With her gaze fixed on the neatly lined-up wall of glasses behind the bar, she finally starts to speak quietly. "Are we going to sit here in silence all evening?"

Oh God, no, that's the last thing I want. I clear my

throat. "Of course not… What do you want to talk about?" I sound a bit like a little boy who feels guilty but isn't sure he's actually done anything wrong.

"I don't know. Do we have anything to talk about?" Suddenly she turns her head in my direction and locks her eyes on me. The blue of her eyes is so light that I can't read anything in them. No flicker, no sparkle. Just secrets.

"How do you see it?" I hold her gaze. We're not strangers who don't know how to deal with each other. We're Lukas and Anna, best friends since childhood. Buddies. Or something like that.

I wait tensely for a sign, and I actually spot one. Anna's hand moves to her ear, her fingers twisting her earring nervously in every direction. "Well… maybe… I think… we should… only if you want to…"

"Yes, I want that." The words rush out of my mouth. This is hard for both of us, that much is clear. So I do what I should have done from the very beginning and say what I'm thinking. "Does it scare you as insanely much as it scares me?"

A relieved smile spreads across her face. "Oh God, yes."

"You start." Maybe that's unfair. But if I had to begin, I still wouldn't know what to say. Because I have no idea what I think, and even less what I feel. So I give her an encouraging nod and who knows, maybe the whole thing will just take care of itself.

"So… um… there's something I have to tell you. And if I don't find the courage for it today, then I probably never will." All of a sudden she's tugging wildly at her earlobe while reaching for her glass with the other hand. She looks a bit like she's trying to drink up some courage, and I'm not sure I really want to know what for. "I'm just going to say it straight out, no frills and no fake understatement."

Her intense gaze hits me, her expression turns serious.

Instinctively, I hold my breath. I can't perceive anything anymore, only Anna's tense posture and the way her chest is rising and falling at a frantic pace.

"I love you."

Of course she does, we've been best friends for so long that it couldn't be any other way. "I love you too!" I say, maybe a touch too relieved, and give her a friendly punch in the side.

She pushes me away at once. "No, Lukas. It's more than that. It always has been." She speaks quietly, but so firmly that I realize in a split second how serious she is. "I've been waiting my whole life for what happened last night."

Her revelation hits me like a lightning strike.

She loves me? In a romantic way?

No. She's clearly imagining that. She's confused, nothing more.

"I would've noticed that," I reply quickly. "How could you have loved me for years without ever giving me even the slightest sign? As close as we were… I would've had to be blind…" I stammer on as countless memories race wildly through my head. I search for moments, touches, and glances. For clues that could've let me see it. But there's nothing. Just unromantic vibes, matey hugs, and innocent kisses on the cheek.

Unlike me, Anna seems to see things clearly. Her hand twitches; she wants to touch me but doesn't dare. "I waited. Other women came along, and every time they left again, I wanted to find the courage to confess my feelings to you. Over and over I failed. I was way too afraid of how you'd react."

Her eyes plead with me, her words echo inside me,

and still I can't understand her. "What changed?" I ask carefully, because that's the only thought I can put into words.

She gives me a gentle smile. Her expression turns almost tender, her cheeks flush. "Last night you made the first move. And the second."

I nod. Even though last night is a blur in my head, I remember that. Whatever the reason it happened at all, the whole thing definitely started with me.

What am I supposed to say next? What does she want to hear, and what am I supposed to feel?

While I'm still searching for words, Anna doesn't seem to have any trouble finding them. "When I woke up this morning, you were gone. The bed next to me was cold. Ever since, I've been asking myself what I'm supposed to make of what happened last night."

She's not alone in that. I could tell her so, but I can't. Instead, I drain my Whiskey Sour in one go and signal to Joe to bring me another. He nods and looks a bit like a Buddhist monk who can read my mind. That's a sign. A sign that my brain has stopped working.

Everything is a mess. My thoughts, my feelings, and my whole life.

I know Anna is waiting for a reaction, but the truth is I can't even look at her. Because I'm afraid of what I might see. And of reacting the wrong way.

Because one thing is clear, after all: if I lose Anna, the last remaining foundation of my life will collapse as well. I can't let that happen.

An uncomfortable silence settles over the already fragile mood between us. I count the seconds, even though it doesn't make any sense. The fact that one of the teenagers from the darts game chooses this moment to turn on the jukebox behind us and of all things picks a booming metal song doesn't help me at all.

"I can't think straight anymore," I finally whisper, my head lowered. Because that's the one thing I really know for sure.

Out of the corner of my eye I see Anna's sad look. Like a wounded deer she huddles on the barstool next to me. "Of course, I get that, of course."

Seeing her like this gives me a sick feeling all over my body. My arms suddenly feel heavy, and a burden spreads across my shoulders that I can hardly carry.

Because it's my fault, I disappointed her. And that even though she was there for me at any time during the darkest periods of my life. What kind of friend am I?

I immediately reach my arm out to her and gently stroke her shoulder. "Give me a little time. To process all of this. To understand it myself…"

Anna cuts me off before I can finish the sentence. "I've been waiting my whole life, a few more days more or less won't make a difference now." All at once she winks at me and smiles. She's trying to spread some good cheer, but I still see the disappointment in her eyes.

There's nothing I want more than to comfort her. Knowing she's unhappy because of me feels like an entire mountain range is lying in my stomach. I'd love to hug her, pull her close and tell her that I feel the same way she does. But I can't do it. I can't promise her anything when I don't even know myself if I can keep that promise.

"Thank you, Anna. For everything," is all I say as I shove my hands under my thighs.

She gives a wistful smile. "Shall we go home?"

I look down at myself. I really shouldn't wear these clothes again tomorrow. Marie hasn't been in touch all day.

The thought of her silence drifts through my head like a dark cloud, turning everything inside me dull and gray.

Still, I stick to it. I'm definitely not going to make the first move to settle our fight. It's her turn to show me that she's ready to fight for this love.

If that's even still possible. If, after what happened last night, there's any way back at all.

On top of my guilty conscience about Anna, these overpowering feelings of guilt now join in. It's obvious. I cheated on Marie. Without batting an eye, I spent last night with another woman.

Damn.

How could that happen?

"Lukas?" Anna's voice tears me from my thoughts. "Should we go or stay?"

I quickly shake my head to drag myself back to reality. "I need fresh clothes and a few other things from the apartment. So I pretty much have to go there, whether I like it or not."

"No, you don't." A proud grin spreads across Anna's face as she straightens up. "It's all taken care of. I was at your place today and packed what you'll need for the next few weeks. Even your weekly planner."

"Wow… um… thanks!" I can't get anything else out. This is great. Actually. This way Marie still has to make the first move. Even so, I feel a burning pain deep in my chest. It wants to convince me that I already miss Marie. That I should go to her and try to straighten out our relationship again.

No. I've been that stupid often enough in the last few months. I don't want to see Marie, and my heart doesn't get a say in that.

"No problem, my dear, I was happy to do it. Last

night you said you needed some distance, so I figured you'd be glad about this." In a good mood, Anna waves Joe over and takes care of our bill. I can clearly see the bar owner biting back a comment as he sorts the bills into his leather wallet. He only wishes us a nice evening and looks at me so intently while he does that it makes me feel queasy.

"Let's go." Anna grabs my hand and pulls me out of the place.

When we step out onto the street together, she doesn't let go of me. And I don't make any attempt to pull away from her either.

Because she's the only thing that still gives my life any stability at all. She's there for me, she only wants what's best for me, and that feels good. With her I'm sheltered and safe.

Caught between relief and sadness, confusion and longing, I trudge along beside Anna in silence. She surely knows that words are unnecessary right now. She's always sensed what I need, and today is no different. The night is dark, thick clouds cover the stars, and even the moonlight barely has enough strength to reach us. Accompanied only by the artificial light of the streetlamps and the headlights of passing cars, we wander side by side through the night.

By the time we reach her tiny apartment, nothing feels strange between us anymore. We're who we were again, and I'm incredibly grateful for that. Without further ado, Anna gets a place ready for me to sleep on the sofa.

"It's been a long day." She makes no move to come closer to me. On the contrary, she has almost left the living room before I can answer.

"Sleep well." A bit awkwardly, I raise my hand.

"You too. And don't forget: tomorrow is a new day." She winks at me.

A warm feeling spread through me as she closed the door behind her.

Anna is great.

With her, even this evening had been bearable. We were able to talk openly and found a solution. Whether I wanted to or not, I immediately remembered how difficult the past few months with Marie had been. How hard I had had to fight, only to lose in the end anyway.

Exhausted, I let myself fall onto the sofa, which creaked under my weight. My thoughts wandered further back into the past. To a time when Marie and I had been as happy as I had never been at any other point in my life.

I saw her in front of me, her honey-blond hair falling into her face. She smiled, her eyes shining with excitement. A lovestruck glow lay on her cheeks. She shone, even more than the sun above us.

"Come on!" she called to me, and marched on along the narrow path right through the grain field. The ears of corn under her palms swayed lazily in the wind. It smelled of summer. And of life.

Quickly I ran after her, caught up with her, and wrapped my arms around her torso from behind. "Stay with me," I whispered hoarsely into her ear. "Forever."

She immediately turned to face me. She didn't have to say anything; I saw everything in her face. "Let's live as if we only had today. I want to enjoy everything together with you. We should swim in the seven seas and climb every mountain in the world together."

I smiled, even though I clearly felt a familiar old fear crawling up inside me like an annoying insect. And yet it couldn't do anything to the butterflies in my stomach. They kept fluttering around happily down there and with every beat of their wings they left only one wish behind: to be with her. "We should," I whispered. Then I kissed her with all my passion.

Never again will I be able to love a person like that. That exact thought shoots through my head like a massive bolt of lightning as I lie here now, so many years later, completely alone on the sofa in Anna's apartment, staring up at the ceiling.

And yet our love failed. Because of life, because of everyday routine, and maybe even a little because of ourselves.

Was it a mistake? That I left, that I stopped trying, that I no longer tried to straighten everything out again?

No. Because where could that have led? Now I'm gone. Away from her, her problems, the mood swings, and the crazy behavior. It's only a matter of time before I feel better and forget her. Little by little she'll disappear from my thoughts. The overpoweringly beautiful image of Marie and Lukas will fade like a photograph in the sunlight. Then the day will come when the memory of her no longer hurts.

And if not? If my heart never goes quiet and my stomach keeps rebelling?

As if in a trance, I reach for my phone. It's silent, just like it has been all day. It's already been more than 24 hours since we last had any contact. Maybe Marie is hurt, but so am I.

I unlock the screen. I shouldn't do that. And even less should I stare at the picture that appears on my phone right afterward.

Marie and me. In a sea of wildflowers.

Gently I let my index finger glide over the photo, touch her cheeks, and stroke her hair. If only there were a way to undo the last few months and pick up again where we were in the time this picture was taken. I'd go to the ends of the earth for that. And a little farther still.

But there isn't. And this photo is nothing but pure poison. It soaks through my body, reaches all the way down to my toes, and spreads in my chest. If I'm not careful, it will kill me.

"It's over. That Marie doesn't exist anymore, get that through your head," I tell myself sternly and shove the phone away from me with a jerk.

Chapter Nine

Leisurely, Alex and I stroll across Schwedenplatz. I guess it's supposed to look like a nice little outing between girlfriends, but it's anything but that. My fingers keep reaching for my ring finger, right for the spot where, four days ago, I was still wearing my most precious piece of jewelry. The engagement ring with the sunny yellow stone is gone. It left me together with Lukas.

"And he really didn't even come himself to pick up his stuff?" My best friend shakes her head in such disbelief that her extra-long cherry earrings dangle all the way down to the corners of her mouth. Encouragingly, she hooks her arm through mine as we walk.

I shrug. My shoulders feel so heavy, as if they were buried under a whole sack of dark soil. That shouldn't surprise me after all those sleepless nights. The moment I close my eyes, my nightmare comes back. I can't bear it, so night after night I lose myself in a mere twilight state between worlds.

Why on earth did I let myself be talked into this city stroll? Every part of me is tired. The people all around us are in far too good a mood, the sun is shining too brightly, and the sky is too blue. I don't belong here, I'm like an ugly foreign body in the busy pedestrian zone.

Alex nudges me gently with her shoulder. "Lukas is scared," she says with utter conviction and even nods vigorously to underline it.

"Maybe." Alex might be right, but that doesn't solve my problem. "But he can't just cut off contact completely from one hour to the next. And then he sends that stupid Anna instead, like he can't even stand my presence for a couple of minutes. When he's the one who behaved so ignorantly that I can hardly find words for it."

Okay, in truth Anna isn't stupid. She's nice, and it was at least as uncomfortable for her as it was for me. On top of that, I'm sure she's there for Lukas right now, which basically makes it impossible to hate her.

"Stupid Anna?" The words leave Alex's mouth a bit too loudly. We look at each other and she bursts out laughing. "You sound like a kindergartner."

I have to at least smirk, and even that is, in truth, a small miracle. The way we stroll across Schwedenplatz, we must be making a very strange impression. The fairy and the misery guts. Alex is laughing like a madwoman and I'm grinning, even though my body language is definitely only telling the story of how desperate I am.

"Come on," Alex says at last, takes my hand, and pulls me along behind her. "Let's get some ice cream."

I'm really not in the mood for that, and protesting would cost me too much energy. "Why didn't he come himself?" My voice is quiet, but Alex's attention is on me immediately.

She stops abruptly and puts her hands on my shoulders. "Why didn't you go to him?"

I push out my lower lip. Does this woman always have to go straight for the wound that hurts the most? "Why should I? Even though I can understand his point of view, he hurt me too much. But even if that weren't the case, it wouldn't lead anywhere. As long as he hasn't worked it out with himself, he won't listen to me anyway. Maybe he doesn't listen to me at all anymore. These last few weeks already felt like I was talking to a wall. And now the wall has even hit back."

"Do it," Alex cuts me off, smiles at me, and pulls me farther across the square. "Go to him and tell him exactly that."

As if it were that easy. Lost in thought, I trudge after Alex and a little later dutifully line up beside her in front of the ice cream parlor. While we wait, I let my gaze wander over the surroundings. It really does seem as if everyone is happy today. A young couple strolls past us hand in hand. They seem to notice only each other, as if they were trapped in a pink bubble.

Watching that is torture. Still, I can't look away. I watch the two of them lovingly hook their fingers together. He lets his thumb glide over her index finger, again and again it wanders up and down, and I'm sure that for her every repetition feels like a little declaration of love.

"And for you, Marie?"

Is that Alex talking to me? I quickly tear my eyes away from the couple. Right, there's my best friend. With a huge cup of ice cream in her hand, she looks at me expectantly with her big round eyes.

"It's your turn," she says insistently, nodding toward the counter.

Obediently, I turn to the ice cream flavors—what else can I do? I block out everything with chocolate, or at least I try to. I order one scoop of yogurt and one of hazelnut.

Only when we leave the ice cream parlor again does Alex give me a critical look. "Listen, this isn't going to work."

"I don't know what you mean," I snap back far too defiantly and pretend I have to focus completely on the ice cream in my hand.

Still, I don't miss the way Alex rolls her eyes. "Yeah, what happened was crap. But what you're doing right now is even bigger crap." She sounds too invested.

"Definitely not." I start walking, wanting to get away from the other people and especially from the couple I can still see on the opposite side of the street.

Alex catches up with me immediately. "Don't be so stubborn, Marie."

"I'm not stubborn at all. Even if I wanted to reach out…" I swallow. How am I supposed to explain this? "There are no words. At least none that would get through to him. First he has to be ready to listen to me."

Her forehead creases. "Is that really right? When was the last time you approached him? How did you react to his opinion?"

She's asking too many questions I don't know the answers to. How could I, we've never had a fight like this before. And this silence that has pushed itself between us over the last four days, as massive as the Great Wall of China, is paralyzing me. It makes me small and immobile; I can't think and I no longer know what's right and what's wrong. It's been almost a hundred hours since we last heard from each other, and every second of it has been pure torture.

"He's not going to understand me." That's it. Nailed it. "No matter what I say, it sounds different to him. It's been like that for months. We've lost our connection."

"Your antennas are still there, you just have to realign them with each other." Alex puts a meaningful note in her voice.

"What if our antennas are broken? So broken they can't be fixed? Or if we tried with great effort to reconnect them, only to realize there's still background noise?" I look at her, searching for help. The ice cream in my hand is already melting. I feel it running stickily over my fingers. Soon it'll drip onto my deep blue summer dress and leave ugly stains there. Still, my attention is on Alex. Because I need something to hold on to. She shakes her head, and the expression in her eyes turns sad.

"If you and Lukas can't make it, then I'll lose my faith in love. You two are perfect. You always have been, and you will be again."

Perfect? What's that? When all you have to do is look into each other's eyes to know what the other is thinking? When you hug and realize that you can be at home anywhere in the world as long as you're this close to each other?

Lukas and Marie. Forever?

"Hey, don't cry." Alex pulls a tissue out of her cut-off jeans and dabs my cheeks dry as if I were a baby.

I swallow, blink, and lift my gaze to the sky. Not a single cloud is in sight. How unfitting. "Maybe we were perfect. Still, I don't know anymore if we're right for each other."

"What are you talking about?" Now she sounds as strict as a teacher. "Of course you belong together. You two are like summer and ice cream, like parties and music. Like Vienna and the Ferris wheel!"

I look at her doubtfully, having no idea what she's trying to tell me.

Now she rolls her eyes with a strained groan. "Oh, come on, it's not that hard. The fact that you two belong together is a law of nature. If you really broke up, the scientists would have to start from scratch to explain the world."

Her enthusiasm is wonderful, and the fact that she can believe in Lukas and me with such conviction makes even me feel a little hopeful. A touch of warmth moves through my chest, loosening the cramped rigidity inside me, softening me and letting me feel again what I had buried beneath it myself.

This longing.

For laughing together with him. For his eyes, the scent of his skin and the taste of his lips. For the feeling of being with him and knowing that that is exactly where my home is.

Suddenly I feel as if my insides are freezing. Because it suddenly becomes clear to me that there might be another version of reality after all, one I haven't wanted to accept until now.

"He's not going to come back to me," I whisper. My voice breaks, but I have to say it.

Alex immediately takes a step toward me and pulls me into a tight hug. I can hardly breathe, yet I wish she would hold me even tighter. Because she alone gives me the support I'm missing.

I let myself fall, and not a second later the rest of me gives way too. The memories flood me, sweep me along and reveal an image so clear that even I can't ignore it any longer. "We have to find our way back to each other. We just have to!"

Alex leans back from me a little and looks deep into my eyes. "That's exactly how it's going to be."

"What should I do?" A spark of hope stirs in me, like a small light in a dark night. It's not much, but at least it's a beginning.

"Text him. Right now." When she nods at me so encouragingly, she looks like one of those bobbleheads. Normally she manages to sweep me along with that, but not today.

"But he needs…" At once I feel my shoulders sag again.

"No, don't think about it. Text him what you feel. Leave your head out of it." She says it as if it were the most natural thing in the world, like it's the easiest task there is. "Go on, get your phone out."

Obediently, I pull open my bag's zipper and rummage out my phone. As if I knew exactly what I was doing, I turn it on and open a text message.

Then everything inside me goes quiet.

"You and I, we belong together. We're not going to let anything stop us, we never wanted that. Forever, remember?"

In black and white I see the words in front of me. Are they right? Do they really say what I'm thinking? Will he know what I mean?

"And hit send," Alex's voice cuts in, as if from far away.

A fierce wave of doubt crashes over me. What if he doesn't reply? If he laughs at my message, deletes it without reading it, or if it only drives him even farther away from me?

Dark veils rise up inside me, stealing the shine from my hope and the breadth from my gaze.

Still, by now I'm sure of it. Not sending this message could let our wall of silence grow even higher.

I only have to press a single key.

But it feels as if I were asking myself to use my index finger to nudge the whole world a tiny bit further around. Frozen, I take a deep breath, hold it, and clench my teeth. I know I have to do it. And I will. As soon as I can bring myself to.

Chapter Ten

"Time for a break," I hear a cheerful woman's voice trill.

I look up from my desk. I was right, I didn't imagine it. Anna is leaning against the doorframe of my office and waving at me happily. With her flowing batik-style summer skirt and loose white shirt, she looks a bit as if she'd stepped straight out of the seventies. Her long hair is piled up in a messy bun, and the faux-leather bag on her shoulder has definitely seen better days.

She smiles at me. And I smile back. If it weren't for her, I really would often forget to have lunch. Hardly surprising, with all the work the junior boss keeps dumping on me just because he has no idea how to do it himself. I quickly push my swivel chair back and heave myself up.

"What tasty thing did you bring today?" Yes, I admit it. The fact that Anna has been supplying me with home-cooked lunches every day this week is nothing short of brilliant. My gaze wanders back to her bag, but today I have to realize with disappointment that there can't be much hidden in it. It's flat. And too small. Still, I stretch out my stiff bones, walk over to her, and watch how with every step I take her smile turns into a radiant beam.

She shouldn't do that. She mustn't look at me like that. So… in love.

"Hey," she says, without answering me. "How's your day been so far?"

"Just don't ask, or it'll ruin my lunch break too." I quickly try to find out if she's hiding something behind her back with her hands.

She immediately raises her arms in an apologetic gesture. "I thought we could go out to eat for a change today. There's a new snack bar that opened out on the street, and we're going to try it."

"I can hardly imagine it tastes better there than what you make." I automatically wink at her.

Her gaze turns wistful at once. I shouldn't have done that. She shouldn't get her hopes up about something when I don't even know myself if I want it.

"Come on, let's go," I say quickly, shove my phone and wallet into my bag, and head out. It's the only way to resolve this situation and get both of us thinking about something else.

On the way to the snack bar, guilt is already gnawing at me. Three days ago, Anna confessed her love to me. I've been keeping her at arm's length ever since. And that even though she's trying harder than anyone ever has to make sure I'm okay. I shouldn't treat her so dismissively; it's terribly unfair of me.

Luckily, the walk to the snack bar isn't far. The smell of bratwurst and fries reaches my nose, and right on cue my stomach responds with a loud growl. The paved area with the standing tables in front of the food stall is crowded. A colorful mix of suit-and-tie types and construction workers, mothers with their preschoolers, and students who are probably skipping a lesson.

"What are you in the mood for?" I ask, shading my eyes from the bright sunlight so I can at least give her a friendly smile.

"One hot dog, please, without the bun and without sauce. But with lots of vegetables." Anna pulls a face that nobody could possibly resist.

Inwardly I shake my head. How can anyone give up the best parts of this delicacy? But that's just Anna; she'll do anything for that steel-hard body of hers. A little embarrassed, I look down at myself. My belly could be flatter, and my arms are too thin. At least I inherited my father's broad shoulders, but next to Anna I look like an untrained amateur.

"You should stop that." Anna's voice pushes into my thoughts. I look up at her and meet a shamelessly smirking face. "Or do you want me to drag you into the gym? We could turn you into a little Hercules." Grinning, she feels up my barely existing pecs. "Yeah, we'd have to add quite a bit there. And here on the shoulders, too. But then you'd be ready for battle."

Her laughter is so infectious that I join in. I savor how light and free this moment feels. It's like Anna knows exactly what I need. "One hot dog, plain. Coming right up," I say with a wink and gently move her hand away from my chest. "Will you go ahead and reserve this table for us?"

"Aye-aye, will do." Cheerfully, Anna turns around and plants her hands possessively on the standing table.

Again I can't help grinning, and again that wonderfully light feeling spreads inside me.

I wish it could stay like this. It would be amazing to live

so carefree, just having fun with Anna and finding a new kind of home in her.

That would be possible. Maybe.

Lost in thought, I step into the line in front of the food truck and a little later place our order. While I wait for the hot dogs, I watch Anna. Barely two meters away from me, she leans casually against the standing table and winds a strand of her dark curls around her finger. Tufts of hair are sticking out of her bun everywhere, as if they had a will of their own and wanted to rebel against the company of the other hairs.

This woman wants to be with me, to kiss me and love me. She wants to be there for me, no matter whether we go through hard or happy times. Our relationship would be like it has been so far, just with one more component added. We'd be a couple and no longer best friends.

Could we be both?

I wish my feelings would say something about that, but they don't. Ever since I forbade them to plant those longing thoughts of Marie all over my body, they've been silent. As if they were offended. As if they were protesting against what just has to be.

Marie was the past. I wasn't even worth enough to her for her to get in touch with me. For four days now she hadn't managed to approach me, even though everything that had happened was entirely her fault. And I definitely wasn't going to crawl back to her. My dear Anna over there could be my future. If I wanted her to be.

"One hot dog with extra sauce, one plain." The loud male voice made me flinch.

I quickly shook the vague thoughts from my head, turned to the man at the snack stand, and opened my wallet. "How much is it?"

Distracted by everything that had happened over the past few days, I slowly searched for the right coins and placed them on the counter one by one.

Every time a coin touched the metallic surface of the counter, I heard a bright click. It sounded similar to the notification tone for messages on my phone. When I put down the last fifty-cent piece, I even heard the sound twice.

Something was wrong here. All at once and without any further warning, my heart took command. I spun around, and my gaze immediately found the standing table where I had left my phone.

It was no longer there.

Even though it was crazy, I suddenly got nervous. As if I were missing the most important thing in my life, my eyes scanned the dark gray tabletop. Nothing. My gaze wandered upward, and I spotted my phone in Anna's hand.

Thank God. Everything was fine. Even though I would rather not admit it, I was relieved.

With an apologetic smile, I turned back to the vendor and took the hot dogs. He just shook his head in amusement and gathered the coins from the counter.

I stride over to Anna because I'm suddenly in a hurry. I know why, but I'm not going to admit it to myself.

"Is everything okay?" I sound excited, even though there's no reason for it.

She takes her lunch back from me and nods. "Sure. Why wouldn't it be?"

"I just thought I heard something. A notification on the phone or something." It's nonsense, but I still study Anna closely. I check her reaction and watch her body language, as if something in me didn't trust her, even though that's of course totally unnecessary.

Anna looks confused. "Yeah, my friend Alice texted.

We're meeting up at the gym later." She bites off a tiny little piece of her sausage and chews on it as if it were a whole mountain of meat.

"All right. I guess it wasn't my phone after all." I burst out laughing, relieved and disappointed at the same time.

"It's quite possible we've got the same notification sound," Anna says with a shrug and pulls her phone out of her crochet bag with one hand. "Do you want me to show you Alice's message?"

I immediately feel incredibly stupid. Our phones look almost identical. It's entirely possible that Anna had hers in her hand earlier. "Nonsense. I was just confused, that's all."

I reach for my hot dog, but before I can take a bite, my movements falter again.

Wait a second, if that was Anna's phone, then where's mine? And who says I didn't get a message too?

This thought shouldn't be giving me this much hope. And even less should I be patting down the pockets of my jeans so frantically. It's quite possible that the first guests are already turning toward me and eyeing me critically. Still, I can't help it. It's this wish I'm not allowed to have that makes my hands move more and more hectically.

Anna notices my panic, comes closer, and lays her arm on mine. "You look pale, darling. What's wrong?"

"My phone," is all I say absentmindedly while my eyes search the ground. I don't see it on the dark gray asphalt either, among all the sneakers, sandals, and elegant leather shoes.

Anna's bright laughter is soothing. "There it is, you idiot."

I look up. Sure enough, there where Anna has just lifted the napkin holder, lies my phone.

I don't have time to pretend everything's okay. I have to get it. And check. Right now.

Because it might be. It could be possible…

I ignore Anna's astonished expression. In a flash I circle the tall table, grab the phone, and turn it on.

There's no message.

In the very next moment I feel as if dark storm clouds are closing in tightly above me. I fight against it, don't want to let it throw me so badly off balance. Still, I'm powerless. The storm of my life that has been brewing relentlessly over the past few months now seems almost impossible to stop.

Marie doesn't get in touch. No matter how much a part of me wants her to. I'd most like to scream at myself, "It's over. Get that through your head already," but I can't do that in front of Anna. So I just press my lips together and shove the damn phone back into my damn pocket.

Chapter Eleven

"He's not answering." I feel my shoulders slump forward.

Shaking her head, Alex takes the phone from my hand. "He's working, you know that."

Of course she's right about that. While she slips my phone back into my handbag, I try not to let it get me down. I only sent the message to Lukas five minutes ago. Still, the waiting already feels unbearable.

"What if he doesn't get back to me?" I ask, my voice hoarse.

Alex comes over to me at once and pulls me into a hug. "He will, I know he will."

Her embrace is warm and pleasant. I want to let myself sink into it, but my tension won't allow it. She must notice that I'm stiff as a board and hardly even dare to breathe. How could I? How could I relax when, in these very minutes, so much is being decided about my life?

"So, how's the photography going?" Alex asks, deliberately cheerful, as she lets go of me again.

No matter how encouragingly she beams at me, even

this topic can't chase away the dark veils hanging over my thoughts. "I've got the equipment together and I've already taken a few test shots," I say. Then I wrinkle my nose for a moment. "But they all suck," I finally admit. Because it's the truth.

My best friend immediately raises her eyebrows in doubt. "I don't believe that. Let me see."

Suddenly I'm embarrassed. I can't let her look at these pictures, they're way too bad. Ever since Lukas left me, I've been missing the inspiration. My head feels too heavy and my stomach too queasy. It's as if I can't really see the beautiful things anymore, as if the world were a terribly ugly place. And that's exactly what the pictures look like too. So I raise my hand defensively. "Maybe another time."

For a moment Alex studies me. She probably doesn't know what to do with me. And I don't know either. I'm still clutching my handbag tightly against my side. So I'll feel it if my phone vibrates. That way I can pull it out right away when Lukas replies. Or maybe even calls me back.

Oh please, he just has to.

I inevitably imagine what my life would look like without him. Sadness hits me instantly, inside I shrink, I'm hardly really there anymore. I barely even notice how Alex links her arm through mine and steers me toward the Danube Canal, as if that could take my mind off things.

"I've got an idea," she chatters cheerfully, as if everything were perfectly fine. "You should take a course and learn how to take professional pictures. What do you think? Should we look one up for you?"

That would be great.

Still, it's impossible.

"A really good course definitely isn't cheap, and money's in pretty short supply for me right now." That's anything but an exaggeration. Paying the rent without help is challenge enough. It's my apartment; I'm the only one who signed the lease. From now on Lukas won't be contributing anything anymore, that much is clear. And in six weeks my unemployment benefits will be cut off.

No. I don't want to think about that as well. The sky already feels like it's about to collapse on top of me. Isn't that more than enough? I force myself to focus on the colorful graffiti on the concrete wall we're walking along.

"You don't know that at all. We'll take a look together, maybe we'll even find something cheap. Or you can pay in installments." She sounds like an overenthusiastic saleswoman from a shopping channel.

Just for her sake I force a smile onto my lips. Because I know what she's trying to do for me. "That's sweet of you, but I also need a few lenses. I can't afford those until next month, and without them the course doesn't make any sense anyway."

"What ever happened to your idea about being a virtual assistant?" Alex just doesn't want to give up.

Involuntarily, I wrinkle my nose, and apparently that's enough of an answer for her.

"Have you actually tried to get any jobs?" She doesn't want to let it go; I can tell by the way she stares at me.

Quickly, I drop my gaze to the unevenly laid paving stones. "I deactivated my profile when I thought I'd be going back to my old job." And since then I haven't reactivated it. Because I'd much rather take photos than design boring presentations or write form letters.

"No problem, then we'll just undo that." Her good mood remains unclouded. Wherever she gets the energy from, a bit of it even spills over to me. "Out with the phone.

Show me the platform. I'm sure we'll find some jobs there you can apply for."

More than happy, I reach for my phone in my handbag. It takes less than a second to see that Lukas hasn't been in touch. But it takes minutes in which Alex is probably trying to get jobs in my name while I digest this truth. His silence sits in my stomach like a hard lump, so heavy that I can't ignore it.

Only a week ago I wanted just one thing: to be happy taking photos. I was full of passion and dreams.

And today?

Not even seven days later I'm afraid that without Lukas even taking photos hardly makes any sense anymore.

What an idiot I am. I was blind and deaf. That's the truth, even if it's hard for me to admit it.

"I screwed it up," I mumble, and already I feel big tears welling up in my eyes. "How could I do that?"

Only a brief moment later the cruel reality overwhelms me. I alone am the one who destroyed everything, while Lukas, like a lone warrior, tried to save the two of us. Today I'm standing in the middle of the burned-out battlefield of our love. I'm alone. And I'll stay that way.

"Hey." Alex takes my head in her hands and lifts it just enough that I have to look her in the eyes.

Through my veil of tears I can hardly see her. But I see one thing: how serious her otherwise so delicately elfin expression is.

"You're going to fix this, got it? I'm here, we're going to get through this!" Her words are insistent and firm, as if no storm and no tempest could harm them.

I'd love to take some of her certainty for myself. Then I, too, could still have hope while my phone stays silent. I don't answer her, because I just can't. Whatever I'd say would be wrong. My gaze fixed on the calmly drifting water of the Danube Canal, I wonder whether the river of time will one day carry away my pain as well.

"How's your grandma doing anyway? Tell me," I suddenly hear Alex say.

That really is a good topic, because at the thought of Grandma at least a smile flits across my face. "She's full of life. Even though I'm sure she misses Grandpa terribly, she's making the best of what she's got."

"That sounds great. Has she discovered any new activities for herself?" Alex links her arm through mine and we stroll on together. I'd rather block out all the laughing people in the café gardens, as well as the little bouquets of wildflowers on the tables. And I don't even want to know if someone is kissing somewhere right now.

"She's a nanny now. And she told me recently that she's thinking about offering a child-care service at her place." Absentmindedly, I watch the murky water of the Danube make its way through the canal. "She probably can't stand the silence in the house."

"Then that's the perfect solution for her." Alex sounds thrilled.

Maybe it is. Or maybe it's an escape. I don't know, but at least Grandma seems to be doing better with it day by day.

"No more brooding, Marie," Alex scolds me, of course immediately noticing where my thoughts are drifting.

"Mhm," is all I say, because there's one thing I can't let go of. If Grandma finds her way without the love of her life, could I do the same?

No. Even imagining it hurts too much. Besides, our situations are completely different. Grandpa is never coming back.

And Lukas? Will he come back?

Without warning, Alex punches me in the side. "That's enough," she says in a playfully strict voice. "This won't do, you seriously need a distraction, and I already know how." A proud grin spreads across her face. "I need new clothes and you're going to help me pick them out."

Before I can even grasp what's happening, she grabs my hand and spins me around. I stumble after her toward the city center and only a few minutes later I find myself in a small boutique. The air conditioning is set so cold that I shiver.

"Go look for some dresses. And if you see anything in turquoise anywhere, let me know." Her insistent gaze lands on me. "Come on now, chop-chop, get to work."

Seriously? She thinks that can cheer me up? With a shrug, I turn to the clothes racks and let my fingers glide over the garments. Scratchy linen and delicate silk, soft faux fur and coarse knit alternate beneath my touch. I see blue, red, and orange, sometimes a bit of green. Two teenage girls are loudly talking about boys, the sales assistant is folding sweaters in bored silence. I stroll on slowly, but after only a few seconds my thoughts start to drift.

If I want Lukas back, I have to fight. I need more than a ridiculous little message. But what could convince him? This is new to me. I've never been the one who had to go to him after a fight.

Even though I already know what I'm about to see, I glance at my phone again. The screen is black. There's nothing. No message, no call. Nothing.

He's mad. Damn disappointed and horribly hurt.

"Have you found anything yet?" I hear Alex call from behind the big round clothes rack.

The truth would be the right answer. Instead, I pull the

first thing I can grab off the rack and hold it up. "What do you think of this?"

"That's blue. I said turquoise. Come on, don't make this so hard for me." With her lower lip stuck out, Alex looks at me accusingly.

I immediately put the blue item back. "I'm sorry. I just can't." I don't get any further than that. But I'm sure she already knows what I'm trying to say anyway.

"Then let's try something else." She still seems confident, and I have no idea how she manages that. "We're going to draw up a battle plan. How does that sound to you?"

A battle plan? For a war that might already be long lost? Nothing stirs in my handbag; there's no ringing and no vibrating. I glance sideways at my watch. I've already been waiting for almost an hour.

"Fine." I nod, because I don't have any other choice, and let myself drop onto one of the softly padded chairs next to the fitting rooms.

Alex laughs. "Here? All right, whatever you want." Amused, she slides onto the chair next to me. "Do you think someone will serve us champagne as well? We could really use some."

Incredulous, I watch as Alex raises her arm to signal the sales assistant. There are only a few people here, but at that moment they all turn to look at us. Quick-witted, I grab her hand and pull it back down. "Are you crazy?"

A satisfied grin spreads across her face. "Ah, so there is someone alive in there after all. Very good, then I guess I've achieved my goal."

I raise my arms as if I wanted to surrender. "Yeah, I get it. You're the best friend in the world."

"Exactly." Elegant as a princess, she crosses her legs and

straightens her back. "Back to you. What do you want to do?"

That's the crucial question. "I have to see him," I say spontaneously, "and make sure he listens to me." A detailed apology is in order. "But how is that supposed to work if he so obviously doesn't want any contact?"

"Just because he doesn't reply immediately after a single text? You don't even know if he's read it yet." She shakes her head in an exaggeratedly conspicuous way. A blonde woman with model proportions and an armful of clothes walks past us and gives us a critical once-over.

No matter how skeptically that bag of bones looks at us, my friend is right. If what she says is true, I'm still allowed to hope, and every part of me longs to do exactly that. As if from nowhere, the shadows inside me recede a little.

It's going to work. Because I'm taking action. I'm doing something instead of just waiting and hoping. In the best case, I even have it in my own hands and can influence what's going to happen. My cheeks start to glow with excitement, I lean over to Alex and give her a conspiratorial look.

"Lukas always needs some time alone, that's how he's always been. After every argument I had to give him a few hours to sort himself out. But by now it's been four days. It's never taken this long before. How much more time should I let pass, what do you think?"

Thoughtfully, she puts her index finger to her chin. "I'd say definitely until he finishes work."

"That makes sense." There are still a good four hours to go. "And then?"

"If you don't hear anything from him, go to him." The words roll off her lips completely casually, as if it were nothing special at all.

Even so, just the thought of it makes me break out in a

sweat. I see him in front of me, his expression hard, his gaze disappointed. He's like one of those rocks on a steep cliff, unconquerable and rough. How am I supposed to get through to him? "I don't even know where he is."

"Oh come on, I've never heard such a lame excuse in my life." She throws her hands in the air theatrically. Her words are so loud that the saleswoman turns around to look at us. She watches us skeptically, but Alex doesn't seem to notice. "You know where he works. Catch him tomorrow morning on his way there. Or at lunch."

I wave it off. "No, he definitely won't like that. We need peace and time to talk everything through, that's not something you can just squeeze in on the side."

Alex wrinkles her nose. She knows how right I am. "That sounds logical. You have to meet him in his free time."

"Exactly, but where is he?" By now the heat in my face is spreading through my whole body. It teams up with my nervousness, and still I know the answer immediately. "Anna. I bet he's holed up at her place."

All at once I feel relieved. I'm sure I'll find him. I just have to think about what I'm going to say to him. In what order and how.

"Then everything's clear," Alex says happily, and I'm happy with her.

"I'll drive over to Anna's place this evening," I say, and already my thoughts are whirling wildly around the upcoming meeting.

It has to be perfect.

So perfect that he has no choice but to give the two of us another chance. Everything will turn out for the better, and my block with photography will dissolve into thin air as well.

Hours later I'm standing nervously in the exposed stairwell in front of Anna's door, trying to breathe. Every single step up to this point was torture, but I held out. Now doubts are crashing over me. My fear of what might come next is far too great.

What will happen when I press the doorbell in a moment? Will it be a new beginning? Or just another ending?

No. I can't do this. If Lukas is here and rejects me, our love would be irretrievably over.

Hasn't he already done that anyway? My message is still unanswered. He's giving me the silent treatment, ignoring me and punishing me. Why should he want to talk to me today? Just because I'm standing right in front of him and he can't push me aside so easily?

Full of doubt, I let my hand sink before it reaches the doorbell. This doesn't make any sense. Nothing makes sense anymore. I want to leave, to run away to the other end of the world. Yet I'm still standing here, unchanged, as if my body had stopped obeying me.

All of a sudden I hear footsteps on the other side of the door. They're coming toward me. It could be Lukas. Maybe he heard my heavy breathing or the restless twitching of my legs and is, right this moment, looking at me through the peephole into the stairwell.

He sees me.

Everything stays still. Nobody moves, not even the world seems to be turning anymore. From my little toes to the tips of my hair, I'm frozen in shock. Even my thoughts are on ice; they can't even circle around anymore.

The door handle moves. In slow motion, the metallic lever tilts down. My heart races. It's pounding so loud and hard in my chest that there's one thing I know for sure.

He can hear it. Every single beat.

What about his heart? Is it calling out to me? Is it pushing him to yank the door open, pull me into his arms, and never let me go again? Or is it warning him to leave it alone? Not to invite me in at all. Into Anna's apartment. And into his life.

The door opens. He knows I'm waiting on the other side, and he still does it. The gap between us grows wider. That's a good sign. All at once, my tension eases. I exhale. He's giving us a chance. I swallow, wipe my damp palms on my dress, and try to smile. That's how I wait until I finally see him.

But it isn't him who appears in the crack of the door.

Anna's wild mane of hair is the first thing I recognize. Then her face, looking at me questioningly. Her perfectly trained body is wrapped in skimpy workout clothes, beads of sweat glittering on her forehead.

What kind of sight must I be, standing here and gasping like I've just run a marathon?

I clear my throat. Breathe out. Open my mouth and close it again. "Hi, Anna," I finally manage.

"Marie? What are you doing here?" she asks me, obviously confused. She folds her arms across her chest and positions herself in the doorway, as if she wanted to block the entrance to her apartment, flashes through my mind, even though that's absolute nonsense.

"Um… so…" The words refuse to take shape, but I can feel how the disappointment forces its way straight into my chest. It hurts. Everywhere. "I want to see Lukas. Is he here?"

Pity is reflected in her eyes, maybe even a touch of helplessness. "I'm sorry," she says with a shrug.

I should go. Say thank you, turn around, and take the

stairs back down. But I don't. Instead, I just stand here as if I didn't know anything anymore.

All at once Anna takes a step toward me and strokes my upper arm encouragingly. "Do you want to come in?" she asks in the tone of a caring mother.

Anna and I, we're not friends. We're more like acquaintances. All these years we've hardly ever done anything all three of us together, and at parties we never really ended up having a proper conversation. Maybe because I was always a little jealous of her. Of her toned body, her symmetrical face, and those great, sweeping lashes. Around her I felt small and unattractive. Still, I'm glad I have her now. I nod and pull up the corners of my mouth as best I can. "I'd like that."

Carefully, I walk down the narrow hallway and follow her into the room that seems to be living room, kitchen, and dining room all at once. It's small and not particularly cozy. The furnishings are functional, but at least bathed in airy, light colors. An impressive collection of those diet protein powder tubs is stacked up in the kitchen. Pictures hang on the walls showing Anna with a beaming smile. In one she's riding a desert camel. In another she's hanging in a climbing harness in the middle of a waterfall. No matter where I look, she's always in motion; there's always something going on with her.

"Lemon water for you too?" Anna's voice pulls me out of my thoughts. I search for her with my eyes and find her standing by the kitchen counter.

I don't like water, but I nod anyway. "Yes, please, thank you."

"Sure," is all she says, and opens the fridge. Next to the lemon juice and heaps of vegetables, I discover a stash of Lukas's favorite beer.

As if she didn't notice how the thought of Lukas gradually makes me collapse in on myself, Anna steers me toward the bright sofa and signals for me to sit down. She herself sits cross-legged on a dark mat on the floor and rests her hands on her knees.

"Okay, then tell me." Her body moves sinuously in every direction while her eyes watch me closely. Not curious and not accusatory, just completely neutral.

Lukas has definitely told her the reason for our temporary break in contact, and still she isn't biased. She seems like a really nice person, and by now I honestly don't know why we never became friends.

I clear my throat. "Like I said, I'm looking for Lukas. You know where he is, right?" The words leave my mouth awkwardly.

"Right now he's still at work. He mentioned something about a special assignment. I guess he has to impress his new boss or something." She stretches her arms up, spreads her fingers, and gives me a crooked grin.

"Do you also know how I can reach him? Where is he living?" Yes, I sound helpless, but I don't care. It's far too important to take a step forward.

"Up to now, exactly where you're sitting." Anna points at the worn-out sofa.

I can't help but smile. I'm relieved, even though knowing where to find him doesn't actually mean anything yet. "I see."

"Can I give you a piece of advice?" Anna asks suddenly. She sounds cautious, almost as if she's afraid of breaking something. She even pauses her workout for a moment to look me deep in the eyes. "I can see how bad you're doing. You're sad and hurt. A breakup like this is very hard."

"For him too?" That's the crucial question. Anna knows

the answer, I'm sure of it. Those two never kept secrets from each other.

She reaches for her lemon water. "Sure. You two were a couple for a long time, nobody can forget that so quickly."

There's nothing in this world I want more than for her to be right about that. "So you think we still have a chance?" I dare to ask. I don't want to open up to her like this, and yet right now she's my best option. Seeking help, I look into Anna's light-blue eyes.

She hesitates, I can see it clearly. Why is she doing that? She doesn't want to tell me the cruel truth. To keep me from breaking down here, right in the middle of her sofa, and never going home again.

"Anna, what do you think?" I ask again, because I just have to know.

"You can never really predict what'll happen in life, I think," she answers cautiously, pursing her lips. Her gaze flicks up to the ceiling for a moment, as if she had to think hard about something. Then she squats down, tucks her head between her upper arms, and lifts her legs off the floor. "So yes, I think there might still be a chance."

Which heaven do I have to beg, where do I have to plead, and whom am I allowed to implore, just so she'll be right? "Do you really think so?"

"Sure." She finishes her exercise and moves on to the next one, as if there were nothing more to say about it.

A thought hits me at once. There's something she can do for me. "I want to ask your advice." My words sound like pure pleading. "You and Lukas, you two have known each other for so long. Please, give me a tip. How do I win him back?" I ask, because I obviously don't know anymore myself.

For a moment she looks as if I'd asked her how I could

quietly bump off my own mother. Then she gives the slightest shake of her head, pushes herself up from her mat, stands up straight, and tenses her muscles.

"You really hurt him," she says, dropping into a deep squat. "Give him a bit of time. I think he needs to calm down first so he can see things clearly again. Don't pressure him, don't bombard him with calls or messages. Give him some space." She's still holding the skier's squat, her muscles not even trembling. "That would be my advice."

That sounds logical. Very logical, in fact. Still, doubts immediately stir inside me. "But how is he supposed to know that there's nothing I want more than to be with him again?"

Anna comes out of her position and strides off toward the kitchen in long lunges. It's as if she can't sit still for a single second. Is it because she wants to be burning calories all the time? "Here's what we'll do: I'll tell him about our conversation. About what you want and about the advice I gave you. That way he'll know, and he'll come to you when he's ready. How does that sound?"

Suddenly I no longer understand at all why Anna never became a friend to me all these years. If we had just had one real conversation, I would have taken her into my heart much sooner. "Thank you, Anna. Thank you so, so much!" Relief brings tears to my eyes and I let them find their way down my cheeks. Because where everything was still dark a few hours ago, a small fire is burning now. It's far away and barely visible, but it's there. And when I close my eyes, I can almost feel its warmth in my chest.

"You're welcome." Anna comes over to me, pulls me into a loving hug, and strokes my back. She's sweaty, but I don't care. She holds me very tightly, and in that moment I know that with her by my side I can make it.

When I pull away from her, I notice how she steals a glance at the big clock on the wall above the TV.

"I've kept you long enough." I push myself up quickly from the sofa.

"I'm on the breakfast shift tomorrow. Unfortunately," she says with an apologetic look. She reaches for my hand once more and squeezes it. "It'll be okay. You just need a little patience."

I nod, because I want to be just as positive as she is. Anna walks me to the door. I'm not floating and I'm not skipping. I don't feel good and certainly not relieved. I'm just a tiny bit more hopeful when I say goodbye. Then I leave the apartment and step out into the dusk of the approaching night.

Chapter Twelve

Accompanied by a long yawn, I stick the key in the lock and turn it carefully. Today is the fifth day that after work I don't go to my old home but to Anna's place instead, and it still feels strange. I can hardly describe how exactly. Dejected. Tired. Muted. Maybe because of Marie, maybe not. My new boss could just as well be to blame, the way he makes every minute at work a living hell. Not only did he get the position I applied for. No, he's also the managing director's nephew and therefore absolutely untouchable.

With a sigh, I slip off my shoes, then wait a moment. I don't really know why, but something in me wants to be alone a little longer. So I lean against the white-painted hallway wall and close my eyes.

I just want to breathe. Not to think and not to feel anything. Slowly I draw air in through my nose.

It smells like peach.

Confused, I tear my eyes open. Is that really necessary? Can't my longing be quiet for once? It definitely doesn't smell like peach in here, that much is clear. I quickly shake my head and make sure to head into the living room, even though I suspect I won't be safe from myself there either.

"Hi, darling." Anna is standing in the kitchen in a baggy tracksuit and turns her head in my direction. Her smile is warm and heartfelt. She's happy to see me, and that in turn makes me smile. "How was your day?" she asks, even though she's definitely noticed my slumped shoulders and exhausted expression.

I let myself fall onto the sofa, the delicate scent of freshly washed pillowcases creeping into my nose. "Pretty good." That's a lie, but what else am I supposed to say? There's nothing we haven't already gone over a thousand times. And talking about it didn't help. On the contrary, it only made everything worse. "Did you have company?" I hear myself ask, as if I didn't have a will of my own. As if part of me hoped I hadn't just imagined the smell of peach.

Anna takes one of the big pots out of the cupboard and fills it with water. "No, I just got home myself," she says with a shrug. "I'm going to cook something great for us, how does that sound?"

I wave it off. "No need, I'll eat whatever's there." Because I don't care anyway; everything tastes the same to me.

With the wooden spoon in her hand, Anna suddenly gives me a stern look. "You're definitely not going to do that." A mischievous grin flashes across her face. "You're going to rest for a bit while I work my magic in here. And then you're going to eat, understood?" Her lovingly serious tone is exactly what I need.

I hold up my hands defensively and can't suppress a smirk. "Before I end up in the pot myself…"

While I only hear Anna switching on the extractor fan and clattering pots, I grab the weekly planner and sink deeper into the sofa. My eyes want to close, but I don't let that happen. They have to stay open so my mind can work. I go through the upcoming appointments for the next few days. I cross out everything that has to do with Marie or the apartment. For good.

So I don't have to deal with the dark feeling rising up inside me, I watch Anna cooking. She loves me, flashes through my mind, as it so often does. My best friend wants to be more than that to me. Four nights have passed since her confession, and I wonder how long she'll keep waiting. Not once has she tried to get closer to me. She has kept her promise, hasn't pressured me, and hasn't asked again. Of course not, Anna wouldn't do something like that.

Maybe that alone is why a wave of affection washes over me now. This woman has only one goal: to see me happy.

Anna is amazing. She would never hurt me the way Marie did.

On impulse, I push myself up from the sofa and walk over to her in the kitchen. Because I want to feel what happens when I'm close to her. I have to know what my heart says, even if it only whispers softly.

"Hey, you're supposed to be resting." Anna brushes a curl from her forehead and purses her lips into a pout.

I only shrug. Right now I can't answer, because I'm busy studying every inch of her face. And feeling what happens when I imagine kissing her.

Am I staring at her? Maybe. Am I fixating on her lips? Absolutely.

Anna's eyebrows knit together at once. "Um…" Nervously, she wipes her hands on the green-patterned dish towel, her gaze dropping to the old-fashioned gray-marbled kitchen counter. Then she awkwardly grabs a spoon and dips it into the sauce simmering on the stove in front of her. "Try it," she tells me.

Obediently I open my mouth and let her feed me. Warm, creamy, and with an indescribably intense flavor, the sauce spreads across my palate. "This is insane." I don't take my eyes off her for a second, and the longer I do it, the more insecure she becomes. Red blotches appear on her cheeks, her breathing turns uneven. I've never seen her like this before.

Yeah, she looks damn cute, standing in front of me like this. Should I just do it? Should I give us both a chance to find out whether this has a future?

Carefully, I move a little closer to her. "I have to warn you, you shouldn't spoil me like this, or one day you'll never get rid of me again."

"Maybe that's exactly my devious plan." With a single step she's right in front of me and puts her hands on my shoulders. "Besides, darling, someone has to make sure you're eating properly. Anything else is something a trained chef like me absolutely can't take responsibility for, you must realize that." She smiles, her eyes searching for something in my gaze, and maybe they even find it.

"Thanks. You're the best." A wave of affection sweeps through my body and crashes over me. It carries me along and makes me wrap my arms around her hips.

She doesn't answer, just nods as if in a trance. Nothing else moves, only her head, and I suddenly feel frozen too. Because I'm trying to imagine how this is supposed to go on. It would be so easy to kiss her, to bury my hands in her hair and feel her close to me. It could happen. And who knows, if I wished for it hard enough, maybe I'd even forget all the things that torment me.

"That's enough now, darling," Anna suddenly says with

mock seriousness. Her doll-like eyes fix on me. "Stop staring at me like that. It's like Big Brother in here."

Before I understand what's happening, she slips out of my embrace. Instantly I feel a little colder, but that only makes me feel one thing all the more clearly.

I want to have her close to me again. I want to feel safe, I long for closeness.

Still, I turn away from Anna. Because I don't know whether it's nothing but pure selfishness. A way to cover up the wounds Marie left behind, the kind I could have with any other woman too. Or whether there are actually romantic feelings for Anna behind my desire to pull her straight back into my arms.

I have to figure that out first. Because I'm only allowed to kiss her if I'm absolutely sure I want to be with her. Anything else would be unfair to my very best friend.

Chapter Thirteen

Have they talked to each other yet?

How many times have I watched the sun set by now and nothing has happened? Ten days have passed since our fight, five days since Anna promised to help me. I haven't had a single sign of life from Lukas so far. Nothing. It's as if I no longer exist for him. As if there were a big dark hole where our love used to be.

It has grown quiet in the apartment, too. It lies before me, dark and cold. Because no matter how brightly the August sun shines outside in the sky, in here everything revolves around one single thing. Lukas is gone. Maybe even for good.

As so often, I wander through our apartment and find memories of him in every corner. There's the half-empty wardrobe in the bedroom. All his winter clothes are still there. I let my fingers wander over the thickly padded jacket with the olive-green stripes and bury my nose in the fleece-lined neck. I can't even smell him anymore; too much time has passed since he wore this jacket.

With a sigh I turn away and slide the wardrobe door shut so I don't have to see the gaping gap inside it any longer. In the bathroom, his half of the shelf under the mirror is empty. Only the thin lime marks on the glass surface are still visible. Carefully I let my fingers glide over the spot where the cup with his toothbrush used to stand. Cleaning the surface of these traces is out of the question. If I did, Lukas would disappear from this apartment for good. So the place stays as it is. As if, just like me, it were also waiting for Lukas to come back.

Just like shortly after I quit my job in the spring, black and gray clouds gather threateningly close together in my thoughts. I know I can't let that happen. And there's only one way to manage that.

I have to get away from here. And focus on what, apart from Lukas, still makes me happy. So I pack my camera and trundle into the city center on the tram.

Once there, I wander aimlessly through the alleys. I have no idea what I'm looking for; I can only hope I'll know it when I see it.

At the edge of the city park, I spot an elderly couple. They're sitting close together on a weathered wooden bench. The man is wearing one of those old-fashioned hats. In the shadow of the brim I make out his brilliantly bright eyes. He looks as if he'd spent his whole life laughing.

In that moment he lovingly puts his arm around his wife. She lets her head drop onto his shoulder. In her face I see a kind of contentment that brings tears to my eyes. That's how we wanted to be. Lukas and I.

At once I see Lukas's youthful face before me, feel how he brushes a strand of hair behind my ear, and hear his words. "Let's grow old and gray together," he whispers lovingly, and all I can do is nod. Because that idea sends a warmth through my body all the way down to my toes. Nothing, absolutely nothing in this world could be more beautiful than that.

And yet today I'm standing here alone, surrounded by passersby who, thankfully, don't notice how I stand rigid with grief in the middle of the green park, silently crying inside.

If only Lukas could see how the elderly couple are quietly giggling together, as if they were teenagers plotting something. Then he'd understand too that we must not give up on our love.

Without thinking about it, I rummage the camera out of my bag and look at the two of them on the bench through the lens. She looks up at him, smiles, and raises her hand to stroke his cheek. At that exact moment I press the shutter, and right after that, once more.

I capture their love in pictures.

A feeling as intense as the sound of a full symphony orchestra spreads in my chest. From there it travels into my stomach, makes my arms tingle, and quickens my breathing. Not for the first time I feel very clearly that photography is right for me. Even though I don't know how I can manage to make a living from this passion, I still have to try. For my sake. For the sake of my later, which becomes my now whenever I press my camera's shutter.

All at once the elderly couple separate, he pushes himself up from the bench and offers her his arm for support. With a grateful nod she takes it and clumsily gets to her feet. For a moment she looks as if her legs can't carry her. But there he is, there for her, even though his body is clearly tired too. I keep capturing the scene with my camera without a break, thrilled by the atmosphere and swept up in the feelings the two have for each other, which are so plainly visible. Even when they turn and stroll away down the birch-lined path, I go on taking pictures as if in a trance. Entwined with each other, they amble along beside the other people who are marching briskly down the gravel paths. They pass dogs, businesswomen, and kindergarten children standing together in groups. When they reach the end of the park, they disappear from my line of sight.

Thoughtfully, I lower the camera. Even though I haven't seen the pictures yet, I can feel they're going to be something special. I recognize it by this feeling that rises up in me when I'm taking photos. This certainty that everything is just right. As I slowly come back to myself from my dream-like state, it occurs to me that I should have asked the elderly couple for permission to take their pictures. So I run after them. I turn into the same alley they went down before, but I can't find them anywhere.

Could they be in one of the shops? I look around and spot a jewelry store not even two meters in front of me. It feels a bit strange, but I still peer through the display window inside.

They're not in there. I should keep looking, but my gaze gets caught on the rings in the display. There's one with a slim silver band. Its elongated, sun-yellow stone is framed by tiny diamonds. They sparkle like stars. I have to swallow, and at the same time I can't look away. The ring doesn't just look like my engagement ring, it's exactly the same one.

Did Lukas buy it here? Or is it actually my ring that he returned?

It's a really stupid idea, but I go into the small shop anyway. Because there's one thing I want more than anything. I need to have the ring with me one more time, just once more I want to feel, even for a moment, what it's like to be engaged to Lukas.

In awe, I look around; everything is glittering and sparkling, a hint of luxury hangs in the air. With careful steps I walk over to the friendly salesman with the graying hair and ask him for this one favor that means the world to me.

Just a few minutes later he's holding the ring with the sun-yellow stone in his hands. Nestled on a cushion covered in light velvet, it's right in front of me, sparkling up at me.

"Would it be okay if I took a picture of the ring?" I ask in a choked voice.

He gives me a gentle smile; he probably sees this all the time. "Of course. Take your time," he adds, as if he can see exactly that I need it.

I feel the pain everywhere in my body. My insides clench so tightly that they're nothing but a single boulder. Still, I take the camera out of my bag and photograph the ring from every angle.

Then I carefully lift it out of its cushion. I must be crazy or an unbelievably stupid sadist, but I can't help slipping it onto my finger. Slowly the cold band glides over my skin until the ring sits perfectly, exactly where it's supposed to be.

I stretch out my fingers, spellbound by the sparkle of the diamonds and the perfect shape of the yellow stone that nestles against my skin as naturally as if it had been made just for me.

All at once I'm absolutely certain: this is how it has to be again.

With every other version of my future, I'll only be half as happy.

I take more pictures, place my hand on different surfaces and finally against my chest. I'll have to see later whether the photos turned out well, but my gut tells me that I need them as a keepsake, no matter what.

"Do you want to have it?" the salesman suddenly asks, cutting right through my thoughts.

With a sad smile, I look up at him. "I already had it," I say, and immediately find myself staring into an uncomprehending face. "It got lost, but I'm going to find it again." Even though it hurts, I slide the ring off my finger and hand it to the salesman. "Thank you for letting me try it on."

"You're welcome." That's not what he's thinking, I can see it clearly. Shaking his head, he tucks the piece of jewelry back into its cushion and puts it back in its place in the display.

With the camera in my hand and a strangely queasy feeling in my stomach, I leave the shop. I keep wandering along the streets and everywhere I go I discover memories of my time with Lukas. I photograph the ice-cream parlor where we met for our first real date, walk on to the club where we first met, and finally even take the tram out to Schönbrunn Palace, to our meadow of flowers behind the Gloriette. It hasn't grown nearly as tall as it was back then, but I lie down in the grass anyway. Just like five years ago, I hold the camera up high and snap away wildly. I take pictures of myself, and even though Lukas is missing from the images, I pretend he's here.

Am I crazy? Maybe.

Still, I can't help it. I want to live the memory, because it's all I have right now.

As I go through the day's collected photos right afterward, I find myself smiling more often than I have in a long time.

They turned out great. Every single one of them is like a little piece of proof: photography and I, we belong together.

And yet this shadow is still hanging over me. It asks me

what I'll do if Lukas doesn't get in touch. How much time I should let pass and how much space he'll need to breathe.

How much longer can my life even go on like this?

Lost in thought, I look at our flower meadow. Two weeks ago I thought I knew everything and could see my path clearly ahead of me. Now my future seems more uncertain than ever before.

I want to take photos, but so far I haven't had any success to show for it. On the contrary, up to today I've only spent money on equipment that I don't really have. My dream of traveling the world suddenly makes no sense without Lukas. And as if all that weren't bad enough, I'll only be able to pay the rent for the apartment for one more month.

Nothing is right anymore, nothing fits together.

Thoughtfully, I pluck blades of grass from the meadow and peel them apart layer by layer. Suddenly I think of the stranger at the water park who has given me so many words of wisdom over the past few months.

If he were here, what would he advise me to do?

"Dreams don't just come true, you have to make them come true." Yes, that's what he'd say. Then he'd look deep into my eyes and I'd feel how right he is.

But even if he's only with me in my thoughts, I know I have to keep fighting. Being happy is a decision, and it's up to me alone to make it.

That's what I'm doing, here and now. I'll stand up for everything that matters to me in this world and I won't give up until I've achieved my goals.

Every day, be as happy as possible. Tell stories with photos that move other people. Dream together with Lukas again.

Those were the three wishes I tied to balloons and let fly

a few weeks ago. Together with Grandma, I watched them on their way to the sky and promised myself I'd make them come true.

There has to be at least one thing I can get under control. At least one part of my life could go on, even if the other one stands still.

The apartment. That's where I'll start. Even though I don't even want to imagine that Lukas won't come back to me, I at least have to make provisions in case he doesn't.

Luckily, the solution to this problem is simple. I'm sure I'll find shelter with Grandma. Like before, we'll have breakfast together, take care of the animals, and bake her unique apple strudels that are filled to bursting. Grandma wants company, and I like being around her. It would be the perfect solution, for her and for me.

In my mind, I put a check mark next to the apartment problem and turn back to my professional plans. I think hard.

What about traveling? I'll probably have to put that on the back burner until I've established myself enough as a photographer to afford it. Or maybe just until I have a few regular clients as a virtual assistant—if anyone ever shows any interest in my services at all. And also until Lukas is by my side again. Because conquering the world without him makes no sense.

And photography? Alex did recommend that I take a course. But wouldn't it be better to work directly for a photographer? While I'm working, I'd learn from a pro and even earn money doing it. On the side, I'll try to land photo jobs. Before long, my money worries could be solved and at the same time I'll be doing what I love.

This isn't how I imagined a "later," but at least it's a start.

I still have to find a solution for Lukas. I have no idea what it will look like, but I can feel that that will work out too. Anna promised to help me. I just have to be a little patient, then everything will be okay again. Because for the story of my life there's only one possible ending. Lukas and I conquer the world together. I capture our memories in pictures and, even though we're constantly on the move, we still have the secure feeling of having arrived.

That's it. That's what I'm going to fight for from now on. I push myself up with new determination and brush the grass from my jeans as if it were the last remnant of my darkness that I finally want to get rid of. With an excited flutter in my stomach and tears of longing in the corners of my eyes, I leave our flower meadow.

This is it. I'm setting off into my new future.

Chapter Fourteen

"Do you need anything else before I disappear to work?" I hear Anna call from the hallway.

I look up from my laptop, which I set up on the kitchen table a few minutes ago. By now she has appeared in the doorway. I don't miss her worried look, but I ignore it. "No thanks, I'm fine," I answer and give her a smile.

She doesn't like that I'm working overtime on a Saturday evening. I still have to do it. Not just because otherwise I'd probably already be getting wasted at Joe's again. No, I need the money, because the costs for the house are breathing down my neck.

The house Marie and I were supposed to move into in November and start a family in soon after. The house that's currently being renovated for a couple in love that, in truth, no longer exists.

Could Anna and I live there? I don't know. Just like I don't seem to know anything anymore.

"You don't look as if everything's all right, darling."

Anna furrows her brow, tilts her head to the side, and studies me searchingly.

I know that all this work doesn't make me any more attractive. The dark circles under my eyes are deeper than ever before, and the other day I noticed how pale my complexion is. Even the first gray hairs have suddenly appeared at my temples, where there never used to be any.

Still, I wave it off. "I'm just a little tired. That's all." As if to prove it, I yawn broadly. "There's not much left to do anyway."

She doesn't believe a word I say, I can see it clearly. Once more she comes back to me and lays her hand on my shoulder. Then she crouches down in front of me and forces me to look at her. "You know I'm here for you," she says seriously. "Anytime. Whatever you need. Tell me about it and I'll do everything I can to help you."

When she looks at me like that, I can't help it. I want to hug her, so tightly it's as if I never intend to let her go again. Because she alone is the one who keeps me grounded. Without her I would fall apart, I'm sure of it. So I pull her toward me and bury my face in the bony spot at her collarbone. "Thank you, Anna. You're amazing. I keep forgetting to tell you that. Thank you!"

In that moment something happens to me, and it feels far too good not to savor it. Her closeness is the only thing that really does me good right now. I want more of it. My lips brush her shoulder and slowly feel their way toward her neck. All on their own, without any conscious decision from me, they reach her chin, her cheeks, then her forehead and nose before I open my eyes again. I'm looking straight into the light blue of her eyes.

There I find longing. But also uncertainty. Gently, I

touch the tip of her nose with mine and give her a grateful smile.

She chews shyly on her lips.

I should just do it. It would be like taking a look into a possible future and finding out how it feels.

Right now I don't want to think about it any longer. So I take her hands and pull her so close that I can feel her warmth everywhere. Then I do what I would never have thought possible just a week ago. My hands glide up along her arms to her shoulders, then over her neck. I touch her pink-tinged cheeks and draw her head closer to mine.

Anna's lips tremble, and probably mine do too.

Am I doing this because I truly want to? Or only because I hope it will save me? Am I about to kiss my best friend so I don't lose her as well, or because I have real, romantic feelings for her?

Whatever the truth is, it no longer matters. Marie is gone. Anna is here. I can make her happy. And me? All I want is a single moment in which I feel only what could be and, in doing so, forget what was.

One last time I look into Anna's eyes before I close mine and kiss her gently.

As carefully as if she were afraid of making a mistake, she returns my kiss. I notice the trembling of her hands as they stroke down my back. Our closeness feels strange, so unfamiliar and at the same time thrillingly new.

Her fingers flutter on to my chest and finally push me away from her. A wistful sigh leaves her mouth. "I hate to interrupt you…" she suddenly says in anguish, lowering her gaze.

Something's wrong here. All at once she's holding me at arm's length, when things between us had just become so fascinatingly different. Uncertain, I watch her expression. It seems closed off. "Is something wrong?" I dare to ask.

At least her gentle smile calms me. She puts her finger on my cheek and traces the outline of my jaw. "No, it's amazing. And beautiful. But…"

"But?" I ask, confused, and kiss her fingertips.

"I don't know where to start." Her hand wanders over my head and comes to rest at the nape of my neck.

She makes me nervous. Absolutely. Still, I have to know what's suddenly going on with her. "Just tell me."

"Okay." She takes a deep breath again, then fixes me with an intense look. "Tell me what this is. With us, I mean. What am I to you, what do you see in me? Are we friends with benefits? Or…?"

She doesn't get any further. She doesn't dare say out loud what has been haunting my mind too ever since our night together two weeks ago. Day after day I ask myself the same question. She's right, it's time I settled on an answer. I want to do it—no, I have to do it. So that my life can move on.

For a moment I listen to my own feelings. I actually find words that feel right. "First of all, you're the dearest person in my life." I kiss her forehead. "And I enjoy every moment with you." My lips brush her eyebrows. "When I come home in the evening, you're there, and I like that." I let the tip of my nose glide along her cheeks. "Spending time with you feels right." Now I look deep into her eyes.

That's the truth, and we both feel it. But is it more than friendship?

I notice the trembling spreading through her body. Tiny little tears form in the corners of her eyes, giving the sparkle in her gaze even more shine. Joy and relief appear on her face, so clearly that my own heart grows warm.

There is someone who loves me. A woman who appreciates that I'm here and who would walk through any fire with me.

I dare to move closer to her and press my lips to hers. We kiss passionately and tenderly at the same time, because it just has to be. Anna's closeness doesn't make me fly, my heart keeps beating steadily in the same rhythm. Still, I feel a deep affection, like a gentle glow in my chest.

Minutes later she pulls away from me, out of breath, and smiles at me. Then she gets up with a conspiratorial expression and walks over to the sofa. She takes my pillow, presses it tightly against her chest, and carries it into her bedroom.

I follow her and see how she pushes her own pillow aside to make room for mine.

"Weren't you going to work?" I ask her with a crooked grin and lean against the doorframe.

With smooth, fluid movements she comes toward me. "All of a sudden I feel sick. I'm hot, I must have a fever." She opens the buttons of her baggy shirt, revealing her cleavage a few centimeters at a time. "Feel."

She guides my hand to her breast. I can feel her heart pounding far too clearly, as if it wanted to gallop away. "It's clear," I whisper, overwhelmed by what's happening here right now. "You belong in bed."

Now I'm the one who opens her shirt further. And with every movement of my hands I forget my inner conflict a little more, until there's only one thing I know for sure: Anna is my future.

Hours later I wake from a light doze. The streetlights outside brighten the bedroom just enough for me to make out Anna's outline. I let my gaze wander over her naked hips, then farther up to the dark curls that fall gently onto her toned shoulder. Carefully I raise my hand and brush her hair back.

"Hey, my love," she murmurs. Her voice is soft, she stretches contentedly and snuggles a little closer to me.

I can hardly resist the weight of my eyelids and close my eyes. That way I feel even more intensely how Anna's warm skin presses against mine. Her closeness still feels unfamiliar, but that will pass with time.

"Well, sleepyhead?" Her fingers tap quickly across my chest and then farther down. She's wide awake, and in an instant I am too.

"I don't see any sleepyhead here," I say without opening my eyes, and reach for her hand to stop her.

She immediately stops whatever she was about to do and nestles her head into the little triangle between my upper arm and my chest.

"Well, if that's how it is, I can finally tell you about last night."

"Are you worried I won't remember it anymore?" Amused, I rest my cheek on the crown of her head.

She bites my collarbone gently. "Honestly, I don't understand where you get these dirty thoughts from. I just wanted to tell you about a completely innocent dream I had."

"All right then, let's hear it," I prompt her, my eyes still closed.

Her fingers start playing with the fine hairs on my chest. "There was a dazzling white beach, deep blue sky, and crystal-clear sea. Just the two of us in a hammock under a palm tree. Someone serving us cocktails and fruit…"

"Mmm… go on, that sounds wonderful."

Suddenly she sits up, and I can feel her hot breath on my chest. "We're bathing in the warm, salty water, watching colorful fish and enjoying the tingling of the evening sun on our skin."

"That's exactly my thing," I say, because I want to keep on dreaming a little longer myself.

"I figured as much." She covers my upper body with countless tiny kisses, all of them so gentle it's as if butterflies keep taking off and landing on my skin.

Carefully I pull her up and open my eyes. By now the dream is over, and we both know it. "It won't work."

Not just because I'm afraid of flying. My weekly planner is full of appointments. Besides, I don't have the money for a vacation, and there's no way Anna is going to sacrifice her savings for me. She would do it, I'm sure of that, but I definitely won't accept it.

With a disappointed expression, she lowers her gaze. "I know that. But that doesn't mean we can't at least go on a short trip."

The way she's looking at me makes it hard to disagree. "That sounds lovely. I just have to see if I can get time off," I say, even though I'm not sure I really want to. Right on cue, a bad conscience spreads in my stomach. I'm in debt; I can't just go and spend money on a vacation.

Anna doesn't seem to notice the battle raging inside me. With a contented sigh, she lets herself fall onto the bed beside me. "Wonderful." Her dreamy expression tells me that in her mind she's already far away. Somewhere, wherever we're going to go together.

My thoughts suddenly start to drift too. I know my life can't stay the way it has been these past few weeks. It has to get easier again, and my decision in favor of Anna was the first right step. If I free myself from more dead weight, I might be able to breathe again. Just as I'm slowly building something up with Anna, I can also get my finances back in order.

Does anyone even need the house anymore?

How could I ever go back there without thinking of Marie? Of her bright, sunny smile, the scent of her skin, and the feeling my heartbeat leaves in my chest when she only looks at me. Of that very special light that surrounds us when the two of us are together, sealed off from the rest of the world as if in a bubble.

But wouldn't selling the house also put the stamp of finality on our breakup?

Stop. These thoughts have no place in my head anymore. I've just now definitively closed the chapter on Marie. It's decided.

But no matter how hard I try and how urgently I lecture myself, I can't stop what's happening to me. Suddenly it turns completely dark inside me as I lie here in the moonlight, Anna in my arms and my thoughts with Marie.

We wanted to be happy together forever. We dreamed of enjoying life to the fullest together and loving each other as if there were nothing more important in this world.

What on earth happened to us? And how could we let it happen?

Not once in the two weeks since our argument has Marie gotten in touch with me. Is there any clearer sign of how little I mean to her?

Hardly.

I'm going to put a stop to this once and for all. I won't allow myself to think about Marie any longer. I have to bury the memories and all the feelings under a protective layer. And trust that, with time, it will become hard enough for me to forget Marie for good.

Chapter Fifteen

The owner of Photo Paradise peers at me critically over the rim of his glasses. "Do you have any experience as a photography assistant?"

Of course he asks that. Everyone does. And no one wants to hear the answer. Tense, I lift my shoulders. "I learn quickly," I say, putting on my brightest smile.

My effort has an effect. Even though he doesn't comment on it, I can tell from the smile playing on his lips how much he liked what I said. The corners of his mouth tilt upward as he turns back to my résumé.

So I'm still allowed to hope, as long as I keep sitting on the hard chair and waiting for his verdict. To distract myself, I look at the many pictures on the wall. I really like the colorful mix of faces, landscapes, and everyday scenes. Even a layperson like me can see how good the photos are. I could learn so much from the somewhat grumpy man with the receding hairline who is sitting across from me, leafing attentively through my documents.

He just has to hire me. This would be the perfect start to

my life as a photographer. And I need the money more than desperately.

Nervously, I wipe my hands on my cotton dress. Should I add something else? "If you give me a chance …"

He immediately raises his hand. "I'm sure of that."

I nod and probably look terribly stupid while I do it. But what else was I supposed to do?

The minutes in which no one says anything pass as slowly as honey. Then, finally, he looks at me again. "All right, Ms. Berger, thank you very much for coming by. I really liked your photos." A smile flashes across his face. That's a good sign.

"It was great meeting you." I sound giddy, but I can't stop the anticipation that's currently spreading inside me. "Being allowed to start here would be an absolute dream."

"You'll hear from me by the end of the week." His smile is promising.

We say goodbye to each other and I do my best once again to leave a friendly and motivated impression. My ambitious expression has an effect; he likes me, I can see that clearly.

As soon as I leave his office, all the tension falls away from me. Even though I know it's nonsense, I send a quick prayer up to heaven. This just has to work out. It has to! The pay is lousy, but that would be fine for now, as long as I could land a few photo jobs or gigs as a virtual assistant on the side.

Striding quickly through the photo shop toward the exit, I rummage in my bag for my phone so I can tell Alex about the interview, just like I promised.

It's not there.

With growing panic, my hand flits between my wallet, pens, the little camera case, scraps of notes, and tissues.

Did I maybe put it on the table during the interview, after I'd shown my new boss a few of my pictures?

Of course. There's no other possibility. I turn around on the spot. The office door is wide open, so I step inside. "Excuse me," I say politely, then my whole body freezes in an instant.

Am I seeing this right? Did he really just throw my application documents into the trash can?

No. That can't be true!

The guilty look in his eyes is answer enough. I can barely hold back the tears that are surging into my eyes.

He doesn't want to hire me at all; he just put on an act. He shouldn't have done that, because in truth that makes him even worse than all the others before him. At least they didn't pretend to be interested and give me false hope.

"Yes?" he asks, raising his eyebrows.

I clear my throat with effort and point at his desk. "My phone." I don't say anything else. I just pick up my cell and turn to leave.

As fast as I can, I leave Photo Paradise. I have to get out of here; I can't stand having my failure right in front of my eyes any longer. This isn't the first time this has happened to me. Nobody wants me, even though I'd practically work for free.

Why? I give it my all, but it's never enough.

"Because you just don't have any talent," a voice suddenly whispers inside me. "You're not a photographer, get that through your head."

No, I don't want to hear that voice. It's not allowed to take my dreams away from me. I've already given too much for them; I even risked the love of my life.

I start walking as if I could shake off my self-doubt that

way. While I hurry down the street, I check my account balance. 1,500 euros, that's all I have left. The unemployment assistance I'll be downgraded to next month won't be enough. No matter how frugally I live, my financial cushion will disappear. I have to do something, or I'll be broke in four weeks.

"That's what you get," I hear my voice say, just as cynical as before. "What did you think? That the world has been waiting for you?"

"Giving up is not an option," I remind myself, to take away the power of the voice inside me.

My head has to stay clear and make good decisions. Besides, it's obviously time to activate the emergency plan.

I dial Grandma's number. Luckily she picks up right away and I can get straight to the point. After all, Grandma can probably already hear from my greeting how upset I am. "I need your help," I blurt out, still agitated from what happened at Photo Paradise.

"Of course, sweetheart." The warmth in her voice does me good. She's my rock and will never let me down. "What can I do?"

"I'm running out of money. Nobody wants to give me a job. I have to move out." The words leave my mouth in short, choppy bursts, and every single one of them hurts. They're proof that I can't get my life together. They also make my dream seem ridiculous, and the fact that I still want to hold on to it even more so. "Can I have my old room back?"

Grandma doesn't say anything. Why not? This answer can't be hard for her. Far too often in the years after I moved out she emphasized how much she missed us living together.

Although I don't even know why, I stop in the middle of

the street. Something's wrong here. "Grandma?" I ask carefully.

She clears her throat at length. "I'm sorry."

Excuse me? What does she mean? Why is she apologizing?

"Your room hasn't been free since yesterday. It was an emergency. I wanted to tell you about it today." Her voice sounds thin, and I know it tortures her to have to disappoint me. "Little Ludwig and his mother moved in with me. There was an ugly fight with Ludwig's father; the two of them had to get out of their house urgently. I thought…"

"I totally understand," I say quickly, because I can hardly bear how bad she feels right now. She wanted to help the two of them, and that can never be wrong. "You wanted some company, the young boy adores you, and he and his mother need a place to stay. It was a great idea."

"But…" comes her contrite voice from the other end of the line.

"Don't worry," I cut in quickly. Then I try to smile, just hoping that makes my voice sound a bit more cheerful. "I'll find another solution. Or I'll get a job soon after all. I can do this."

"If you really want something, you can achieve anything," I hear Grandma say, full of conviction. "Otherwise I'll help you out a bit financially too."

Definitely not. With her small pension she can barely make ends meet herself. "That's sweet of you, but I'm managing. Really." With every word my voice gets thinner, but I hold it together.

Grandma mustn't hear my despair. I don't want that. Now that she's finally able to again, she should be laughing. Because I don't even know what to think or what else I could say right now, I gather my strength one last time and say goodbye in a tone as if everything were perfectly fine.

Dejected, I let the phone slide back into my bag. I wish I were as convinced as I just pretended to my grandma. But I'm not. For almost three weeks I've done nothing but wait.

For work, any kind. And for Lukas.

This waiting is driving me crazy. I know I have to be patient, but for how much longer? Will anyone even hire me or book my services? And won't Lukas forget me rather than forgive me, the longer we don't see each other?

I need a place where I can think in peace. So I head in the direction of the water park.

I hadn't been here in over two months. Still, the moment I arrive, it's as if the surroundings suddenly come into sharp focus. Even though the sun is already weaker now that September has begun, it still has enough strength. Maybe it's the same with the love between Lukas and me, shoots through my mind as I stroll to the spot where I've already realized so many things. That's where I want to search for my path. It's there; I just have to find it. That's the only thought I'm allowing myself.

My spot by the lake is empty. No wonder, it's Wednesday lunchtime, most people are at work or taking care of their children. That's fine by me; the more peace and quiet I find here, the better I can think. With my gaze fixed on the picturesque surface of the water, I try to let go of my thoughts. Then I close my eyes.

Right on cue, the butterflies appear that have become my faithful companions over the past few weeks. Whatever happens, they're with me and never let me forget where my new heaven is waiting for me. Where they're fluttering off to now, I see Lukas and me. We're sitting here together by the lake, holding hands. I let my head sink onto his shoulder, he kisses the crown of my head.

"Do you see the swans over there?" he whispers.

I look around and spot them on the opposite shore. Silently, they drift on the water. The two of them seem so familiar with each other, as if they knew everything about one another and understood each other blindly.

"Once they've found each other, swans spend their whole lives together." His voice sounds wistful.

I move closer to him. "Just like us," I say, and I feel all over my body that this is the truth.

Even if I'm sitting here alone today, longing for Lukas to be close, it is and remains the only way. We have to find each other again. No matter how long it takes, I'll be strong.

Like a time-lapse, the months since my spontaneous resignation run before my eyes. Once more I feel the doubts and all the hatred. For myself and for the world. The weeks that were so dark I could no longer believe I would ever see light again.

I wanted to give up. To let myself fall and stay forever in that place where black and gray fought for dominance. But then so many magical things happened. Things I never would have thought possible.

That's how it will be with Lukas, too. Everything in life has its time, and our time will come again. That's what I have to believe in.

With a deep breath, I open my eyes and let my gaze wander. Across the line of trees on the opposite side of the lake, along the shore to the improvised jetty, and on to the path I took to get here.

Then I see him. All at once he's there, without warning and without announcement. The stranger who brought this magic into my life. The man I never wanted to see again just a few weeks ago.

I want to make up for that mistake, so I give him a friendly nod. He raises his hand and comes closer.

"Good afternoon," he says with stoic calm when he reaches me. "May I sit with you?"

I immediately make room for him. "Sure. It's great to see you."

"I've been waiting for you every day." There it is again, that warm voice I could just sink into. His deep blue eyes cast a spell on me.

I study him with interest. But there's no mischievous grin and no crinkling at the corners of his eyes to be seen. No hint of a smirk and no playful glimmer in his gaze. "Really? Every day?"

He lets himself sink down onto the grass beside me. "Have I ever lied to you?"

He hasn't. I shake my head.

"You see." As if that settled everything, he fixes me with a meaningful expression. "How are you?"

"Good." I smile at him automatically.

He doesn't accept that; I can see it in his face. "Many people ask each other exactly that question every day. And most of them aren't interested in an honest answer." He pauses meaningfully, wanting to see if I understand what he means. "It's hardly surprising, then, that the answer is always the same, even though it can't possibly be true. No one feels good every day." His hand finds my upper arm. "When I ask you how you are, I'm prepared to hear the truth. So: How are you?"

He's so right. In all our lives this question is nothing more than an empty phrase. We ask each other how we are even though, deep down, we don't really care. We just want to hear that everything's fine. There's no room for sad, worried, or negative feelings. The stranger is different; he always has been.

I smile at him gratefully. "A lot has actually changed since our last meeting. Today I can hardly understand why it took so long. But everything in life has its time, doesn't it?" I say, and I can hear myself how frustrated I sound. How could it be any different, when one time refuses to come and the other already seems long gone?

He nods. "That's exactly how it is. What has time brought into your life?"

"It made me recognize my dream. I found what I'd been searching for far too long and far too desperately…"

"…the moment you had actually already given up the search," he finishes my sentence.

He can't surprise me anymore. Not after everything we've already been through together. "When I stopped searching, the solution to my problem suddenly came to me as if on its own. Without any effort at all."

A satisfied smirk spreads across his lips, and I even think I can make out pride in his expression. "Do you want to tell me about your dream?" he asks, letting his gaze wander absentmindedly over the lake lying before us in perfect calm.

I don't hesitate for a second. Because I know every answer I give will be fine with him. "I take photographs. And it fulfills me in a way I never would've thought possible."

Abruptly, he turns back to me. With his eyes he demands my full attention. "If that's really the case, tell me why you're so downcast."

He knows. He can see that alongside the happiness

there's still melancholy in me. Right now I'd most like to hug him. Just for the fact that he's here.

"Yes, I found my dream, but I can't manage to live it. I'm doing my best, but it doesn't seem to be enough. I fight, I fall, I drag myself back up again. Then I keep fighting. And fail again. On top of that, I lost someone along the way, and I don't know if photography will ever be able to fill this emptiness." That's it, and speaking it out loud gives it a different kind of weight. Depressed, I chew on my lower lip. "The love of my life left me. Ironically, at the very moment my dream started to become reality."

He immediately shook his head, as if what I was saying wasn't the truth. "Everything in life has its time," he reminded me in a gentle voice. "If this man really is the love of your life, your time will never be over."

Yes. Every fiber of my heart, every muscle in my body and every inch of my skin wanted to believe that. Still, that time didn't seem to want to come. "I want to trust in that too. But I've been waiting for weeks for him to get in touch. Or for anyone who appreciates my photos. For nothing." I lowered my gaze. "Maybe it's time to accept the way things are," I said tonelessly. I probably wasn't a gifted photographer in the making after all, and Lukas might never forgive me.

At first he didn't answer. He waited until I looked up at him. He surely saw the pleading in my eyes; he knew what simply saying it out loud did to me. "I don't think that." He sounded utterly convinced.

How could he be so sure? How could he assume I still had the strength to keep fighting? "What am I supposed to do?" My words sounded so weak.

His hand came to rest on my arm. Where we touched, I felt all his strength. "Believe in yourself and your dreams.

Never stop fighting for them, no matter how hard it is for you. Don't forget that true love is the greatest treasure we have. Many people search for it their whole lives; you've already found it. Fight for the person who belongs with you like no one else."

"It's not that easy," I murmured thoughtfully. How was I supposed to fight for my dream of being a photographer when I was running out of strength? And how was I supposed to reach Lukas when he needed distance? Anna had made that clear, and if anyone knew for sure, it was her. She'd known him longer than I had and saw the situation clearly. He didn't want to see me, didn't want to hear my voice, didn't want to touch me.

"Sometimes you only find the way by putting one foot in front of the other." The stranger's voice pushed into my thoughts.

"Just start walking and see where you end up?" That was supposed to be right? I looked at him doubtfully. "I could ruin everything that way." I was already on the brink of financial ruin. And my relationship with Lukas definitely couldn't withstand another encounter full of misunderstandings and arguments. "My life is already as fragile as a glass sculpture. One wrong step. One thoughtless word…"

He shook his head, just a little, yet it was enough to make me fall silent. "Sometimes there are no words," he said then, sounding as profound as a Buddhist teacher, "it's gestures that make clear what you want to tell someone."

What did he mean by that? Lost in thought, I gnawed on my lower lip, but my mind stayed blank. "What kind of gestures?" I asked bluntly.

"The ones that come from right here." He points at my chest. At once my heart starts beating a little harder, as if his words were giving it strength.

In a trance, I look at him. With a warm smile, he pulls his hand back and pushes himself up from the ground.

He wants to leave. And I sense that it would be pointless to try to hold him back. Because he has told me everything I need to know.

So I thank him in farewell and watch him until he disappears between the bushes.

Then I turn back to the lake and try to understand how I can go on from here. Even though the stranger is gone, my heart is still beating with full force. And suddenly I'm sure. It knows what to do, in life and in love. It probably has always been that way. I just finally have to manage to really listen.

Chapter Sixteen

A long day is behind me, work has drained every bit of strength I had. Tired, I stroll through the alley to Anna's apartment. When I feel like this, it's as if I don't have any energy left to keep my protective shell up. Then, all at once, I sense that I could never call the apartment building I'm heading toward my home. While the sun disappears behind the city's buildings, casting long shadows across the sidewalk, I notice how much I miss that feeling. And that, even though this coming home had already taken on a new note months ago. Flat and a little bitter.

It's not because of Anna, because I hadn't had a home with Marie for a long time either. Anna took me in and is there for me. In every situation in life, no matter what happens.

Having someone like that is anything but a given gift. Maybe it'll take a few more weeks before I gradually start to feel at home here too. At least that's what I try to tell myself as I fumble the key out of my pocket.

When I reach the apartment building, I hear someone

running down the outside stairs. Anna's dark, tousled head is the first thing I recognize. Then her teasing smile.

"Hey, my love." She looks like she's walking into a candy store after months on a diet.

Adorable is the word that rushes through my head as she comes closer and cheerfully loops her arms around my neck. She rises up onto her tiptoes, I bend down to her.

When we kiss, the world doesn't slow down. But it doesn't have to. There's something comforting about it, and that's enough.

Smiling, she pulls away from me again. "I was hoping we'd run into each other."

"Me too," I confirm, even though I'm not exactly sure why.

Maybe to see the radiant smile that spreads across her face in that moment. "It was worth waiting until the very last second. Totally worth it." She kisses me again, passionate and exuberant. "But I'm already damn late."

"Work's calling, huh?" I ask with a crooked grin, because I can see exactly what's going on in her head. She's thinking about skipping out again to spend the evening with me.

As if to prove it, she pushes out her lower lip and dips her chin. When she looks up at me like that, I can hardly resist her. Because I know what she'd like to do with me right now and how it feels when she does it.

"You've got this," I say anyway, because today I need to be by myself. The day was exhausting and I need a break. From everything. So the thoughts about work, money, and decisions in my head finally stop spinning so fast in circles that I can't get hold of them.

With an exaggerated sigh, Anna rolls her eyes toward the sky. "I guess I don't have a choice. Take care, my love."

She kisses me one last time, then turns to go. "There's a surprise waiting for you in the fridge," she calls back to me as she walks briskly down the street.

She cooked for me. Again. And I'm sure it's one of my favorite dishes. A guilty conscience gnaws at my stomach. She gives everything for our relationship and I don't give enough.

With a long yawn, I trudge up the stairs and a few minutes later step into Anna's apartment. I slip off my shoes and walk on into the kitchen.

In the fridge I find a bowl of chocolate mousse. For that alone I should love Anna. Before I dig in, I really need different clothes. I have to get out of this shirt with the tight collar and these uncomfortable jeans. So for now I just grab a beer.

On the way to the bedroom I take a big swig and enjoy the warm, slightly dull feeling that spreads through my body right after, so much that I immediately lift the bottle to my mouth again. By the time I reach the wardrobe, I've emptied half the beer. Pleasantly buzzed, I pull out a fresh T-shirt and reach for a pair of sweatpants. Under the soft fabric my fingers touch something hard.

What's that?

I shake out the folded pants. That's when I see it.

The ring box.

It lies there in front of me like a memorial, and I hardly dare to touch it. Still, I can't help myself, I have to open it. Slowly I lift the lid, and after just a few seconds my heart stops beating.

The ring is actually here with me. It must have been, ever since Anna picked up my stuff from Marie's. This whole time it hasn't been on the finger of the woman it was once meant for.

All at once it feels as if a world is collapsing inside me. Because I realize what must have happened.

Marie gave Anna the ring. She doesn't want it anymore, just like she doesn't want me anymore.

She doesn't love me anymore, she has closed the book on us, as if our relationship had been nothing more than a stopgap solution for her.

Had she been putting on an act all these years, while I, like some love-struck idiot, was convinced she was the one?

What am I thinking? I can't let that get to me. "You don't care about Marie. You don't care, you don't care, you don't care!" I harshly remind myself.

Then I let myself sink wearily onto the bed and drain my beer in one long gulp. Thick fog gathers in my head, but I still keep ordering myself, in a military tone, to forget Marie once and for all.

I have to. I'm going to keep walking my path with Anna; it's the only right thing to do.

As if a part of me had just been waiting for this moment, many of the questions that had occupied me for so long suddenly receive an irrevocable answer.

Not only Marie, but the dream house too is now definitively a thing of the past.

I have to unwind the purchase. Tomorrow it'll be the first thing I take care of. Together with the house, I'll leave behind even the last little bit of Marie. A new life will begin, because that's just how it has to be.

Anna will be part of this life too. And I even already know how it's supposed to start.

I grab my phone right away. "I'm in. Let's go on vacation," I type in a message to the new woman at my side. That's what she wanted, after all. And this way I can at least give her a little bit of what she wants so badly.

It takes less than a minute for her reply to come in. "Oh yes, let's do it," it says. She's added a big grinning smiley after it.

I know how happy she is, and that alone should make me at least a bit happier too. Whether it really does, I don't know, but one thing is absolutely clear: going away with Anna is my best option. The farther I am from Vienna, the better.

"Anna is my future," I tell myself, and for the first time I'm sure that it's actually the truth.

There's only one more thing I have to do. I open the folder with the photos on my phone and delete, one by one, all the ones that show Marie. With every additional picture that disappears into nothingness, I feel better. When I finally delete the wallpaper of the two of us from my phone and replace it with one of Anna, I'm able to breathe freely again for the first time in months.

Chapter Seventeen

Sometimes there are no words. It's more the gestures that make clear what you want to say. That's how the stranger put it a few days ago. And as if his sentences were still echoing inside me, they've stayed with me ever since. I brood and ponder, but nothing I come up with is good enough. Not for Lukas, because for him it has to be something special.

Lost in thought, I stroll through the city park. Even though the early autumn is showing its coldest side this morning, I wanted to come here. I drop down onto one of the weathered wooden benches, my gaze wandering over the trees that will soon be completely bare. Only now and then do I see people walking along the paths. The crunch of the gravel has something calming about it. Wisps of grayish-white fog cling stubbornly to the ground. They veil the brownish patches on what was once such a lush green lawn.

As so often in the past four weeks, my hand automatically reaches for my ring. Once more I remember the cold feeling that suddenly spread from my hand up my arm and straight into my heart when I took it off.

I pull the camera out of my bag, because at least this way I can look at pictures of the ring. Even though I don't know what good that's supposed to do—if I've learned one thing, it's to listen to my intuition.

As if I were reliving last week's photo tour in reverse, I scroll through the pictures. Our wildflower meadow, which still barely shows any sign of autumn. It isn't quite as overgrown as it used to be, but I still managed to capture the mood. My own longing is written all over my face. Where the warm golden tone of the sun touches my forehead, you can see deep lines. In the corners of my eyes I spot a suspicious glimmer.

I go further back and find pictures that show the façade of our club. There, to the right of the oversized wooden entrance door at the jutting bit of wall, is where we stood. With aching feet and heavy eyelids. But I couldn't feel any of that back then. It didn't matter, because only the two of us counted.

Next, the red plastic chairs in front of the ice-cream parlor catch my eye. They're still the same ones, just a little more faded. I know exactly that this is the spot where we sat, because under the tabletop we carved our initials. Not in that boring way, it doesn't just say L + M. No, it's more like a logo, two letters joined together. As close to each other as we were ourselves. I photographed that too, and right now I'm looking at the picture. A heaviness settles over me, even though all the photos convey lightness and joy. A longing joins it. So intense that I can't feel anything else. Not the cold that keeps creeping up my legs through my pants, not the wind that's picking up more and more, and not how stiff my fingers have become as they curl around the camera body.

I go further back and arrive at the old couple. Looking at the pictures feels as if someone were dealing my heart the death blow.

"Wherever you are, that's where I want to be. Forever," I hear Lukas say. That's what the shots show me. That's exactly how the two of us could be. In forty years, or in fifty.

If Lukas could see these pictures. How they line up like a gallery of our life together, showing our past, present, and a possible future. If he could understand that they express exactly the story I'd most like to tell him myself. Then I could tell him everything without a single word.

That's it!

That's the gesture I've been looking for. I'm going to put the photos together into an album. That way Lukas can understand everything. Not just how happy we were, but also what I think, how sorry I am, what I wish for us, and that photos aren't just a ridiculous hobby. No, pictures that manage to tell an entire story are more than that.

An excited tingling spreads through my stomach, because all at once I know this is exactly right. I'm so nervous I can hardly sit still. I spring up from the park bench, carefully slip the camera back into my bag, and set off for the nearest copy shop with glowing cheeks and full of anticipation.

Once I get there, everything goes quickly. I don't have to think long; the pictures fall into the right order as if by themselves, the background designs are quickly found. I work so intently that I forget everything around me. And in fact, the little album I'm holding in my hands a few hours later doesn't contain a single word. The photos alone tell a story, just the way I'd wished.

In the middle of the plainly furnished copy shop, between humming machines and busy students, I pause for a moment. With the smell of vending-machine coffee in my nose and a kind of hope flowing through my veins like pure gold. I suddenly become aware of all this, as if I were waking up from a trance.

Now only one thing matters: the album has to get to Lukas, and it has to be directly. One look at the digital clock above the copy shop counter is enough for me to know what to do next. In a little over an hour he'll be taking his lunch break. I certainly won't ambush him, because I still want to respect his wish for distance. I'll leave the album in a sealed box on his desk. When he comes back from lunch, he'll find it and then…

Whatever happens, it just has to be something good. That alone is what I want to believe in as I trundle to his company on the tram and, from sheer excitement, barely register what's happening around me.

When I step into the café across the street from his workplace a little later, I feel a bit crazy. Only a few old people are playing cards at the big round table in the middle of the room. Otherwise, not much is going on. I pick a seat by the window from which I have a clear view of the company entrance. If Lukas hasn't changed his habits, he'll be coming through the tinted glass sliding doors in twenty minutes.

I don't take my eyes off the company entrance, I'm so fixated on it that I don't notice anything that's happening here in the café. The tablecloths could be cream, dark green, or bright orange, if there are any at all. It could be a waitress or a waiter from whom I order a fruit tea. Whether it's warm or cold in here and whether my armchair is comfortable or uncomfortable, I don't know. All I know is that every time the glass doors across the street start to move, I flinch instinctively. And that my pulse starts racing. For a moment my breath catches and maybe even stops altogether. Until I see who's leaving the company.

Lukas doesn't show.

"Come on, take a break," I mutter, as if I were a witch trying to conjure him from a distance.

As if on command, the sliding doors across the street glide open again. Restlessly, I shift around on my chair and even catch myself sending up a quick prayer to a heaven I'm not sure even exists.

There's Lukas.

He doesn't see me, and I'm far away from him. Still, all at once my heart pounds so hard against my chest that I can feel my pulse in my ears. Beads of sweat form in my palms, and I'm short of oxygen because I can't seem to breathe.

I could jump up and run to him. We wouldn't have to say anything. It would be enough to look at each other to know that we belong together. He could put his arm around me, I would smile at him. Then we would kiss, and we would both know that everything between us has to be all right again.

Still, I hold back. Because there's one thing I know for sure: it's his wishes that matter. Not mine. And he needs distance to get a clear view of things. The fact that I ignored his needs was, after all, the main reason for our crisis. At last I have the chance to show him that I've understood that. Whatever he wants, I'll give him.

So I just watch him as he trudges along the sidewalk. He looks tired, the way his shoulders slump forward. As if he had used up all his energy. Every step he takes seems to cost him even more strength.

Immediately I'm reminded of myself. That must be how

I looked when my days were dark. Only his jacket, which hardly reaches around the little belly he used to have, doesn't fit the picture.

If he looked to the side now, he could see me. But he doesn't. His eyes are fixed on the ground, as if there were nothing worth lifting his head for.

If hearts could really break, mine would break now. Because seeing his pain so clearly is worse than any torment I have to endure myself.

There's nothing I long for more than to be there for him. Even so, I let him go and watch as he disappears on the horizon. It won't be long now before everything is all right again. I cling to that thought as I spring up from my chair, press the money for my tea into the waitress's hand, and leave the café.

A few forced breaths, that's all I manage before I'm standing where Lukas was just a few minutes ago. I enter the company building. Reception is unmanned, so I seize my chance and march straight to Lukas's office. My steps echo down the wide hallway. I press the package tightly against my body. From the outside it looks inconspicuous, but inside it my whole world is hidden. I swing around the corner at speed, and suddenly I'm standing in the middle of his office.

There's no one here but me. I cross the room and set my treasure down on Lukas's desk. He was just sitting here. Maybe that's what tempts me to stay for a moment. Or maybe it's the idea that he might unexpectedly come back and be happy to see me. I don't know. I stare hard at the desk, as if I were searching for clues, for something, anything, that might give me hope. But I don't find that here. On the contrary, over there, next to the withered plant, something is even missing.

The photo of the two of us. He's made it disappear. Just as I'm supposed to disappear from his thoughts.

With all my strength I fight against the awful feeling spreading inside me. I can't let it take away my hope. Love always finds a way. That's what the stranger said, or something like that. And that's how it just has to be.

I turn away quickly. I should go. Right now. And yet I'm standing here as if I were set in concrete, wanting to take something with me. Just a small dose of Lukas. Something I can hold on to.

I must be crazy, unhinged, or completely insane. Anyone who could see me would probably call a psychiatrist. But no one is here. So I do it. I bend down and let my nose glide over the fabric of the backrest of his office chair. Right there, exactly at the spot where his neck usually rests. A second later, it happens. I can smell him. The invisible scent molecules find their way into my nose and, as if on command, unfold their incomparable effect. I feel a bit like a recovering alcoholic eating a rum ball.

I want more of it. More than just a delicate trace of Lukas.

I want all of it. I want to nuzzle right at his neck, wrapped in his arms, surrounded by his warmth. For this one moment I surrender to the fantasy and experience it all as if it were really happening.

"Marie?"

The voice is far too muffled to reach me. I let it bounce off, somewhere far, far away.

"Marie!"

I feel something on my upper arm. It's shaking.

"Hey."

Like a loud bang, the voice yanks me back. My gaze

jerks up and I recognize Lukas's closest coworker. "Bernd," I stammer, unable to form a full sentence.

His forehead creases. "You okay?"

I just about manage to nod. "Uh… yeah…"

"I'll get you a glass of water, you're white as a sheet." He looks at me doubtfully and steers me toward his office chair so I can sit down.

I immediately wave him off. "Thanks, but I have to go," I force out, shake his hand off my upper arm, and head out.

"What did you want, anyway? Should I tell him something?" he calls after me as I stride toward the hallway, as fast as my legs will carry me.

"No, you don't need to say anything," I answer quickly, then turn around one more time. "Please don't."

His understanding nod tells me he's reading my pleading expression correctly. And that Lukas has told him about our breakup. I raise my hand in farewell and disappear from the office. I quickly walk back the same way I came and turn right as soon as I've left the company's sliding doors behind me. That way I won't run into Lukas, and that's the most important thing right now.

Only once I'm sitting on the tram does my tension ease. A heavy tiredness washes over me. I feel as if I've just taken part in one of Anna's hardcore triathlon competitions.

Even so, I smile. Because I did it. The package is delivered, hope is alive.

Chapter Eighteen

With my phone pressed tightly to my ear, I step into my office. "Great, that sounds fantastic. I'll see you later then," I say to Anna, who's almost impossible to stop on the other end of the line. Seeing her so full of anticipation for our vacation makes me happy too. We're leaving today, and I only have to hold out for less than four hours until then.

Grinning with delight, I end the call and march over to my workstation. Even though I was only gone for a short while to grab a bite to eat, it looks completely different here than before. Someone has actually dumped a whole pile of documents and folders on my desk.

Do all of these have to be dealt with today? Please no.

"Is there a problem?" Bernd's head pops up over the partition between the desks. He smiles in amusement.

"Is this a gift from our new deputy department head?" I sigh, gesturing broadly at the chaos on my desk.

Bernd rolls his eyes at the ceiling. "What do you think?! The junior boss is living up to his reputation again."

Conspiratorially, he leans toward me. "You'd do the job at least a thousand times better than he does."

I wave him off; I really don't want to hear any more about it. The fact that I didn't get the position, even though I'm much more qualified, is still gnawing at me anyway. "Let it go," I reply weakly. "I guess I'd better get to work, right?" As if my body doesn't want to cooperate, suddenly every single one of my muscles turns tired. I drop into my chair and painstakingly pull myself closer to the desk.

"Hey, Lukas, wait a second. There was something today..."

"No time to chat," I mutter, focusing on what's in front of me. I unlock my PC screen and enter the password.

Bernd might still be mumbling to himself. I don't listen. I've only got a good three hours to at least chip away at part of the mountain of work. So I open the first file and start checking the incoming deliveries.

When I switch off the computer, exhausted, just under three hours later, I've managed barely half of everything the junior boss dumped on me. My desk is pure chaos; I can't leave it like this. While I stack the files neatly on top of each other, my thoughts are with Anna and our vacation together. In less than an hour the train to the south leaves. Even though we'll be on the road for a long time, it'll be worth it. We'll spend an entire week on Italy's coast. I can finally sleep in again, have long breakfasts, read newspapers, and just do absolutely nothing. I can let go of my obligations for a few days and don't have to worry about anything.

Everything will be great, I can feel it. With a liberated smile on my face, I gather up the pens scattered across the desk and drop them into the drawer. Calculator and ruler follow, as do sticky notes and stapler. When I'm almost finished, I discover a small package under the file with the unprocessed supplier contracts.

Where did that suddenly come from? Curious, I reach for it. But before I can grab it, my phone rings. The real estate agent is calling, finally.

“Ms. Molinger, thank you very much for returning my call,” I say, making an effort to sound friendly.

“What can I do for you?” She sounds rushed. In the background I hear high heels hammering on the pavement.

I don’t need to look at the time to know I’m already in a damn hurry. So I’d better get straight to the point. “I have to withdraw from the house purchase. I’m very sorry.” I sound completely convinced. It’s as if I’m shouting the final death sentence for my relationship with Marie out into the world. And that’s a good thing.

Suddenly the background noise on the other end of the line falls silent. “Are you sure?”

“Absolutely.” To buy myself some time, I wedge the phone between my ear and shoulder and keep tidying up. I push the keyboard straight on my desk and line up the files in a row.

“I’ll have to coordinate that with the seller. Give me a few days to check whether a withdrawal is possible,” Ms. Molinger says, sounding contrite.

What does she mean by that? Of course that’s possible; no other option is even up for debate. But instead of saying so, I just politely ask her to get back to me about it soon, and quickly say goodbye.

I don’t have any time left; Anna is already waiting for me at the station. So I give my desk one last critical look so I won’t get scolded by our insane junior boss when I get back. Apart from the unfinished files and the unopened package, everything looks good. I mentally put those two things right at the top of the to-do list for my first day back at work after my days off. Then I take my jacket from the coat rack and head out.

The vacation can begin. Finally.

Chapter Nineteen

The ticking of the kitchen clock reminds me how time passes. Second by second, hour by hour. With every passing day, a little more of my hope disappears. It leaves me. And where it used to be, nothing but longing spreads.

It devours me. Slowly. From the inside out. And as I stand here at the kitchen window, watching the autumn wind tear the golden-yellow leaves from the trees, I wonder how much longer I can wait.

I don't know.

Abruptly, I turn away, grab the two wineglasses on the counter, and march over to Alex, who is waiting for me in the living room.

Sitting cross-legged on the sofa, she's looking through the photos I took in the park the other day. "What took you so long?" she wants to know, her eyebrows drawn together.

I set the glasses down on the coffee table and join her. I don't answer her question; instead, I at least try to smile at her. "How do you like the pictures?"

"The mood in this one is fantastic." She holds up one of

the shots of the little pond. A layer of mist lies over the surface of the water, the tips of the tall reeds are covered in dew that glitters mystically in the light of the morning sun.

I remember the moment I took it. And in fact, it was above all one thing: fantastic. "I'm glad to hear that."

"You absolutely have to keep at this," Alex says with an encouraging nod.

Everyone thinks so. But nobody wants to buy the pictures. And nobody wants to hire me either. "Over the past few days I've traipsed through every bridal shop in Vienna and asked if I could leave my flyer there. You know, the event photography offer." I sound dejected, and I am.

"That's a good idea." Alex sounds enthusiastic, and I'd love nothing more than to hug her for it. Because she's the only one who reacts to my initiative like that.

I take a big sip of my Muscat. It's from the last bottle we had left. The last wine from Lukas's parents. "In every single shop I gave it everything I had, but only three even took the flyer. I left the rest in copy shops and cafés. What else was I supposed to do?" This isn't working. No matter how hard I fight, I keep losing. "I knew it wouldn't be easy. But I never imagined it just wouldn't work at all. How am I ever supposed to make enough money to live from photography? Or any at all?"

See? Lukas was right. Photography is nothing but useless daydreaming. My voice is back and, as so often, it's trying to make everything even worse. As if my situation weren't already bad enough.

I quickly focus on Alex. From the way she's furrowing her brow in thought, I know she's hatching something. "You need contacts," she says finally, "a real network where people help each other out."

I can barely suppress a snort. "Sure, no problem, that kind of thing is totally easy to get."

Alex refuses to be put off by the ironic tone of my voice. Excitedly, she squirms back and forth on the sofa. "What about that photography course we talked about?"

"I could definitely meet someone there. But..." Lost in thought, I reach for my glass again.

Alex nods so vigorously that it must almost make her dizzy. "Absolutely. Just imagine it. Your pictures are already great, and with professional help they'll be incredible. The course will also help you get into the right circles."

What she says is absolutely true. I wish her enthusiasm could sweep me along, but there's still something holding me back. Sadly, I lower my gaze. "I can't."

She's at my side in an instant and lays her hand on my upper arm. She even gives me a little shake, as if she wanted to wake me up. "Anything is possible, you just have to do it."

Of course, it's that simple for her. "I can't even afford the rent for this apartment anymore." The thought settles on my shoulders, heavy like a thick coat. Every day my bank balance shrinks further, no matter how hard I try to save. I can't crash at Grandma's, something I've skillfully pushed aside over the past few days. And right now I don't even want to think about the fact that this problem will soon catch up with me again.

Out of the corner of my eye I see Alex shrug. "Then you just move out, so what?!" she says, as if it were the easiest thing in the world. "This environment isn't good for you anyway."

Can she tell that I haven't really slept in a long time because that same recurring nightmare keeps creeping into my nights? On an endless loop, Lukas hurls my heart out onto the street and there's absolutely nothing I can do about it.

I take a deep breath and lift my gaze. I look straight into her elfin face and I know I really wouldn't have to say anything at all. Still, I do. "You think he's not coming back?"

What leaves my mouth is no more than a hoarse whisper, but the words carry everything in them.

What had so far only been in my thoughts and my heart is now spoken aloud. Maybe it's the truth, but I still want to refuse to accept it.

"I don't know." She looks helpless as she tilts her head to the side and looks at me with pressed lips and a sad expression on her face.

"By now four whole days have passed since I left the album in his office. Why isn't he reacting to it? How can it be that he doesn't understand what I'm trying to tell him with it?" Shaking my head, I drain my glass in one go. Not that it would change anything about the situation, but at least it makes my stomach feel a tiny bit warm.

Instead of answering, Alex shrugs. Then she gives me a forced smile. "I want you to take this course, you hear me?!"

How sweet of her to try to distract me. Still, I shake my head. "I can't afford it."

"Has no one gotten in touch with you about the virtual assistant jobs? I applied for at least twenty positions in your name."

Now I'm the one who shrugs. "Three of the companies were interested, but they weren't even close to being willing to pay an acceptable rate."

"So what? You have to make a name for yourself first. Take the jobs, deliver excellent work, and be happy as long as you stay under the additional-earnings limit for unemployment assistance. The clients will give you good reviews, and that'll increase your chances of getting better jobs." No one can resist her enthusiasm, not even me.

Smiling, I reach for my wineglass. "I probably should do that," I say, even though I don't really feel like taking on any of the three jobs. I need the money, so I'll just have to get through it. "But the course still won't be possible."

"Yes, it will." Her determined expression tells me she's plotting something in her head. "Just move in with me temporarily. You can sleep on the couch for a few weeks. You help me a bit with the rent, you work, and you take your course. More money will start coming in soon enough, and then you can look for a new place."

I fix my gaze on her even though tears are welling up in my eyes, making the world around me disappear. What she's saying sounds so simple. But in reality it's anything but. "If I move out of here, it'll really be over." That's it. That's the truth, and it feels blacker than the darkest night could ever be.

"What's between you and Lukas will never be over." The words leave her lips softly. There's a certainty in them that reminds me of the stranger at the water park. "Because you belong together, and nothing and no one can change that."

I let myself fall into the soft cushions of the sofa, grab one of the purple pillows, and press it tightly to my chest. "If that's true, why don't I get so much as a sign of life from him?"

"It'll come, trust me. And in the meantime, you're just going to make the best of it. You're going to sign up for this course." She sounds like my grandma when she used to tell me off for not cleaning my room. "Come on, what are you waiting for?"

"But…"

Now she even nudges me, her index finger poking into my upper arm over and over again. "No backtalk, understood?"

She's actually managed to get me to at least grin at her a little. She's probably spot on, and her offer to let me stay with her if the worst comes to the worst will save me. Today is September twelfth. Lukas has only two more weeks to get in touch before I have to cancel the apartment for good and look for a new tenant. "Thanks, Alex. And if it happens at all, it wouldn't be for long, I promise."

I don't have to say anything more; she knows what her support means to me. We wrap our arms around each other, and she strokes my back encouragingly. "It'll be okay. You can't just switch off love because you want to. Not even your Mr. Control Freak can do that. I'm sure of it," she murmurs into my hair.

There's nothing I want more than for her to be right. Because otherwise I'd have to give up this apartment. The place where Lukas and I had been happy for so long would then be history. Moving out would mean the start of a new life I never wanted. It would definitely be a setback, but it still wouldn't be over. Because it's not allowed to be over.

Chapter Twenty

"Hey, sleepyhead."

My ears registered Anna's voice and even the gentle rush of the sea in the background. Next to me a hollow opened up, and I rolled onto my side without resistance.

A cloud of the scent of salt water and sunscreen reached my nose, soft lips touched my mouth. That felt nice, wonderfully warm and relaxed. Despite my tiredness I noticed how a contented smile spread across my face. With my eyes closed I savored the moment that surrounded me halfway between dream and reality, and lazily stretched my body. Finally on vacation. There were no obligations, only rest.

"Come on, it's breakfast time." Anna's voice pushed into my half-sleep.

The bed vibrated.

"Mmmh… in a minute…" I yawned broadly and reached out my hand for her. There was an arm; I pulled it toward me. Willingly, a few seconds later, she snuggled up against my chest. I slid closer, my nose touching her hair.

Her fingers wandered over my stomach and then farther down. "Wake up, my love."

There was no way I could go on sleeping like this, absolutely not. The first days of vacation had already shown that the bundle of energy beside me wouldn't give up until I opened my eyes. So I did the same today. Slightly dazed, I blinked at her.

"At last… You're going to sleep the whole day away." She seemed so jittery, as if she had downed an overdose of sugar.

I rubbed the sleep from my eyes. "We're on vacation," I grumbled, pulled the thin blanket up to my chest, and watched Anna throw her arms dramatically into the air.

"Exactly, we're on vacation. You have to experience it. You can sleep at home." With a cheeky grin Anna bounced up from the bed and danced energetically through the simply furnished hotel room. Her curly head swung in time, she yanked her oversized T-shirt up to her hips, which she rolled in a seductive circle. "Look where we are. It's absolutely amazing!"

Strictly speaking it's only Bibione, but I don't want to spoil her fun. "Yes, it is," I say, sit up in bed and stuff a pillow behind my neck. "Your energy is a bit too much for me right now. Let me wake up properly first."

All at once there's a suspicious sparkle in her eyes. Like one of those hot dancers she comes toward me. "You want to wake up? Really wake up?" She's already kneeling on the bed and leaning over me. "Well, if that's how it is, I know something," she breathes in my ear, and a moment later she's getting to work with her mouth.

It feels so thrilling that a tingling spreads through my body from that spot. I wrap my arms around her hips and feel my way up under her T-shirt. I only get to see her satisfied smile for a fraction of a second, because in the next moment she's on top of me, kissing me with full passion.

Not a second after we pull away from each other, Anna looks at me with her bright, lively gaze. "Breakfast?"

Where on earth does she get all that energy from? I'd much rather stay in bed, but I know I don't stand a chance against her. So I nod, let her pull me out of bed, and watch, shaking my head, as she disappears toward the bathroom with the liveliness of a young deer.

She closes the door behind her, and suddenly everything is quiet. Only the rush of the shower can be heard, and only now do I notice how good this silence feels. This is my version of a vacation. I pull on a T-shirt, amble over to the small balcony of our room and lean far over the railing to see the sea. It lies completely calm before me, a warm breeze carries the salty air to my nose. Seagulls circle in the radiant blue sky. I take a deep breath, and then another. This day is going to be great; we'll get comfortable on the beach and really let our minds unwind. That, and nothing else, is exactly what I need.

Despite my good intentions, I already feel rushed again half an hour later. I haven't taken a single sip of my coffee when Anna comes back from the breakfast buffet.

"Oh man, I could easily stay here another three weeks," she says and sits down at the table opposite me. Full of anticipation, she slices a banana into her plain yogurt. "Too bad we're running so late. We've already wasted half the morning."

Wasted, how? "Oh, come on, it's not a big deal." I shake my head and turn my attention back to the daily paper. That's one of the best things about vacation: having the time to read every article in detail. At home I manage, if anything, just the headlines. But here I can spend hours on it. And the weekly planner is finally on pause, and I can do nothing but what I feel like doing. Wonderful.

"I did some more research on what we could do. There are interesting day trips, or we can go surfing. What do you think, do you still remember how to surf?" Anna chatters away so cheerfully, as if she doesn't even notice that I'm absorbed in my reading.

I look up at her and watch how eagerly she tops her healthy breakfast with a load of fresh pineapple.

"So what? Are we going surfing now, or have you forgotten how?"

"I don't know. Why?" Without waiting for an answer, I lower my gaze to keep reading. The article about the impact of air travel on the environment is extremely interesting.

"We could also take a class, if there is one." Anna's voice almost cracks, then it goes quiet for a moment. Is she scrutinizing me? I don't dare look up. "Or we could play a bit of table tennis, I saw some tables over by reception."

This isn't going to work. For her sake alone, I suppress a sigh and lower the newspaper. "All right, I guess I'll have to postpone this till later."

A satisfied grin immediately spreads across her face. "That sounds perfect, my dear. So, what do you think?" Devotedly, she puts a big spoonful of her muesli in her mouth and chews it with a rapt expression.

What was this about again? I try to remember, but I can't. "What am I supposed to think about what?" I ask, and even I notice the slightly annoyed undertone in my voice that I don't want there.

"About what we should do today, of course." She looks at me as if I were a Martian who doesn't know her language.

I'm probably doing exactly the same thing right now.

"Relax," I answer, because that's exactly what vacations are for.

"What, you just want to lie around on the beach again?" Anna's incredulous look makes her eyes seem even bigger than they already are.

I shrug. "Sure, that's why it's called a relaxing vacation, right? Because it's about relaxing." That's logical, so why does she look so surprised?

Disappointed, she pushes out her lower lip. "That's what we've been doing for the last four days. It's too boring for me," she mumbles.

For Anna there can never be enough action. She's a bundle of energy, not just at home. I immediately think of the many vacation photos that decorate the wall in her living room. They show Anna trudging up a mountain in snowshoes, nimbly climbing a rock in short shorts, and proudly stretching her arms into the air at the summit cross. Not a single photo shows her lying on the beach. "Hm," I say thoughtfully, because I can't think of anything better. "You've always been the adventurous one of the two of us."

"Exactly." She tucks a lock of hair behind her ear and looks at me expectantly. "It's such a waste not to see anything of a country when you're already there."

It is. Just not when the vacation has only just started. And not when the last few months have been so exhausting that I don't have any energy left in me. "You know, I'd be glad to just do nothing for once. At home everything has been happening one thing after another lately. Work really drained my batteries." Carefully, I reach my hand out to her. I don't want to disappoint her, but I still see how the smile slowly disappears from her face.

She looks at me, seeking help, deep lines furrowing her forehead. "So what now?"

Seeing her like this makes my stomach clench. Still, I can't give her what she wants today. "Give me this one day to rest," I say, and stroke the back of her hand with my index finger. "Please."

"Okay, I'll head out on my own today. But starting tomorrow, we'll only do things together." It's not a question, more a statement.

Whether I like it or not, I'm strangely relieved. Not just because I have a whole day to myself, but also because she gives in. We'll work it out. In everyday life we function well together, and even on vacation it'll work out sooner or later. "Good. I'll relax on the beach, you can give free rein to your urge to explore. In the evening we'll meet up and have pizza together. How does that sound?" I try to sound cheerful. Still, there's this feeling of tightness that's wrapping itself around my throat.

Anna doesn't seem satisfied either. "Sounds perfect, my love." Exaggeratedly cheerful, she pops a big piece of pineapple into her mouth. While she's still chewing, she shoots up from her chair. "See you later," she says with her mouth full, and just a few seconds later she's gone, without kissing me goodbye.

For a moment I watch her go. Then I take a deep breath and reach for my newspaper. I can finally read it in peace. I treat myself to a sip of aromatic Italian coffee and, with a contented sigh, immerse myself in the article. This is how a vacation should be.

Chapter Twenty-One

With a friendly smile, Peter, the best course instructor in the world, says goodbye to the group. "I wish you a great week and lots of fun taking photos. Next time I want to see five pictures from each of you on the topic of Shadow and Light."

The other participants immediately start applauding. Naturally, I join in. Even though the session that just ended was only the third of ten, I'm absolutely thrilled. Signing up for this course was the best decision I could have made. And I can hardly believe that today's three hours are already over. Peter almost seems embarrassed, the way he keeps running his hands through his medium-length mop of hair and adjusting his horn-rimmed glasses. Then he claps his palms together and imitates a Japanese bow.

Fascinated, I watch him turn away to prepare the room for tomorrow's course. Even though he's dressed entirely in black, he doesn't radiate any sadness. On the contrary, you can tell that, despite his young age, he has already gained a lot of life experience.

That's the kind of photographer I want to become.

With a hint of melancholy, I stow my camera in its case and slip it into my bag. While excited chatter starts up all around me, I let my gaze wander in search of Peter again. He's busy taking our pictures down from the pinboard, handling them as carefully as if they were real treasures.

Peter is simply great. Not only does he know an incredible amount about photography and is a fantastic teacher, he's also really, really nice. I'm convinced he'll have answers to all my questions. So I quickly say goodbye to the other course participants and congratulate them on their successful pictures. Then I head over to Peter.

"Hey," I say a little breathlessly when I'm standing in front of him. "Do you have a moment?"

A warm smile spreads across his face. "Of course." As if he wants to give me his full attention, he carefully sets the photos in his hand aside. "What's up?"

"I love your course," I burst out, full of enthusiasm. And it's worth every one of my hard-earned euros as a virtual assistant.

"You're a good student too." His approving nod is exactly what I need. "So talented and full of passion."

Almost embarrassed, I bite my lip. Because what he just told me is so important for my future. "I want to be a photographer." There's a matter-of-factness in my voice that even surprises me.

The last time I said those words, all I got back from Lukas was pure incomprehension. In an almost mocking tone, he wanted to know if I'd lost my mind.

Peter is different. There isn't the slightest trace of doubt and not a bit of confusion in his expression. "That's fantastic." He leans against the edge of the table. He studies me intently through his large glasses.

I can't help but beam at him. "What should I do so I can finally make money with my photos?" That's the question that has been on my mind for so long. I absolutely have to get my finances under control, and what I want most is to take pictures. There has to be a way to combine both.

Suddenly his expression turns terribly serious. His usually smooth forehead is furrowed with countless little lines. "First of all: it's damn hard to make a living from photos alone. You need perseverance and a really thick skin."

Even though his words hit me right where they shouldn't, I nod. "I've got that."

His friendly smile returns. "Come on, let's sit down." With his hand, he points to the chairs we stacked in the corner before the class.

I follow him, and we sit down facing each other. Then he leans toward me, even though he already has my full attention. "Tell me what you like photographing most."

I don't have to think about that for long. "Landscapes and faces. I love capturing moments that tell stories. Mood pieces, so to speak." Even I notice how excited I sound. But just thinking about what I feel when I take photos like that makes me happy. My cheeks are probably even glowing while I beam at him as if there weren't a single shadow in my life.

Over the next thirty minutes I learn everything that's important for me. Peter gives me links to platforms where I can upload my pictures and maybe even find buyers. He also promises to bring books to the next class that will help me. The excitement inside me grows with every second until it has reached every corner of my body.

"And you think I can really pull it off?" I ask at the end and send up a quick prayer at the same moment.

He leans back in his chair, crosses his legs, and puts his index finger to his chin. He looks a bit like one of the great thinkers of antiquity. "You have talent." An uncomfortable pause of silence follows, and I can feel there's more coming. So I wait until he has cleared his throat at length and continues. "But that alone won't be enough. To be successful as an artist, you don't just need talent and technical skill. You also need twice as much luck on top of that." He shrugs. "Out there are thousands of photographers. They all have talent and know their craft."

The first shadows creep into my enthusiasm. Still, I don't want to let it get me down. No, if there's one thing I know, it's that you have to fight for your dreams. "I want to try anyway."

He looks relieved. It's strange, but I feel as if I've already passed the first test. His open smile shows me that he's happy for me. "If that's the case, I have something else for you. Just a moment."

I watch as Peter marches over to his leather shoulder bag and pulls out a sheet of paper. That's exactly what he hands me a few seconds later. Photography Competition, I read in the heading, and I'm instantly captivated. "That sounds interesting."

"There are lots of competitions like this. You submit your pictures and can win prizes. In this one it's a scholarship. See, it's all written here," he says, pointing his finger at the text.

"We want to support up-and-coming, talented photographers and enable them to devote themselves fully to their creativity," I read out loud. That sounds absolutely fantastic. A little further down I find the amount of the grant. "Three thousand euros?" I whisper in awe. "That would be… amazing!"

As if he wanted to dampen my joy, Peter raises a warning hand. "Don't let that distract you. Focus on which pictures you need for the application. Look at the jurors' own work, research what set the winners of previous calls for entries apart. That's the only way you'll have any chance at all."

I rummage out my notepad and write his tips down right away. "Got it. What else?"

"Only pick photos that are perfect. Loads of photographers enter these competitions. Everyone wants the scholarship and they're all good. Don't make any lazy compromises, understood? Any photo you even slightly doubt has no place in your application portfolio."

"Perfect photos, already noted." I beam at him, full of energy and motivation. Because I already know I'll do everything I can to submit the best shots.

Out of nowhere I suddenly see a path for myself that had been hidden until now. With this scholarship I could not only solve my housing problem, but also do something else. A real dream could come true!

"What if I used the money to travel to India and take photos there?" Without thinking about it any further, I've said my plan out loud and made it that bit more real.

Right now a thought settles in the middle of my chest and radiates more warmth from there than a crackling fireplace. I can feel everywhere that I'm on the right track. And I know for sure that my wishes will come true.

All of them.

I can travel and take photos. Only Lukas is still missing; then my happiness would be complete.

"I'll definitely keep my fingers crossed for you." Peter's voice pushes into my hopeful thoughts, his hand patting my shoulder encouragingly.

With all the joy I'm carrying inside me right now, I beam at him. Without him I wouldn't have found this path. "Then nothing can go wrong now." I throw my arms around him exuberantly. "Thank you. For all your help!"

We say goodbye to each other and, even before I leave the building, my mind is already racing. I need great photos, a safe place to sleep until I leave, and Lukas. India is a chance for both of us to live, for at least a few weeks, exactly the life we dreamed of so intensely years ago. I'm going to show him how much it means to me, and without the distractions of everyday life he'll feel how much he still longs for it too. Getting on a plane will be a challenge for him. But for the heaven that's waiting for us in India, he can do it.

It's time to turn this dream into reality. Lukas hasn't reacted to my photo book so far, but I'm not going to let that stop me anymore. I'm going to drive straight to Anna's apartment and talk to him there. Because I don't want to sit around doing nothing any longer. Dreams don't come true by themselves, you have to make them come true. That's what the stranger at the water park taught me, and that's what I want to believe in.

Half an hour later I'm standing in front of the apartment building with the stone-gray façade and the exposed staircase. The next few minutes will decide my future, but I still don't stop. I don't take a deep breath, I don't collect myself, and I don't hesitate for a single moment. Full of energy, I sprint up the steps and press the doorbell for Anna's apartment.

I wait.

There isn't a sound from inside. I ring again, then knock on the door.

Nothing.

Lukas isn't here, but that doesn't mean I'm giving up. I immediately pull my phone out of my pocket and dial his number.

I don't even hear the dial tone; the call drops. "The person you are trying to reach is temporarily unavailable," a friendly female voice informs me.

He hasn't changed his number, has he? Is this how he's trying to keep his distance from me because he thinks he can't bear even to hear my voice?

No. That's not how this works. He's going to have to talk to me, at least once. So I open an email and write him a message at his work address. I let the words pour straight from my heart, unfiltered.

"You and me, forever. That was the deal, and for me it still stands. Our love means everything to me. The two of us can be happy together, and I'm sure you feel that too. We should finally talk. For hours or for days. In rain and in sunshine. Just tell me when and where. I'll be there."

With trembling fingers I send the message and with it all my positive energy. Then I turn around and leave Anna's apartment building to devote myself to my other mission for my later: perfect photos.

Chapter Twenty-Two

If I had a choice, I wouldn't enter this building. My skin is still tanned and my energy reserves are full. But I can all too clearly feel how everything in me resists slipping back into everyday life.

Still, I force myself to keep putting one foot in front of the other. Because it has to be done. That's just how it is, you have to work to build something for yourself. Nothing comes from nothing. That's what my mother preached my whole life. And damn it, she was right. Yesterday afternoon the real estate agent told me that reversing the house purchase is possible, but it won't be easy. The seller insists on compensation; otherwise he won't release me from the contract. I'll probably only get half the down payment back, and I also have to pay the agent's fees. All in all, that's around 35,000 euros that I'll never see again. I clearly need money, and this is exactly where I can earn it. I cling to that knowledge as the sliding doors of the company building glide apart in front of me.

The familiar smell of cleaning products hits me, and the

receptionist gives me an encouraging smile. I give her a quick wave and head for the office.

Bernd seems to have been waiting for me there in eager anticipation. "Thank God you're back!" He immediately grabs two folders, comes over to me with them, and presses them into my hands. "With kind regards from the junior boss. I'm supposed to tell you that these complaints have to be dealt with by nine o'clock."

"What a stroke of luck." I can't suppress a sigh. Ever since the boss's nephew has been in charge here, every day has felt just as heavy as the folders in my arms. "I'll of course take care of that first so he doesn't have another one of his fits."

"I wanted to give you a heads-up, but it only would've ruined your vacation." Bernd shrugs, then suddenly studies me with furrowed brows. "You don't look particularly rested."

So it's that easy to see. As if everything were perfectly fine, I wave it off. "The alarm clock, you know."

With the folders in my arms, I march over to my desk and let myself fall onto the chair. First I have to push some documents aside just to be able to put the folders down at all. That's a damn big pile of work waiting for me here, and yet my thoughts inevitably wander back to the vacation while my computer boots up with a soft whir.

It was only supposed to be a few cozy days by the sea. With plenty of time to relax. It would have been perfect if the two of us hadn't had such different ideas of what a vacation means. I know Anna did her best to fulfill my wishes, but she still didn't manage to just spend the days relaxing with me.

"I'm bored," I hear her grumble in my memory yet again, and at once I relive the moment from a few days ago.

Everything could be perfect. A wonderfully refreshing breeze blows around my nose, I hear the sound of the sea and children laughing. It smells of sunscreen and popsicles. This is the very definition of a vacation, and I want only one thing: to enjoy it in complete peace. With a contented sigh, I open my magazine.

I haven't read a single page when I already notice Anna slowly sneaking up to my deck chair. As soon as she's beside me, she starts drawing circles on my chest with her index finger.

"Mmm," I say, trying to keep focusing on the text.

The circles she traces on my upper body grow larger and larger. "You can rent pedal boats over there."

"Anna, let's just relax a bit more today. Look how beautiful it is here. The sea is calm, the lounger is comfy, and the temperature is just perfect for doing nothing." I reach for her hand and stop her movements.

"As you wish." Grumbling, she pulls away again, presumably back to her own lounger.

I breathe a sigh of relief inwardly and keep reading. The article about the devious business with clothes from the used-clothing collection is just way too gripping.

"I'll go ask over there if we can still join the beach volleyball game," I suddenly hear Anna say. She sounds as if she's standing right next to me.

"Mhm." I nod a little, my gaze flicking over to her for a moment. She gives a forced smile, turns around, and walks away.

The peace that finally surrounds me is wonderful. Luxuriously, I make myself comfortable on my lounger and do what I actually want to do: just let my soul dangle.

I can't help but sigh again today at the memory. Even though we both tried, in the end we didn't find a good compromise for our different energy levels. The longer the vacation went on, the more I gave in for her sake. If I had gone along with everything on Anna's activity program in the last few days, I probably wouldn't have been able to relax at all. Involuntarily, I shake my head at the thought of our rushed day trips. Then I quickly turn to the computer, because it's better to focus on my job.

The password field appears on the screen. As I type it in, a strange feeling comes over me. This is probably the end of my vacation. And I don't know if that's good or bad. Basically, it doesn't matter anyway. Work is calling; that's all I need to know.

Over the next few hours, file after file goes through my hands. I write notes, answer at least some of the emails that have come in, and expand my task lists. As usual, I make phone calls and reach agreements. Only when my stomach protests loudly do I realize that the morning is long gone.

Tired, I let my gaze wander across the desk. At least part of it is done. If I quickly scan the rest, I can continue efficiently this afternoon. I reach for the green folder. These are the galley proofs, all of which still have to be checked today. That goes right at the top of the to-do list for later. I place the folder directly next to the computer keyboard and grab the next one. As I pull it toward me, a small package suddenly appears.

I remember immediately. It was already here before my vacation, but I didn't have time to take a closer look at it. Curious, I reach for it and see that it has neither sender nor recipient. Someone must have put it on my desk personally.

I cut through the tape and fold back the flaps of the box. It's probably a promotional gift from a supplier. Without much interest, I look inside. But what I discover inside catapults me instantly into another universe.

There's a picture of Marie and me.

By reflex I close the flaps of the box and press my hand down on the top as if I had to keep the contents from getting out to me. The package is from Marie, that much is clear. It's the first sign of life from her. For thirty-six days now there's been bitter silence between us. Why is she getting in touch now? And why is she doing it in this strange way? I don't know, but one thing is clear.

It's too late to make anything right. She's left me hanging far too long.

I have to ignore the package. Lock it away or, best of all, throw it out right now. Still, I can't. Not without at least seeing once what Marie wants to show me. But just imagining opening it makes my chest tighten. My palms turn clammy, even the skin under my glasses is damp.

In a reflex I shoot up from my desk chair.

"Is everything okay?" Bernd sticks his head over the partition between our desks. "You've turned a bit pale," he notes matter-of-factly.

I can't pay any attention to Bernd right now. Because I'm staring at the package. And I could swear the thing is staring back. It's ordering me to open it. It wants to force me to look inside.

I shouldn't give in. Not now. And not here.

Still, I feel how my carefully suppressed longing overwhelms me and, seemingly without effort, robs my head of command over my body.

"I'll be right back," I force out, and immediately afterward I look into Bernd's uncomprehending face.

Explaining it to him would be going too far and would also take far too long. Pressing the package tightly against my upper body, I leave the company at a run. My legs steer me of their own accord to the tram that takes me to a place where I never wanted to be again.

Behind the Gloriette at Schönbrunn Palace. To our meadow of flowers.

The minutes seem endless until I'm standing in exactly the same spot where Marie and I promised each other five years ago that our love would last forever. The surroundings have hardly changed; even today the grass has grown tall. Spattered with white, blue, and yellow dots, it lies before me. It looks wild and overgrown.

Maybe I'm crazy, but I march to the exact place where we lay back then. There I let myself sink to the ground, breathe in the intensely scented air for a moment, and then, with trembling fingers, open the box.

Like a fragile treasure, I take out what's inside.

It's a photo album.

And already what I see on the first page drops a whole boulder into my stomach. There's a picture of the club where Marie and I met. There, leaning against that pillar, we waited together for a taxi. We were so absorbed in looking up at the starry sky and wondering how far away it might be that we forgot everything around us.

I feel exactly the same way today. I forget where I am. Page by page I leaf through the album and let my fingers glide over the paper wherever Marie's sunny expression is captured.

She hasn't written a single word in this album, but that isn't necessary. I know what she wants to tell me. She's showing me the story of our love, and when I look at this past in the pictures, it just looks beautiful.

Perfect.

Marie and I were perfect.

Could we ever be that again? After everything that's happened?

I flip to the last page. There I find a picture of Marie. She's lying completely alone in the meadow of flowers, exactly in the spot where I'm sitting right now. Her eyes are asking me the same questions I was just asking myself.

Seeing her like this hits me right where I no longer wanted to be vulnerable. In an instant I can't ignore my doubts anymore.

My life has come off the rails; nothing fits together anymore. And no matter how hard I try to hold the shards in place, I just can't do it.

Anna is a great person, but deep down I still don't know if I'll ever be able to love her the way she would have deserved. I haven't been passionate about my work for far too long, and this damned urge to get everything right all the time is like a golden shackle around my ankle. It forces me to keep going, no matter whether I like it or not.

A good life. That's all I ever wanted. And what did I get? A friend who will probably never again be the best friend who used to be by my side. An ex-fiancée who refuses to be pushed out of my heart. A dream house that turned out to be a nightmare. And a job that keeps getting heavier, with a boss who's making my life hell.

I let my hands sink into my lap and my head fall back. Thick tears well up beneath my closed eyelids, and there's absolutely nothing I can do to stop them.

Because there's only one truth left. I've lost everything that ever mattered to me.

Chapter Twenty-Three

With a wistful tug in my chest, I sort through the photos carefully lined up on the living-room floor in front of me. For the scholarship application I'm only allowed to choose five pictures, but that seems impossible. I started the selection before the sun had climbed over the horizon outside the living-room window, and even though it's now high in the sky, I'm still nowhere near finished. The last bit of coffee in my cup has gone cold, and I'm more unsure than I've ever been in my life.

They have to be the right photos. But which ones will convince the jury?

I pick up the picture of the elderly couple in the city center and search it for flaws. Is there anything distracting in the background, are the lighting conditions right, is the perspective correct? I go through all the aspects I learned from my course instructor Peter. The horizon isn't as straight as it should be. I could still correct that, but the sky also looks flat because there are no clouds. It's not good enough, I decide, and put it on the stack of pictures that won't make it into the portfolio. At least the ones that don't show people I'll upload to the online platform and hope that a buyer turns up.

With a heavy sigh I look around once more. Just as it did hours ago, my gaze comes to rest on one of the old pictures of Lukas and me in the flower meadow. I've reworked them all, and although the quality of the original material wasn't the best, there's something there that no one can deny. A moving mood. Stirring and full of love.

Seeing the two of us like that makes me soar and crash at the same time. Because it reminds me, with brutal clarity, that the waiting has already gone on far too long.

Today is September 23. Fifteen days have passed since I dropped the album off at his work. Eight days since I sent the email. Lukas must have seen the photo book long ago and read my message long ago. And still he doesn't get in touch. Did he even open the email? Did he ignore the album and just throw it away?

At once I see it in front of me, lying in a gray trash can with bent corners. Next to newspapers, banana peels, and empty plastic bottles.

For him, the two of us are the past. What we had doesn't mean anything to him anymore.

My stomach cramps as if it wanted to drown out the pain that travels from my heart through my whole body. And the why that echoes through my head like a sound breaking against smooth rock walls.

I know I can't let that happen. Nothing in me is allowed to give in, neither my body nor my thoughts. I decided to fight, and that's exactly what I'm going to do. I have seven days left until I have to cancel the lease for good. A whole week in which everything can still turn out well.

As if I were sending a signal by doing it, I slip the photo of Lukas and me in the flower meadow into the application portfolio. I'm counting on the two of us, and that will never change.

Suddenly everything is easy. The remaining four photos fall into place on their own. I'm going to submit the entire series I shot behind the Gloriette five years ago.

In the first picture, Lukas's face is bathed in the golden glow of the autumn sun. In the background stretches lush green, sprinkled with white and violet dots. The second photo is of the two of us, smiling into the camera. In the next one Lukas turns his head toward me. *Wherever you are, I want to be.* That's what he whispered in my ear back then, and that's exactly what the photo captures. The fourth picture shows us kissing. In the last one you can only see the sky and a small patch of our meadow.

I can't help but sigh, because the memory of that day is anchored so firmly in my heart that it feels as if I were there all over again.

As I carefully slip the photos into the application folder, I make a decision. For weeks I've followed Anna's advice and given Lukas time. I've sent messages and even tried to reach Lukas without any words at all. Still, it hasn't done any good.

My gaze jerks to the time display above the TV. In a little over an hour Lukas will go on his lunch break. That's when I'm going to catch him. We just have to talk, and I'm sure we'll find solutions. No matter what happened, the two of us belong together.

Quickly I write the address of the scholarship office on the envelope and head out. I want to show Lukas the photos and tell him what they could mean for me. Only then will I take them to the post office.

A little later I leave the apartment and walk to the tram stop. On the way I suddenly hear my phone beep.

It must be Lukas. He's getting in touch because he finally read my email!

With trembling fingers I pull the phone out of my bag. Sure enough, the little white light is blinking. I take a deep breath once more, then turn the phone on.

A new email pops up. But it's not from Lukas; it's from Mr. Altmann, one of my clients as a virtual assistant.

"Many thanks for your fantastic work. At last, Eco-Design has a professional company presentation with unique images. Thanks to you, we're now able to approach new customers with our eco-friendly office furniture. Once again, I'd like to apologize that, as a start-up, we weren't able to pay more for your work because of our tight budget. I still hope I'll be allowed to get in touch with you again if needed."

A smile flits across my face. Not just because Mr. Altmann's email is so sincerely friendly. I took the photos for the flyers myself. The fact that he points them out is a sign. A sign that my dreams can come true, even if I'm only taking tiny little steps.

On the tram ride to Lukas's company, an overwhelming anticipation of seeing Lukas again spreads through my whole body. But even while I'm waiting once more in the little café, a kind of nervousness joins it that I've never known before. Fidgety, I slide back and forth on the wooden chair, my fingers refuse to keep still whenever I lift the teacup to my mouth. I choke every time I try to drink something. My gaze keeps darting between the clock, the sliding doors at the entrance to Lukas's company, and the letter for the scholarship office.

Exactly twelve o'clock.

My documents are still there.

The glass doors don't move.

Any moment now it has to happen. I'll be as close to Lukas as I haven't been for far too long.

Shouldn't I be getting dizzy, with my eyes moving this fast? I have no idea, I only know that I can hardly bear the tension anymore.

My mind is blank. Whatever happens when we're standing face to face, one thing is certain: I'm already at a loss for words. I don't know what I want to say to him, and even less what I'll do. Should I try to take his hand? Am I allowed to kiss his cheek, or should I just smile at him?

Fear and longing eat their way through my insides, push into my chest and take my breath away. They paralyze my legs and make my arms go rigid. Cold sweat gathers on my back.

How much longer until he comes out? How long?

Two minutes past twelve.

The documents lie unchanged beside me.

The sliding door starts to move.

Now it's time. Eyes wide open, I stare through the café window at the other side of the street.

I see the doors glide apart. Someone steps out of the dark interior onto the street.

Lukas.

All at once everything happens in slow motion. He moves his right foot outside, endlessly slowly, the left follows. I, on the other hand, sit glued to my chair. My body has stopped obeying me; nothing works anymore.

A serious expression lies over Lukas's face. He looks tired and used up. As if he had forgotten what joy is. As if he no longer laughed, cried, or even lived at all. Seeing him like this hurts me. I want to go to him, have to help him and comfort him. That's what my legs finally understand. They push me up from the chair and start running.

When I reach the café entrance, I see Lukas turn right. He walks down the street, moving away from me. I rush after him blindly. At the edge of the sidewalk I stumble, save myself from falling at the last second, take a deep breath, and run on. With my eyes fixed only on Lukas, I step onto the street.

A car honks. Tires screech.

That's not going to stop me. Because by now he's already almost at the next side street. At the corner I suddenly spot Anna. She's waiting for him. I lock my eyes on the two of them, stumble, pull myself together, and keep running.

Now Lukas walks up to Anna.

He takes her in his arms.

The two of them kiss. Like lovers!

I'm unable to move. I can't see, hear, or taste anything anymore.

That's impossible. Anna is like a sister to him.

In an instant I feel as if my nightmare has become real. It's exactly this one scene that has haunted me night after night since our breakup. Lukas smashes my heart onto the ground with a happy grin while I'm far away, absolutely unable to do anything about it.

It's entirely possible that my knees give out, my arms go numb, and my body grows weak. Maybe I sink to the ground and hit the asphalt with full force. I don't know, because there's only one thing I'm still aware of: Anna and Lukas turning the corner into the next alley, hand in hand.

The image in front of my eyes grows more and more distorted until the two of them disappear completely.

A second later, everything around me goes black. I give in because I suddenly don't have the strength to keep fighting.

Chapter Twenty-Four

So here I am. Right in front of the apartment building that was my home for the past four years. Behind this dark-painted wooden door, two floors above me, down the hallway to the right, in the apartment with the number 15. Right now, the woman I could never have imagined living without might be waiting for me there.

I try to breathe calmly, but I can't. The longing for Marie weighs far too heavily on my chest. At the same time, I can hardly bear the guilt I feel toward Anna. The fact that I even came here is terribly unfair of me. If she knew about it, her whole world could collapse. And with it our years-long friendship, in which she never once let me down. Just thinking about it makes my throat tighten. It feels as if someone is wrapping a cold silk scarf around my neck and pulling it tighter and tighter.

In spite of all that, I'm here. With an envelope in my hands that might change my future forever.

Because of Joe and what he advised me to do.

Full of hope that it would take my mind off things, I

went to see him alone at his place a few days ago. In my memory he's once again bracing his hands on the marble counter of the bar right in front of me and looking at me intently.

"Vodka or whiskey?" he asks, tilting his head to the side.

Even if Joe hadn't already known me for years, my situation would still be obvious. Anyone who goes for a drink alone right after work on a Friday probably has problems. That's just how it is. "A beer is enough for now," I say, trying a grin. Whether I pull it off? I don't know.

While Joe turns around to grab one of the large glasses from the shelf, I instinctively reach for the stack of newspapers laid out for lonely guests like me. I take the first one I get my hands on because I strangely don't care what I read. I just want to be distracted so I don't have to keep thinking about Marie's album and her message.

So this is what I've come to.

Good journalism doesn't interest me anymore. I don't care that on a Friday afternoon the best I can come up with is numbing myself with alcohol at Joe's so I don't have to feel what I clearly can't deny any longer.

I'm stuck. As if I had blindly driven my life off a nicely paved road onto a gravel track, then onto bare ground, and finally straight into a swamp. The wheels are spinning beneath me, and the more strength I put into fighting it, the deeper I sink.

"A large beer and a shot on the house," I suddenly hear Joe say, and I watch him set the drinks down in front of me on the dark bar.

I take the shot first, whatever. It burns surprisingly hard on the way down my throat, and everything inside me tightens for a moment. But then my stomach feels wonderfully warm and my head pleasantly dull.

I want more of that. "Would you bring me another?"

Less than a minute later the next high-proof drink is in front of me. I knock it back in one go and push the empty glass back across the bar to Joe with an insistent nod.

His questioning look meets mine. "Alcohol isn't a solution," he says seriously.

"But when you drink, you forget the problem." I heard that line somewhere once, and never have I been able to feel how true it is as much as I do in this moment.

Joe leans across the bar toward me. "It's time to get it off your chest. Don't you think?"

"Is it that obvious?" I press my lips together, because just saying it out loud turns the warmth in my stomach into heaviness.

Still keeping his eyes fixed intently on me, Joe nods. "And not just since today."

Of course not, I know that too. Should I tell him about it? What would that accomplish? He definitely doesn't have an answer to the questions I don't even know yet.

"You're unhappy," he goes on relentlessly.

Absolutely.

His forehead creases. "Why?"

Because of the whole damn world. "Everything's spinning out of control," I say hesitantly.

These are my first attempts to explain to anyone at all what has been happening to me since my breakup with Marie. I used to be able to talk to Anna about anything. But since we became a couple, that's no longer possible. Knowing what's going on inside me since I got Marie's pictures and, most recently, her email would hurt her. So badly that our friendship would be destroyed forever. Of course I kept my emotional chaos to myself and tried to deal with it on my own.

Joe waits patiently for me to go on. I can see in his features that he only wants to help me, so I dare to move a bit closer to the truth. "Marie and I…" I can't help but swallow, "…we broke up."

A fleeting smirk crosses Joe's face. "That was hard to miss, with how close Anna and you have been these last few weeks."

Are we really? "Physically maybe, but…" The words tumble uncontrollably out of my mouth, and suddenly there are many more. All of them push to get out, finally wanting to be said and heard. "Anna is great. An amazing woman. I should be able to love her with all my heart."

All at once Joe's expression turned serious. "You can't force love."

"Why not?" I sounded like a toddler who simply doesn't get what he wants.

Instead of answering, Joe just shook his head. Then he braced both hands on the counter and looked at me intently. "If you want to be happy, you have to listen to your heart. No matter what it's about. Our mind keeps trying to make us believe it knows what's good for us. In reality, it has no idea. Absolutely none."

Today, three days after my conversation with Joe, as I stand absentmindedly in front of my old home, I still don't understand his words. Because everything I've learned in life so far is that my mind has to take the lead. It knows what to do, it can structure tasks, plan the right steps and thus ensure a sensible life.

Still, I came here. As if a force had taken possession of me that I can't get hold of.

I could do it. Just ring the bell and see what happens. Maybe Marie would open the door for me. She'd be surprised, but she'd smile at me. Invite me in. Offer me a place on the sofa. Just like she described in her email, we could talk everything through. And who knows, maybe we'd move closer to each other, inch by inch. Until we find each other again.

Hesitantly, I turn the envelope in my hand. No matter how beautiful the idea of making up with Marie is. What I brought with me is something I can't give Marie in person. Not only because I couldn't bear it if even a single detail of reality weren't exactly the way I'd just imagined it in my fantasy. But also because I don't know how I'd ever be able to look Anna in the eye again if that actually happened.

It would be better to make the envelope disappear, because nothing else makes any sense anyway. Before I do that, I want to look at the contents one more time myself. So I sink down onto the stone steps right in front of our front door. The ground is cold, but I hardly feel it. All my focus is on the envelope, which I now open one last time.

The photos I pull out of the envelope are by far not as nicely prepared as Marie's. I just stacked them loosely on top of each other, because the moment I decided to answer her, I couldn't wait any longer. And because she'll understand even so. If there's still a connection between us, she'll know this isn't about beauty.

Marie showed me what she thinks with her album. The shots I was about to drop in her mailbox until a few minutes ago were supposed to show her what I feel.

There's a picture of our dream house. A close-up of a splintered wooden slat on the porch. It looks jagged and hurt. In my mind it stands for everything we ever wanted and still lost.

The next picture shows my overflowing desk at work. In front of the pile of documents and folders I placed a digital clock. It's 8:00 PM. Next to it are several empty coffee cups.

Only the dry rim of brown liquid on the bottom of the ceramic is still visible. It's dark outside the window.

I can't go on. A sharp pain that bores right into the middle of my chest keeps me from continuing. I have to get out of here. Quickly, I shove the pictures back into the envelope and seal it. I push myself up from the cold floor, take a deep breath, and march off.

Without any intention on my part, my legs suddenly carry me to the mailboxes. As if I were no longer able to control myself, I slide the envelope into the slot a few seconds later.

I absolutely shouldn't let it go.

What if Marie interprets the pictures the wrong way?

And what if she doesn't?

I never would've thought it possible that questions like this would ever occupy me. After all, we used to understand each other blindly. That's what we lost somewhere between her resignation and our breakup. We cut the connection between us, and there's no rational reason why she should now draw the right conclusions from the photos.

She might think they're full of reproaches and accusations. But there's only one thing I want to show her with the pictures: how hurt I am. And how disappointed I am about everything that happened. That I feel trapped. In my work life, with the house, and also with Anna.

Maybe this is a test. For me. For her. For both of us.

Do I even have any other choice than to let go of the envelope in my hand? If I don't, we'll never find out whether there's still a way for us.

My heart knows the answer, or at least that's what Joe claimed. And I feel so clearly that Marie wants it. The old Marie. The Marie I don't even know still exists.

So I do it. It's a small movement, my fingers open only a

few millimeters, then the letter sets off on its way. Along with all my hope for a life I just can't let go of. Because even my mother's admonishing voice, which is explaining to me on endless repeat in this very moment that dreams have no place in reality, can't change that anymore.

Chapter Twenty-Five

A monotonous beeping is the first thing I notice. Then the warm cloud my body is resting in. The back of my hand feels as if a bug is sitting there, sucking on me. The sharp smell of disinfectant lets me guess where I am.

I open my eyes.

"Welcome back."

My gaze wanders in the direction the friendly voice came from. Next to me, a woman is fussing with thin plastic tubes. Her hair is tied back in a ponytail, she's wearing a simple blue shirt and smiling at me. The way her full cheeks lift when she does makes her look almost motherly.

"How are you feeling?"

"What…? Where…?" I can't manage anything more. Because with even the slightest movement my head hurts as if bombs were exploding up there. I want to raise my hand to lay it on my forehead, but that seems impossible. It's heavy, far too heavy. The only thing I can do is look at the nurse, silently asking for help.

"You collapsed. The doctors will tell you more details."

She lays her hand reassuringly on my upper arm. "I'll open a window for you, some fresh air will definitely do you good."

Even if I'd like to nod, I can't. The friendly nurse disappears from my field of vision and I don't even try to follow her with my eyes. I also ignore the other two patients in the room. Because that's not important right now.

Even though my head is nothing but pain, I want to remember. What happened, and why am I here?

Of course. Lukas. And Anna.

I've lost the love of my life for good. That's the only thing I can still think about. Exhausted, I close my eyes. Darkness spreads inside me. Tears push out from beneath my closed lids, so forcefully that I don't even try to hold them back. I cry silently to myself, desperately searching for something I can still hope for.

Suddenly, one of the doors of the hospital room is flung open with a loud noise. The trampling of countless shoes can be heard.

"All right, let's have a look then," says a deep male voice. He sounds stressed. And as if he has absolutely no desire to be here.

Stealthily, I wipe away the tears that keep gathering at the corners of my eyes and open my lids. A group of men and women in white coats, armed with notepads and stethoscopes, is standing in front of my bed.

"Who's presenting her?" asks the man with the graying hair and the thick horn-rimmed glasses.

A young, strikingly attractive woman steps forward. "Marie Berger, twenty-five, admitted with syncope and a laceration on the right temple. CT shows indications of a lesion. Wound care, administration of antibiotics and painkillers, regular monitoring, and bed rest." She rattles off the facts without emotion. Dozens of pairs of eyes stare at me as if I were a penguin in a zoo. I feel a bit like a number that gets called, gawked at, and processed.

"How are you feeling, Ms. Berger?" the gray-haired man wants to know, turning to his documents at the same time.

I'd shrug if I could. "When will I be discharged?" I force out, because I don't care about anything else. I have to get to Lukas, need to hear from his own mouth that it's really over between us.

His brow furrows as he focuses on my medical file in his hand. "The medication should start working soon, but your lesion has to be monitored. In a few days we'll see how things look."

Before I can say anything, the group turns around and moves on to the patient in the bed next to mine. A man around forty who apparently broke his leg. The cast goes up over his knee and is covered in children's drawings. He must have a wonderful family. A loving wife and kids who visit him every day.

I quickly look away. I have to focus. Even though my head can barely hold a coherent thought, I search for my phone. I had it with me when I collapsed, so it has to be here now. I find it in the bedside cabinet next to the bed, together with my handbag and the application folder for the scholarship. I pull it out immediately and dial Lukas's number. Even if it could go badly, I have to talk to him.

Just like the last time I tried, I don't even get a dial tone. I don't have any other choice. I grit my teeth and call Anna.

"Marie! How are you?" It's absurd how friendly she sounds. If I didn't know better, I'd think she was happy I called.

That manipulative snake. From the very beginning she

lied to me, fed me false leads, and only pretended to be my friend. Why on earth didn't I see through her much earlier?

"How could you?" I ask, my voice choked, and I'm sure she knows exactly what I mean.

For a moment she's silent before she clears her throat. "How do you know?"

"Is that really important?" I try to pull myself together, but I can't. My tone is cold. "Why, Anna? Tell me."

"Because I love this man like no other person in this world. I'm the one who wants to be there for him. I give him everything he needs." She sounds like a mother desperately trying to protect her child. "You had your chance and you let him go. Try to understand, I've waited so long to be with him. He finally belongs to me and there's nothing you can do about it. Accept it."

Suddenly I hear Lukas's voice in the background. "Anna?"

"All right, Alice, we'll meet tomorrow on the track," Anna says all of a sudden, and in the very next second the connection cuts off.

So that's how it is. Lukas has absolutely no idea what's going on. She's showing him what he wants to see, just like she did with me.

How can she claim she loves him and treat him like this at the same time?

But who am I to judge her? Didn't I do something similar myself?

Alongside all the self-hatred that's spreading inside me right now, at least one thing is immediately clear to me: I can't be the one to tell Lukas what's really going on behind Anna's façade. He wouldn't want to hear what I say. On the contrary, he'd think I'm just his lying ex-girlfriend who wants him back by any means necessary.

Because that's what Anna will put in his head, I'm sure of it.

I need a different solution. But no matter how hard I think about it, I can't come up with anything else I could try. The album was a failure. He never answered the email. He seems to have blocked calls from my phone. Everything points to him not wanting any contact with me.

Suddenly a terrible thought rises up in me. What if he's happy with Anna? What if she really gives him what he needs, and does it far better than I ever could?

I shouldn't let this thought wrap around me like thick, black fog. I should keep believing in our love and in the fact that everything can be okay again. I shouldn't stop fighting for all my dreams. But right now I no longer know where I'm supposed to find the strength for that.

Melancholic, I pull the blanket over my head and let my feelings run free. I'm very quiet so I don't disturb the other patients in the room. And that alone makes me feel even lonelier than I already do.

After a sleepless night I feel numb inside. A new doctor claimed during rounds earlier that the extent of my lesion was unchanged. I nodded politely, because it doesn't really matter anyway. Then I'll just stay here; out there, there doesn't seem to be much good waiting for me anyway.

Thoughtfully, I look at the white-painted ceiling of the room. I search for stains and cracks, for uneven spots and eyesores. There's nothing; I'm the only eyesore here.

The one who can't get anything right. The one who's about to lose everything because she's chasing after something anyone would call a crazy pipe dream.

The scraping sound of the door reaches my ears, and I instinctively look over. It's Alex, and she seems to have brought everything I asked her for.

"Wow, you really had quite a fall there," she says by way of greeting and sets the duffel bag with the clean clothes and toiletries down next to my bed. "What on earth are you doing. I take my eyes off you for one second and you throw yourself in front of the next car."

Having her here feels good. Because she lets me know I'm not completely alone. "Which once again proves that I'm lost without you." I try a crooked grin. Thanks to the painkillers slowly dripping into my vein, I even manage it.

Alex comes closer right away. "Good that you're finally seeing that for yourself." As carefully as if I were a fragile little chick, she wraps her arms around me. When she lets go again, she can't hide the worried look in her eyes. "Marie, why didn't you get in touch sooner? You do know I'm here for you anytime, right?" Gently, she brushes a strand of hair out of my face.

"But everything's fine." I lie, and I don't even know why.

Nothing is fine. Neither on the outside nor on the inside; I'm wounded everywhere.

"You've been here since yesterday at noon and only called me today. Me, your best friend!" The reproachful undertone in her voice shows me how worried she is about me.

"I'm sorry," I say quietly and bite my lip. The truth is that yesterday I wasn't in any state to have visitors. Not after my phone call with Anna.

For a moment she lifts her elfin chin, then she looks at me intently. "What happened?"

The warmth in her gaze and the genuine concern in her voice feel like big, soft bandages laid over my wounds. I immediately tell her what happened on the sidewalk in front of Lukas's workplace and about my phone call with Anna.

"Now I'm here and I have no idea what I'm supposed to

do next," I finish my recap and press my lips together to keep them from trembling uncontrollably.

Alex is obviously at a loss for words. "That bitch," she just mutters, over and over again.

I raise my hand defensively. "She only wants what's best for him." Unlike me, I think silently. I behaved selfishly and didn't even notice what he needed. Not for the first time, I wish I could turn back time and undo all of it. The misunderstandings and the silence. The hesitation and the white lies.

Alex forces a smile onto her lips. "So we need a plan. What could it look like?"

"If only I knew." Thoughtfully, I nibble on my lower lip. "Lukas doesn't want me anymore. He's done with our love. I have to manage the same." Just saying it is hard for me. Because it can't be like this. Because my happiness might never be complete without this one man.

I see the doubt on Alex's face. She can't believe this is really supposed to be the end, just as little as I can myself. "And what about your dream?" she asks, and I know exactly what she's doing. She's trying to take my mind off things.

A tired smile flits across my face. It lets me know I'm not completely lost. That there's something that can at least partially fill the emptiness Lukas has left inside me. "I have an idea for that."

"Seriously?" Her eyes light up, and she immediately scoots closer to me so she won't miss anything.

"I'm going to give notice on the apartment." Saying it feels as if I'm pronouncing my own death sentence. But it has to be done. Lukas isn't coming back. Deep inside I feel that there's only one way left for me. As much as possible of my later has to become my now; I owe myself that. "Still, I might not even take you up on your offer to stay with you."

Fidgety, she squirms back and forth beside me on the bed. "Why?"

I give her a furtive grin. "I'm doing that photography course you found for me. It's amazing. And the instructor is just brilliant."

Her eyebrows draw together. "You mean, you and this guy, you…?"

"No!" I shake my head, but quickly stop again. "Ouch." Instinctively, I put my hand on my forehead.

"And then what? Finally tell me about your plans." All of a sudden she looks like one of those governesses in old movies, strict and uncompromising.

Of course I don't want to torture her any longer, so I tell her about the competition, the photos I picked out for it, and my idea of using the scholarship money to travel to India. Even while I'm speaking, I notice how my cheeks are glowing with excitement.

"You look damn happy when you talk about taking photos, you know that?" Alex suddenly asks, sounding terribly sentimental.

Just as sentimental, I now look into her radiant blue eyes. "Isn't that what life is about? Not waiting for later and spending your time as happily as possible? Who knows how many days are left?" I don't even let the wish to experience all of this together with Lukas surface. Because just thinking about it hurts too much.

"Absolutely right. I'm keeping my fingers crossed that you win, of course." Alex is at least as excited as I am.

"First the photos have to be submitted." I nod toward the nightstand. "I was going to do that, but then…"

Alex reacts immediately, jumps up, and opens the drawer of the rolling cabinet next to my bed. As if she's found a treasure, she holds the envelope up in the air a second later. “Consider it done.”

I smile gratefully. And at the same time, I start calling on all the luck in the world to be there for me when the jury picks the winner. Because I can’t bear to lose my dream of photography as well.

Chapter Twenty-Six

She doesn't get in touch. That's all I can think about as I open the case with my darts and check that the flights are sitting right. Thoughtfully, I tug at the colorful plastic fins and wonder if Marie misunderstood my photos. Two days have already passed since I slipped the envelope into her mailbox. She must have found the envelope and seen the pictures.

Still, my phone stays silent. There's no email, no message, and no call.

I feel a bit like I'm carrying sacks of wet sand on my shoulders. They push me down, make every step heavy. With an effort, I let myself drop onto the barstool.

"Rough day?" Joe slowly wipes the counter in front of me with his dish towel in circular motions.

I wave it off. "I'm fine, just tired."

"Mhm," is all he grumbles, then he pauses and studies me for a moment. There's something in his gaze that unsettles me. He probably wants to know what happened after our last conversation. All at once, the corners of his mouth lift and he gives me a friendly smile. He wants to cheer me up, at least that's what it looks like. "Your head's screaming too loud, huh?"

Of course it is.

Because it has to.

If it were quiet, the longing for my old life would take over. This life doesn't exist anymore, it booms in my head now. Marie's silence is the final proof of that. "Could be," I answer hesitantly and reach for the beer glass.

Before I can take a sip, Anna steps through the entrance on the other side of the room. Like a whirlwind that sweeps everything along, she comes toward me. Her flowing mane bounces up and down steadily like a lion's.

"Hi, my love." She doesn't just say the words, she sings them. On top of that, she puts on a burst of radiant energy. It takes her less than a second to loop her arms around my neck and kiss me so passionately that Joe behind the counter is probably losing his breath right along with me.

I gently free myself from her clutches. "You're in a good mood."

"Yes, I am. Come on, let's play." She rubs her hands together. "Or are you afraid of losing to me again?"

That cheeky expression gets me every time. I have to laugh, and a bit of my burden evaporates. "You wish." I give her a friendly pat on the shoulder. Just like I used to do in the past. Back when we were still best friends. It feels right, and good. Unlike everything else. "Ladies first," I say and follow her to the dartboard.

Not even a minute later Anna's darts land squarely on triple twenty. All three of them. She does her typical victory dance and gives me a challenging grin. "Well then, show me what you've got."

After three games I have to admit defeat, whether I like

it or not. Today she beat me by a mile; I didn't stand a chance.

"You've been practicing in secret," I say in mock offense as I put my darts away again.

Anna brushes a kiss onto my lips and strokes my cheek. "You just don't have any talent, that's all, my dear. Don't take it so hard, not everyone can be a champion."

That's Anna. As if she were missing a filter, her thoughts tumble straight out of her mouth.

"But there are other things you're pretty good at," she murmurs in my ear and presses herself closer against me. As if her mood had suddenly flipped, her fingers wander across my chest. With her tongue she traces the outer edge of my earlobe.

Guilt overwhelms me at once. Thinking of the envelope I dropped in Marie's mailbox two days ago, I swallow hard. Anna stood by me even in times when no one else wanted anything to do with me. She defended me and fought for me. How can I behave so pathetically toward her now? "Let's have another drink," I say quickly, so I don't have to think about it anymore.

Instead of pushing out her lower lip like she usually does, she gives me a conspiratorial look. "Gladly." I can clearly tell she's up to something. Her blue eyes are sparkling, she keeps brushing her hair out of her face, and all of a sudden she seems nervous.

"Is everything okay?" I ask instinctively, and right after that I wave Joe over to us.

Anna just nods in silence. But while we order, she's conspicuously reserved. And even after Joe has been gone for quite a while, she still seems to be searching for words.

I want to help her, so I make the first move. "What's going on, Anna? I can see you've got something on your mind." Gently, I lay my hand on her forearm and give her an encouraging nod.

"We should look for a bigger apartment together," she blurts out all of a sudden, and I can't shake the feeling that she suddenly looks at me with relief. "I mean, that tiny cave we're holed up in right now is just too small for two people in the long run. Don't you think so too?"

The words leave her mouth far too quickly, almost as if she'd been holding them back for quite some time. Now the dam seems to have broken, and her torrent of words can't be stopped.

"We should look for something closer to your work, with an extra room and a big kitchen. Or move into one of those cool lofts. You know, the ones where the bathtub is right in the middle of the room. An apartment with a garden would be nice too." Her enthusiasm could sweep me along if it weren't for the heaviness that comes back right now, the one I can't shake off. It doesn't belong here, I'm doing everything I can to smile it away, but it's still there. "I think about 800 square feet would be good, if we get a basement storage unit with it." Thoughtfully, she presses her index finger to her chin. "Or could we make do with 750? What if we move into the house? After all, it'll belong to you soon, and it doesn't make any sense to leave it empty, does it?"

She looks at me expectantly. I have to answer, even though I have no idea what to say.

Move into Marie's dream house? Together with Anna?

An absurd idea. Back then I would've asked her in a situation like this if she was on drugs. We would've joked that her brain wasn't working right. Then she would've nudged me gently with her elbow. Together we would've laughed until our stomach muscles were one big cramp.

And now? Now I'm afraid of reacting the wrong way and knocking down the last supporting pillar of my life.

"Um…" I say, just to get anything out at all, and run my hand through my hair. Should I tell her that the reversal of the house purchase is already underway? I could probably still stop it. If I wanted to.

"I get it, you need to think about it." For a moment a deep crease forms between her eyebrows, then she gives me a forced bright smile. "No problem, darling. You'll end up realizing that moving into the house is the best plan ever anyway. Of course I'll pay rent, that'll help you with your mortgage too." She seems so convinced of her idea that not even a volcanic eruption right next to us would shake her. "Think about it. I'm just going to slip away for a moment."

Only when Anna turns her back on me do I feel like I can breathe again. My head is spinning. My best friend wants to take the next step in our relationship just six weeks after my breakup with Marie.

Can I even do that? Would moving in with her not at the same time mean letting go of Marie for good? And hasn't that, in truth, already happened long ago?

My head feels heavy, I have to prop it up. My hand reaches for the half-full beer glass as if by itself. I drain it. In a single gulp.

"Heart or head, that is the question." The words come from Joe, who has silently joined me and is looking at me with a knowing expression.

I furrow my brow and wearily raise my empty glass. "Would you bring me another one, please?"

"That's not going to help you," he says, but he still takes the glass from me.

I don't want to hear that. Not at all. "What makes you so sure?"

Fine little lines formed around his brown eyes. "There's always a tomorrow."

Maybe, I thought silently to myself, and still it was today that was making my life so hard. With Anna everything should have been great, and yet it felt wrong to plan my future with her. I was still trapped in Marie's arms, with my thoughts and most of my body. And that even though she was farther away from me than ever before.

"In the end there's only one thing that really matters." Joe's voice pushed its way back into my thoughts. In a matey gesture, he put his hand on my shoulder.

I looked up at him, my gaze landing right on his face. He seemed dreamy and a little wistful. And there was something in his eyes that made me believe he knew exactly what he was talking about.

"What thing do you mean…?"

Before I could finish my question, Anna whirled toward me, seemingly out of nowhere. Beaming with joy, she wrapped her arms around my back and laid her head against my chest. "I just had a brilliant idea. We're going to drive out to the house together and imagine how we'd furnish it. Then the decision won't be hard for you at all. It's going to be great."

No, it definitely wasn't. But I could never tell her that. "Sounds good." Just like that, the words left my mouth. So this was how far it had come. I was lying to her. Even if I only did it so I wouldn't hurt her, it was wrong.

Anna was great. We were on the same wavelength and were a team that always had each other's backs. So why did the thought of choosing her completely feel as wrong as the off-key notes of an out-of-tune guitar?

My gaze wandered to Joe, who pointed his index finger

at his heart. Exactly at the spot where my own chest was tightening painfully right now.

"Still, give me a little more time, please." As I spoke, I pulled Anna closer to me. After all, I could clearly see how happy she was, and I wanted it to stay that way.

"If I have to." All at once her lips become thin lines. "But not for too long, promise?"

"Promise," I say. Then I go ahead and order another beer after all. And a shot on top of it. Because I feel like I need the hard stuff especially badly right now.

Chapter Twenty-Seven

Grandma looks at me with a mixture of admiration and disbelief. Just a moment ago she was sitting relaxed on the visitor's chair next to my hospital bed, now she straightens her back. "You want to sell all your possessions? You'd be giving everything up."

I shrug; that has to be enough of an answer. Of course I know this really is the end. Still, it's unavoidable, at least that's what I've been telling myself for days now. The thought makes me shiver; I pull the blanket a little higher and bury my hands under the white sheet. "What else can I do?"

"I understand that you need the money, but…" Now she falters, as if she doesn't know how to address the sad truth about my plans.

I'm taking off. Leaving everything behind. Lukas, Vienna, the apartment, Alex, and her too. India will be my new beginning. If I win the photo competition, because that's what this future depends on. "Why wait any longer?" I ask, looking Grandma straight in the eyes.

Nervously, her fingers play with each other. "If you really fly to India, will you ever come back?"

There it is, the crucial question. "I don't know," I answer, and that's the truth. "Besides, it's not even clear yet whether I'll go at all. If I lose the competition, this dream could burst too."

"I'm sure all your wishes will come true." Grandma seems so convinced that her mood sweeps me along. And yet she's wrong. One of my wishes will probably remain unfulfilled forever.

"Someone once told me that you should follow your heart. That you mustn't wait for *later*, that you should enjoy your life to the fullest and do what makes you happy." I sound sentimental, I can hear it clearly. "Lukas doesn't love me anymore, I have to look ahead."

At once, Grandma's hand slips under my blanket and finds my fingers.

"I might never get over losing him. But that doesn't mean I can't go on, right? That I can't follow my own path to at least find happiness where it's still waiting for me. Just like you." That's the prettied-up version of what's going on inside me. It's what I force myself to believe, because I simply have to. While I speak, I feel tears gathering in my eyes. Longing and grief mix together, past and future collide and run salty down my cheeks.

Grandma pushes her chair back, and just a few seconds later she leans over me. Very gently, she rests her head on my shoulder. "You'll find your way," is all she says; she swallows all the other words, I can hear that clearly. "I'm going to miss you very much."

I quickly smile at her. "We'll always be connected, no matter where I am."

"I'm sure of that." Grandma blinks suspiciously often, then exhales loudly. "How can I help you with your plan?"

I see the warmth in her encouraging expression and pull her into my arms. I hold her tight and then tighter still, and I have no intention of letting her go again anytime soon.

It doesn't take long before she starts flailing her arms. "Marie, I can't breathe."

I loosen my embrace, her bright red face appears in front of me. "Sorry, I guess I got a bit carried away." I hastily wipe the tears from my cheeks and try to manage a smile. "So you want to help me?" I fix her with my gaze as if I could conjure her into agreeing. "And you're ready to do absolutely anything?"

"Anything," she breathes, as if she were my ally in a secret mission.

"I'm going to be stuck here for a few more days." With a small hand gesture, I indicate the bare hospital room we're in. "From here I can't look for a new tenant or sell my stuff."

Grandma nods. "Got it, I'll take care of it. My new roommate knows her way around the internet, together with her I can manage that." Suddenly the optimism vanishes from her face. "And what about the things that belong to Lukas?"

"When Lukas moved in with me, we bought new furniture together. There's hardly anything left of his other things," I say thoughtfully. I ignore the pain in my chest.

A smile flits across Grandma's face. "Let's do it like this: I'll sell the furniture. I'll give half of the proceeds and his personal things to this Anna."

"That sounds like a plan." I can't help but swallow. Because in my mind a picture of Lukas and Anna appears.

The two of them are gazing adoringly at each other and look almost disgustingly happy.

What drove him of all people into her arms? Had there already been more than just friendship between them before?

I strain to remember a situation that would explain everything. But I can't find one. There were no passionate looks, no goosebump moments, and no touches that hadn't felt like those between siblings. And yet the two of them are a couple now.

"Is there anything else I can do for you?" Grandma's cheerful voice pushes into my thoughts, and that's probably a good thing.

"You're already doing more than enough." I have to force myself a little, but I still smile at her. Where there's light, there's always shadow too. That's definitely how the stranger would put it. What if my shadow is Lukas and photography is my light?

If I had known, in the moment I quit, how my life would change, would I still have done it?

I don't know. I only know one thing for sure: the answer to these questions depends on the outcome of the photography contest.

Chapter Twenty-Eight

More and more often I run away, because I can't shake the feeling that I can't stand being in Anna's apartment. I'm at Joe's, at work or, like today, at my parents' winery. Here in the spacious eat-in kitchen I can still feel a sense of home. There's the cozy wooden corner bench where I used to sit when I was four. And the curtains with the hand-crocheted lace on the small windows. There's even a picture I painted of our family when I was five still hanging on the wall next to me.

My mother is sitting across from me at the kitchen table. Thoughtfully, she sips her coffee, then looks at me intently over the rim of her cup. "People sometimes change without warning." As if it were nothing special, she shrugs. "Be glad it turned out this way. Who knows what…"

I quickly raise my hand. "I know." I know exactly what she's about to say. That things with Marie and me would have ended badly. Or that she would only have used me. It's hard for me to look her in the eye, so I focus on the floral pattern of the linen tablecloth. It looks old-fashioned, but it fits this rustic kitchen perfectly. "She didn't even try to get in touch with me for weeks." I keep the thing with the photos to myself. They would be an open goal for my mother.

Her strained exhale doesn't bode well. "That just shows you how far she's drifted off on her self-discovery trip. I know this, I know exactly what's happening to her."

Of course she does. "Got it," I say, so as not to dig any deeper into the subject. At the same time I wonder what I'd actually hoped to get out of this conversation. Encouragement? Help making a decision? No idea.

"Your Aunt Ulrike was just the same." She pauses for a moment. I look up at her and see in her face that the memory still hurts her even today. "No one could save her. From her own dream that she threw herself into blindly. She thought she was going to be a star, but all that was waiting for her was a deep abyss."

"You still think about her a lot," I say, and in truth my mother doesn't have to answer that at all. For years we hardly talked about her sister's story. Maybe now is the right moment to see behind my mother's façade. And maybe her experience will help me to forget that…

No. Forgetting is unimaginable.

"Ulrike and I were a team. Together we stole cherries from the neighbor's garden. We wore the same hairstyle, and whenever one of us did something wrong, we took the blame for each other. She was the best sister I could ever have wished for." All at once my otherwise so resolute mother seems melancholy. She lowers her gaze to her coffee cup and looks as if she were searching there for answers to questions that have never stopped circling in her head.

I want to help her, so I clear my throat carefully. "You lost your connection to each other." Just saying it out loud is hard for me. Because that sentence applies to Marie and me as well.

Lost in thought, she shakes her head. “To this day I don’t understand it. We never kept secrets from each other. But she hid her joy in singing from me, as if she were ashamed of it.”

Once again I’m reminded of Marie. For weeks she didn’t tell me what was wrong with her. She kept me at a distance, even though I clearly noticed how bad she was feeling. A sense of heaviness settles on my shoulders. I should have been there for her more, asked her about her thoughts more often, and been open to her answers. “You sensed it, didn’t you? But you were afraid to dig deeper and find something you didn’t want to know.” The words leave my mouth of their own accord.

“Look around you,” my mother says, spreading her arms. “This here is real life.”

I know exactly what she’s talking about. She means the roof over our heads, the warm radiators, and the full refrigerator. She’s thinking of the hard work that makes all of that possible, and of her own obligation to keep the winery at least in the condition it was in when she took it over.

“Dreams have no place in reality. Fortunately, you understood that early on and have acted accordingly ever since. Ulrike should have seen it too.” My mother’s fists clench, her knuckles standing out. She looks a bit as if she were fighting against the helplessness of her memories.

Just like I am. Because that was exactly what I had tried to explain to Marie as well. “She didn’t want to understand,” I murmur absentmindedly, “and instead started secretly losing herself in her own world.”

Damn. It couldn’t be clearer. My mother and I share the same fate.

"Did you ever forget her?" I dare to ask. My voice sounds thin, as if it might shatter under the weight of my fear.

My mother's expression suddenly hardens, as if her muscles were cramping because the same thing is happening inside her. "Ulrike disappeared from my life, and I don't even want to know where she is now or what she's doing." She looks at me out of her blue eyes and brushes the gray-streaked bangs from her forehead. Then she just shakes her head in silence.

So that's how it is. Part of me wants to know whether at least over the years it has gotten better, but I still don't ask her. Because I might not like the answer. Because it could show me that I'll never be happy again in my life.

"What if you had allowed yourself to dream with her? Just a little?" I don't know where the words suddenly come from. Only that their origin lies hidden deep inside me. And in the moment I speak them, I realize how long I've been carrying them within me. And how much I'm hoping that this is a solution.

My mother just snorts contemptuously. "Dreams," she says, and she sounds as if she were uttering a nasty swear word.

"Did you never have dreams? Even small ones?" There's something in me that won't let go of me. Even when I refuse to let it rise up, it forces its way to the surface. I know exactly what wants to get out. Something I spent years strenuously pushing into the shadows because it was obvious it mustn't come to light.

"I don't have time for that kind of nonsense." She forces the words out harshly, then grabs for her coffee cup in a fluster and raises it to her mouth with trembling hands. "And neither do you, Lukas. Don't you start thinking like that again. We both know where that led with you back then."

She's right. I shouldn't.

"You have a good life," I hear my mother say with utter conviction. "Be grateful for it."

"I am," I confirm reflexively, just as I did when I was a teenager whenever my mother reminded me of that fact.

A good life, it echoes in my head. That's more than many other people have.

"Just look at what you've made of yourself," she adds now, as if she doesn't believe me. "You've got a good job that keeps you financially secure. And you've got Anna. She's a great woman."

And she would do anything for me, I add silently. Even if she can be demanding sometimes, she's always there for me. I shouldn't want anything more from my life. I have to be content.

It's better if I don't tell my mother that three weeks ago I applied to reverse the house purchase. She might misunderstand, and suddenly I no longer know myself whether it really was the right decision.

Right on cue, my familiar despair washes over me. Because I no longer know what's right. I know my path, and yet it's as if I'm standing at a crossroads, asking myself which direction I should take.

In my mind I see the situation before me in vivid images.

I turn my head to the right. Anna is there. She's standing next to my desk at the office, smiling at me and positioning the swivel chair so that all I have to do is sit down. On the computer screen I see the house we could soon be living in. A good life, my mother would call it. A good life.

Even so, it's not hard for me to tear myself away from the sight and turn my head to the left. There's a winding path. It leads into a jungle that could be just as dangerous as it could be paradisiacal. Marie is there. She's dancing along the path. She doesn't look at me or urge me to come with her. Instead she laughs and sings. She looks happy. Even without me.

Marie and her dreams probably don't need me. Anna and the good life, on the other hand, are waiting for me.

It should be easy for me to decide. And yet I stand motionless at this crossroads, looking alternately to the right and to the left.

Where should I go?

I don't know, even though I'm usually the one who has all the answers in life. Maybe that's exactly what's knocking the ground out from under my feet now, as if my intersection were suddenly struck by an earthquake.

Chapter Twenty-Nine

Maybe I shouldn't be here. Because I should know myself what's best for me. Because I should feel which decisions are right. Still, I came here to the water park. Straight from the hospital, from which I was just discharged after a five-day stay.

I couldn't go straight home. Back to those four walls that are probably hardly habitable anymore. Grandma not only found a late-deciding freshman as a new tenant, she's also already packed up a lot and sold almost all the furniture. In two days I have to hand the key over to the landlord. The thought of it makes me shudder. It feels like an ending, and that's what it is.

Lost in thought, I stroll along the gravel path. September is almost over, the first harbingers of winter are spreading. On the reddish-brown leaves, droplets of water sparkle in the autumn light like tiny little diamonds.

Instinctively, I take my camera out of my bag and try to capture the dewdrops in pictures. I don't manage it. Of course I don't.

Because I can't manage anything anymore. Without Lukas, only half of me is left.

And that's how it will stay.

Disappointed in myself, I wander on to the lake. If there's one thing I can hope for, it's to meet the stranger. So I send a quick prayer up to heaven as I approach the spot where he's already helped me with so many questions.

He isn't here. Of course he isn't.

Is that a sign? That I have to manage on my own? That I should feel for myself what's right and wrong?

I want to try, set down the travel bag with my hospital things and sit on it. Staring stubbornly at the calm surface of the pond, I force myself to conjure up various new versions of my future. But all I ever see is the one where I travel and take photos with Lukas. It's as if my heart doesn't understand what my head keeps drilling into it so insistently.

"Namaste." A well-known, warm voice reaches my ear.

He's here. Thank God. I turn to him and can't do anything but beam at him gratefully. Just because he's here. And because he's looking at me with that wise expression on his face.

Of course he realizes immediately what's going on. He tilts his head. "You've fallen," he says, and I know he's not referring to the half-healed wound on my forehead.

"Because I tried to fly," I answer just as ambiguously. Strangely enough, it feels as if that says it all.

The stranger only smiles. "You should hold on to that. No matter how often you fall. Get up, spread your wings, and dare a new attempt."

How easy it sounds coming from his mouth. As if it weren't frustrating to keep slipping back. As if, in the last seven weeks since things ended with Lukas, I hadn't run out of strength to pick myself up again and again. "I do that. But with every new attempt I fall harder." By now only my passion and my friendships are left. I have no money, no apartment, no job, no love. I don't say it out loud, but there's no need.

"Many people dream of flying. They imagine how beautiful the world looks from above; some even feel how they seem to glide weightlessly through the sky."

"That's not the problem." My vision is perfect. I see everything clearly; I just can't have it.

Suddenly he turns to me, catches my gaze and holds it with an intensity I feel all over my body. "You've found your dream. That was your first step toward happiness."

"I thought I'd made it," I say absentmindedly. "I was sure I'd left the hardest part behind me." My thoughts drift back to spring, when doubt and lack of drive robbed me of all joy in life. It was the worst time of my life, at least that's what I thought back then.

"It was only the beginning." A smile spreads across his lips. How can he say something so devastating and still look so content?

Of course I was naive. Again. "I still have the whole road ahead of me. With all the stones lying there. And the potholes. The dirty puddles and the uneven ruts." Just saying it out loud feels like torture. "What if I've already used up my strength? What if I can't make it along the way?"

"Then you'll never fly either."

I wish he weren't so mercilessly honest. At the same time, I know he's right.

"We only see those who've already made it. Happy and content, they glide through the sky and look as if they don't even have to make an effort to do it." Carefully, he reaches for my hand, and I know that what comes next is an important lesson. "What we don't see, however, is how many times these people fell before they were able to fly. How many times they failed, how many times they were depressed, and how much effort it cost them to keep trying again and again despite all the setbacks."

All at once I understand what has happened to me over the past few weeks. I thought it would be easy. I thought that all it took to follow my path was a passion for photography. "Dreaming of the sky is only the beginning. Getting there, no matter how long the journey takes, is the end," I murmur absentmindedly.

How could I ever have believed the world had been waiting just for me?

The stranger moves closer to me, our arms touching. I feel his warmth and immediately feel safe. "Believe in yourself the way no one else ever would. Don't wait for a sign, be brave."

My head comes to rest on his shoulder as if all by itself. The glitter the golden rays of the sun leave on the surface of the lake blinds me. I close my eyes, watch the points of light dance behind my lids, and take a deep breath. I know what he wants to tell me. "India has to come true," I murmur, a smile on my face that must be shining even brighter than the sun above us.

The land of red earth and colorful fabrics, my camera, and Lukas. That's my dream, and it can't depend on luck or coincidence any longer. I have to do everything I can to make it come true.

We sit close together by the lake for quite a while longer. We stay silent, because everything has already been said anyway. While the stranger listens to the birds chirping, a plan takes shape in my mind.

Just waiting for the scholarship approval isn't enough. I'm going to book a flight today. With my parents' free miles, I might even get away without paying extra if I'm willing to accept long layovers. That'll save my travel budget. I'll also get my rental deposit back. The rest of the money will come from the scholarship, I'm sure of it. And if it really doesn't work out, I'll work as a virtual assistant in India too. It will cost me time, but for my dream it's more than worth it.

And Lukas? I won't leave without at least having talked to him. No matter what Anna claims and no matter how hard she tries to keep the two of us apart. I want to tell him what I think and read in his face for myself what he feels. I want to lay my hand on his chest and feel whether his heart still beats for me.

The thought of being close to him again after so many weeks overwhelms me. I feel as if I'm standing with my arms spread wide on the highest mountain on earth, with a view that makes everything worldly seem very small.

The notification tone of my phone yanks me back into reality. And even though I can't possibly know, I'm sure that something amazing has just happened. Maybe there's a message from Lukas waiting for me, maybe the photography contest committee is getting in touch. Full of confidence, I pull my phone out of my pocket. A new email in my inbox catches my attention.

"Inquiry," it says in the subject line, and my fingers immediately start to tremble. Clumsily, I open the message. It's true! What I didn't even dare hope for a few hours ago has happened.

Someone wants to book me as a photographer for a baptism.

This is it. Proof that it's going to work out, even if it's

only the tiniest bit. With the payment I couldn't even live for three days here in Vienna, but in India I'll definitely get by for two weeks.

Suddenly I notice that the stranger is watching me. There's a knowing smirk on his lips. He gives me a nod, but that wouldn't even be necessary, because I know it perfectly well myself.

It's the beginning of something good.

Chapter Thirty

It's Friday afternoon, the watch on my wrist says it's only 2:30 PM. I know the work on my desk is piling up. There are orders that need to be entered and a thousand other tasks the junior boss has dumped on me. Still, I didn't want to stay any longer. Of course it's wrong, but this work makes less and less sense. And I don't enjoy it anymore either.

With a deep sigh I push open the front door to Joe's. It's noticeably quiet today. Apparently only a loser like me wants to spend a golden autumn day like this in a bar. Together with a group of teenagers playing pool in the back of the bar. A smell of home and security wafts toward me. It would be great if that could distract me, but without at least a beer that's not going to work. I head straight for the bar.

As if he'd been waiting for me, Joe grabs a beer glass and fills it. By the time I've made myself comfortable on the stool right at the bar, my beer is already in front of me.

"Thanks, you know exactly what I need." I sound just as worn out and tired as I feel. The stress at work would be enough on its own, but the whole thing with Anna and Marie is finishing me off. And the fact that Anna has put a hike in the weekly planner for me tomorrow is also clouding my outlook for the weekend.

"Life doesn't have to be like this, you know?" The sad sound of Joe's voice makes me prick up my ears, but I still don't say anything. Because I wouldn't know what to say. Instead, I take a big gulp of my beer.

As if his hands need something to do, Joe starts straightening the glasses on the bar top. Then he takes a deep breath and turns to me. "Can I tell you a story?"

"Sure." I wish I sounded more enthusiastic, but I gave up hope that anything could distract me a long time ago.

"Twenty years ago my life was different. When I look back now, it seems crazy to me, but back then there was so much I didn't see." Suddenly his face takes on a wistful look, maybe even melancholy. As if he can't quite grasp it himself, he gives a slight shake of his head.

I immediately feel a little uncomfortable. Stories that start like this often have a terrible ending. Still, I don't interrupt him, because hope overwhelms me. What Joe is about to tell me could help me. And I clearly need help.

"I only wanted one thing: to make a career. I was ready to do anything for that." Lost in thought, he reaches for a glass and pours himself a beer. "After graduating in business administration, I started working for a management consultancy. I worked around the clock, and it paid off after just a few years." There's irony in his voice, a contemptuous snort leaves his mouth. "I thought I was a winner. Money, prestige, and power were my trophies." His intensely sad gaze meets mine. He shakes his head. "But in reality I had lost everything."

Until a few months ago I probably wouldn't have understood what he was talking about. Today I can empathize with him.

Because I know what it's like when everything looks fine on the outside, but inside there's nothing but emptiness.

"Then I met a woman. She shone from within in such a special way that I don't have the words to describe it to you. I fell in love with her on the spot."

That sounds great. "It was what you were missing." Stubbornly, I try to ignore the stab in my chest.

"Still, I didn't get it. At least not the way I should have." Thoughtfully, he runs his index finger along the rim of the beer glass. "She never said anything, never wanted to force me to work less, and she was never angry when I showed up late to her performances or didn't turn up at all."

"Work is important; after all, it's the basis for a good life." The words slip out of my mouth all by themselves. Of course I know I'm repeating one of my mother's sayings. But at least it's one that's beyond dispute.

He looks up from his beer glass, his intense gaze meets mine. "That's what our mind talks us into."

I immediately remember our last conversation. Our head doesn't know what's good for us. Only our heart does. Those were his words. "You mean we shouldn't believe it, not even in this case?" I ask, sounding downright shocked.

He doesn't answer, but takes a deep breath to continue his story. "I wanted everything, and that's what I got. Every second of my days was scheduled, crammed full of obligations and tasks. When I came home late at night, I was tired. Still, I wanted to spend time with this incredibly amazing woman by my side. It didn't take long before I couldn't really sleep anymore. In the mornings my jaw hurt because at night I'd clenched my teeth so hard that the muscles in my face cramped."

I see how heavily the memory weighs on his shoulders. He bites his lip, a watery sheen lies over his eyes.

"One day my body just stopped working. And suddenly it didn't matter how hard my head tried to fight it. This guy here…" His index finger moves to his forehead. "…couldn't do a thing."

For a moment he looks at me intently, and it's as if time stands still. As if we weren't here in Joe's Bar and as if things suddenly mattered that usually hardly have any value in our society.

"We humans are stupid," he says with a wistful smile. "We dominate every last hidden corner of this planet, yet everything loses its meaning if our hearts don't get what they so desperately need."

Is that true? I don't know, but one thing is clear: I have to hear the end of his story. I have to know how he still managed to become the balanced person I've known for so many years now. "What happened next?" I ask, instinctively holding my breath.

"In the mornings I couldn't get out of bed anymore. Apparently from one moment to the next my legs no longer wanted to move."

That's the truth, I see it in his eyes. Still, I can hardly believe that something like that is possible. "And then?"

"My beloved smiled at me, kissed my forehead tenderly, and asked me to close my eyes." A soft expression comes over his face. I can see all his love for this woman, and also what the memory does to him. "I had no choice anyway, so I did it. Right after that I felt her lie down close beside me. Her arms wrapped tightly around me, she began to sing. It was the melody of Leonard Cohen's 'Hallelujah,' with different lyrics."

Immediately, I have the song in my head, with all its intensity.

"She sang about the meaning of life and about dreams. About vocation and about happiness. With her very special voice she told me about the transience of the moment and the beauty you can only recognize when you're completely in touch with yourself. Long after she hummed the last notes, we lay silently next to each other. My body forced me into inaction, and that was, in truth, the only thing I needed." That sounds strangely esoteric. He sounds a bit like Marie, and that's exactly what scares me. Still, I don't say anything and let him go on. "Then she asked me a question. And it's exactly this question that I now want to pass on to you. Don't think about it, just let it sink in and listen to the answer your heart gives you."

I nod. Maybe because I feel as if he's throwing me a lifeline that could help me get out of my swamp. Maybe because by now I'm so desperate that I'd give anything to get my life back on track.

"If you knew that today was your last day – what would you do? Where would you want to be and who would be with you?"

That's just…

"No. Don't think," Joe admonishes me.

Has he noticed that rejection instantly built up inside me? That my mind already wanted to negate the very question?

"Okay, I'll try," I suddenly hear myself say. "How can I switch off my head?"

A broad grin appears on Joe's face. "That's easy. When the word *but* starts to form in your thoughts, your mind wants to take command. In that moment you have to stop it. There is no *but*."

Absentmindedly, I nod. "*But* doesn't exist. Got it." Even as I speak the words, I'm full of questions. What will happen if I cross but out of my life? Will I actually be able to do that? Once more I turn to Joe. "What did you say to your wife back then?" I ask curiously. Maybe there's a clue in his answer, even just a small one.

"If today were my last day, I wouldn't want anything more than to stay lying here and listen to you sing. Those were my words, and that was the moment I realized that my life up to then had been meaningless and empty." He sounds as if it had been very easy for him to see that. As if he had immediately been full of certainty and hadn't had any unanswered questions.

My head doesn't get it, but somewhere in my chest I feel warmth rising up inside me. What is that supposed to mean? "And you actually went through with it?"

Joe nods. "Not for a single day have I regretted the decisions I made back then. Quitting my job was right, this bar here was right. And spending as much time as possible with the love of my life was the best thing I could have done."

Something hurts him, I can see that clearly. At the same time he seems so convinced that I want to believe him. All at once, doubts overwhelm me. They wrestle me down and pull at me.

What if Marie was right? What if we really had been living our lives wrong up to now?

No. The world is just the way it is. No one can simply drop out and only ever do whatever they feel like. There are obligations, bills, responsibility, and saving for the future. All of us are forced to move in step with society.

If we don't, we lose.

"What are you afraid of?" Joe looks at me expectantly.

There it is again, the question he already asked me once

months ago. Back then, when my relationship with Marie was falling apart irreversibly. I know what he wants to hear from me, I already knew it back then. But only today am I ready to answer him honestly.

Exhausted, I look up at him. "I had a dream once too," I say quietly. It's as if I'm afraid someone might hear me. And that even though there isn't a single other guest in Joe's anywhere in sight.

In a split second the memory floods me and there's nothing I can do about it.

Once more, in my mind, I wander through my home village in Burgenland, searching for stories. I see the neighbors whispering about me behind their hands. And I hear my mother's voice, warning me to stop this nonsense and study harder for school so I'd have a chance at a decent job later on.

I have to clear my throat to be able to go on. The thought of telling Joe my story puts a heavy feeling in my stomach. Still, I want to do it, because by now I'd do anything to get my life back on track.

"When I was a twelve-year-old boy, I wanted to be a journalist. Not a normal newspaper reporter, but someone who uncovers real scandals and secret schemes." A wistful sigh leaves my mouth. "I even put out my own newspaper. Today I know it was full of clumsy sentences and poorly researched reports. But back then…"

"Back then those few sheets of paper were your whole world," Joe finishes my sentence.

With my lips pressed together I nod, because I can't manage anything else right now. The wound I suffered back then sits far too deep and has never really healed. Instead, I drain my beer in one go and signal to Joe to bring me another.

"Where did your world disappear to?" he wants to know as he sets the glass down in front of me not even a minute later.

I can't look at him; I just stare at the white foam. "Into the neighbors' trash cans," I answer, shaking my head, and although that alone would be bad enough, I wish that were all.

But it isn't. There's more.

"The adults laughed at me, my school friends turned away from me. No one wanted anything to do with the idiot who wasn't interested in video games or soccer." As if it had just happened, I feel the disappointment all over again. "They denounced me as if I were a criminal. And they shunned me as if I had anthrax. Still, I couldn't let go of my idea of journalism. On the contrary, the fewer friends I had, the more I buried myself in working on my newspaper." Only Anna stayed faithfully by my side. She went through that hard time with me and was always there for me. I owe her everything. And so much more.

"It was your dream, of course you fought for it. That was right and good." Joe sounds convinced, but he has no right to be.

Because he doesn't know anything, absolutely nothing.

Involuntarily, I slam my fist down on the counter. "No," I say, with my own mother's sternness in my voice. "It was wrong. I didn't just make a laughingstock of myself, I made my family one too." There it is again, that feeling of guilt I just can't shake.

Joe keeps looking at me, still unimpressed. "A village community can be relentless."

I barely hear his words, because I'm trapped in my memory. In that one day when I buried my dream of becoming a journalist so deep inside me that it should never have been able to catch up with me again.

"It was the tenth of February, the evening before my thirteenth birthday. Snow lay on the hills. My mother was bottling wine in the utility building. She wore a thick jacket and those gloves that only go up to the middle finger joints."

I had come under the pretense of wishing her good night, but in truth I wanted her to hold me. To feel safe and cared for, just for a moment, when the rest of the world was constantly against me. But I keep that truth to myself; it doesn't matter here.

"She was on the phone and at the same time was filling one bottle after another at record speed. She must have been so distracted that she didn't notice me standing in the doorway, shivering with cold. And that was a good thing. Because if she had seen me, I probably never would have found out."

"Who was on the phone?" Joe asks, as if he knows it's important.

"My grandma." I prop my head in my hands. By now it's so heavy I can't hold it up any longer. "The two of them were discussing how they could beat that nonsense with the newspaper out of me. At first I was angry because they didn't want to stand by me. I was my mother's child, after all; she had to want me to be happy!"

The memory hits me with full force. And suddenly the parallels between myself and Aunt Ulrike are clearer than ever before. She went through this hell too. No wonder she left the village. She was able to; I wasn't. I was only twelve. All the disappointment and anger flood over me again now, fifteen years later.

"Then something happened that I'd never experienced

before," I whisper, my voice choked. "My mother, the strongest woman in the world, suddenly seemed nothing but fragile and small." Lost in her sadness, she filled one of the wine bottles so full that the pale yellow liquid splashed up into her face. A few strands had come loose from her ponytail and stuck damply to her temples. But the biggest drops running down her cheeks were as clear as a mountain stream.

I draw a shaky breath and force myself to let the air escape my lungs very slowly. It's the only way I can keep the memory from sweeping me away.

"In that moment I knew I had to stop. I was the disgrace of our family, and my mother suffered from it more than she ever wanted to show me." That's it, the story of my guilt, which never wants to let me go, even though I've pushed it away from me so stubbornly all these years. "Someone who chases after their pointless dreams is nothing but an egoist who hurts other people," I add bitterly. That was what my mother had already gone through with Aunt Ulrike, and back then I was about to do the same thing to her.

Only now do I manage to look up. I look straight into Joe's face and can hardly believe what I see there. He's smiling. "Like Marie?" he then asks me on top of everything else.

"Like Marie." Even I can hear how hard my words sound, but they're true, after all. How could I ever go back to her as long as she doesn't understand what she's doing to me?

All at once Joe tilts his head to the side and studies me conspicuously long. "Isn't each of us chasing something?" I want to say something right away, because that answer is easy. But he doesn't allow it, just raises his hand and signals me to wait a little longer. "What is it you're chasing?"

The good life.

"And aren't you being selfish while you do that?" is the next thing he wants to know.

Am I? I don't know. I don't know anything anymore, except that it finally has to stop.

"Your heart knows the answer." Joe gives me one last nod, then he turns and disappears around the corner of the long bar. As if he'd told me everything I need to know.

I'm left on my own. With a half-empty glass of beer, a loudly protesting head, and filled with a longing I can't understand but can feel everywhere inside me.

Chapter Thirty-One

It's time. The moment I was still afraid of this morning at the hospital is now directly ahead of me. I set my travel bag down on the sidewalk and let my gaze glide up along the cream-colored plastered wall. All the way to the two windows that belong to the apartment that has been my home for the past six years.

Home. Isn't that supposed to be the place where you arrive and immediately feel safe? The place where dreams can take flight and longings are fulfilled?

If that's the case, then the sixty square meters up there on the second floor can't be my home any longer. And in three days they won't be. I'll find a new place to stay—at Alex's for the next three weeks, then in India. And after that, somewhere in this world.

I don't know what's waiting for me up there. Grandma has already sold a lot and stored some of my personal things in her shed. The apartment will surely be empty. And cold.

With a wistful sigh, I feel for the apartment key in my

jacket pocket, hoist the travel bag onto my shoulder, and set off. I stop at the mailboxes. As soon as I unlock the slot, a pile of flyers and envelopes with bills spill out at me. And the magazines Lukas always gets shortly before the end of the month.

Reading the articles was his favorite pastime. Every time he got his hands on the fresh issues of his favorite magazines, he was barely approachable for hours.

It's strange that he doesn't have them sent to his new address with Anna. Do they not mean anything to him anymore?

Lost in thought, I slip the magazines into my handbag and reach for the rest of the mailbox's contents. Even though I hardly dare hope for it, I notice the tension spreading through me even as I touch the stack.

There could be something in there that will decide my future. A letter from the scholarship office. With an acceptance.

For a moment I send a quick prayer up to heaven and let out a shaky breath. Then I do it. I take the stack in my hands.

On top lies a flyer, that can go. Underneath, an envelope.

A shiver runs down my back and makes its way all the way to the tips of my toes.

This could be it.

In slow motion, I turn the envelope to see the sender's details.

My insurance company. Great.

The tension leaves my body, and I can't do anything to stop the disappointment that takes its place inside me.

"Believe in yourself the way no one else ever would." Over and over I repeat the stranger's words in my head to keep myself from imagining the worst while I go through the rest of the mail.

Suddenly I freeze. There's another envelope.

I hurriedly look for the sender, but I can't find one. There's no postmark either. Someone must have put the letter into my mailbox personally.

Weird.

In a matter of seconds a fierce nervousness overwhelms me, even though I have no idea where it comes from. It could be anything in there; maybe it's just a party invitation from one of the neighbors.

Still, my fingers shake uncontrollably as I tear open the envelope to see what's inside.

They're photos.

Of Lukas.

I don't know if my heart is racing or standing still. If I'm gasping for air or holding my breath. Are my knees giving way or the muscles in my face? I have no idea, and basically it doesn't matter at all.

What I'm holding in my hands now is a sign.

Lukas and Marie, forever. That's what we swore to each other. And if there's one thing I know with unshakable certainty, it's that this is how it will be. The photos prove it, even though they carry so much sadness that my eyes fill with tears.

I recognize our dream house, which looks just fantastic in the panoramic view. The next pictures are close-ups of a splintered wooden slat. Lukas is showing me the view behind the beautiful façade, and I know what he's trying to tell me with it.

He has also understood that not everything that looks beautiful from the outside actually makes you happy.

The picture of his desk fits that, too. He still works too

much, as always. I wonder if he's already asking himself where that's supposed to lead him.

I'm sure he is. Because the next photo shows his face. I can read everything in his eyes.

He's unhappy. And he feels lost.

Seeing him like this sends a sharp pain straight through my chest. Because it's my fault that he feels this way. I should have taken him along on my journey from the very beginning. For far too long after quitting my job I hid from him what was happening to me, and that's the only reason he couldn't understand my change. I left our shared path and forgot to take him by the hand so he could see which paths life has to offer us, too.

It's not too late to change that. Because for Lukas and Marie it will never be too late.

On the spot, I turn around and set off. My destination isn't the apartment, and certainly not Anna's place. No, I'm going to look for Lukas at his company. There, where Anna can't sabotage our communication. Today is Friday, the clock shows a little after four. I'm sure I'll find him at the office. And once I'm standing in front of him, nothing will be able to stop us anymore.

Chapter Thirty-Two

Monday morning. Again. It's still dark outside, yet I'm already entering the office with a steaming cup of coffee in my hand. I can hardly suppress a yawn, but that doesn't matter. No one sees me here anyway, no one's around and that's a good thing. Because I have no idea how I'd explain to anyone why I show up at work before five in the morning.

Of course I have a lot to do, the junior boss doesn't miss a thing. Even if I worked 24 hours a day, I wouldn't be able to get through the workload. But that's not what's keeping me up at night.

Not tonight. Not last night, and probably not in the nights to come, either.

It's Joe's words from last Friday that keep circling in my head and still don't lead to any insight. Ever since our conversation three days ago, they've been tormenting me, and at the same time they make me believe that I'd only have to find the right answers to be happy again.

I stubbornly keep trying, but it doesn't work. Not yesterday either, when Anna and I had breakfast together. It could have been nice, with relaxing music in the background and fresh, homemade rolls on the table. Still, it felt strange. Whenever she was distracted, I watched her out of the corner of my eye. As if I were some lunatic. As if I really believed I could see something in her face that would help me.

But there was nothing.

Now and then a frown, sometimes a smile.

"What's wrong?" Anna asks once more in my memory and draws her eyebrows together.

I quickly shake my head. "Nothing really." I should say more. Maybe. Or maybe not. I have no idea, because in my head there's no room for anything but this one question.

If today were my last day, what would I do? Would I want to sit here and have breakfast with Anna?

"Come on, tell me."

Does her request sound urgent?

As if she wanted to know at all costs what's going on inside me and definitely wouldn't give in as long as I don't tell her?

Or am I just imagining it?

Heavens.

My brain has stopped working!

"Yesterday's mountain hike is still in my bones. I really need to rest today." I force a crooked smile onto my face; I can't manage anything else. Then I quickly take a sip of coffee so I don't have to keep talking.

There it is again.

An almost imperceptible twitch of her eyebrows. She knows I'm lying to her. She knows it. Still, she stays silent, lowers her eyes, and abuses the egg-white omelet on her plate with her fork.

Even though nothing at all happened at breakfast

yesterday morning, the memory of it weighs heavily on my shoulders as, here and now, I push my desk chair back. All my life, Anna was my refuge. The place I went when I didn't know what to do anymore. But I can't do that anymore. Because I'd have to tell her that I'm not sure if what's going on between us is really what I want. Within seconds, her world would lie in ruins.

Damn.

Damn. Damn. Damn.

All at once I'm even more tired than I already was. I sink down onto my desk chair, because there's only one thing that can help me.

My job, which doesn't leave any room for my private life.

If I throw myself into work now, I won't be able to think about anything else. It gives me a few hours of normality. I don't want anything more than that, but I don't even seem to be getting those. Because when I set my coffee down on the coaster, I discover a sheet of paper that someone has wedged under my keyboard.

If this is another harebrained order from the junior boss, then…

Even though I'd rather ignore it, I reach for the note, pick it up, and unfold it.

I'm wide awake in an instant.

This isn't from the boss.

I recognize Marie's handwriting. She was here. Right here, where I'm sitting now. It must have been Friday afternoon, while I was getting wasted at Joe's to feel good just once again.

Instinctively I crush the paper in my fist and focus on the office window, behind which everything is still dark.

So here it is, her answer to my pictures. It's late. I put the envelope in her mailbox seven days ago.

Is she as agitated as I am? Does she also not know what's right and how things are supposed to go on?

Right now I'd most like to ask her that. And on top of that I want to know what she'd do if today were her last day. She'd probably wrinkle her little button nose for a moment and smile at me in that incomparable way of hers. Then she'd say that it doesn't matter at all what we do on our last day, as long as we're together.

The thought makes me swallow, but even that can't stop the warm feeling that's spreading through me right now. I mustn't allow myself thoughts like that, because they'd only make everything even worse than it already is.

Indecisively, I knead the paper in my hand. There's no one here but me. I could read Marie's words and, no matter what they do to me, no one would see it.

But I would feel it.

And what if I don't do it? I could just make the letter disappear and feel better for that reason alone. That would be great. But if I've learned one thing in the past few weeks, it's that it doesn't work like that.

I have to do it.

So I press my lips together and unfold the paper with trembling fingers.

Dear Lukas,

Today I found your pictures in the mailbox, and I didn't want anything more than to be with you right away. All the way here I imagined what it would be like when I showed up in your office doorway.

You look up from the screen. You recognize me. You smile. I walk toward you. I don't take my eyes off you for a second. And nor does my heart. We don't say anything, and we don't have to. Because we can feel everything we need to know.

That was the plan. But when I got here, the office was empty.

This letter may not be perfect, but it's my only way to reach you. Because I've been trying for weeks. Because I have to tell you something. And even though I still don't know how to put it into words, I finally want to do it.

When we met, we both had a dream. Maybe we didn't take it seriously. We thought it was just fantasy, nothing more than a pleasant way to escape everyday life in our minds. Over the years we forgot it. We jumped into our hamster wheel and worked ourselves to the bone. Days, weeks, and months rushed past us so fast that we no longer saw anything of the world. As if we were passengers on a high-speed train, we didn't really experience anything.

Only when Grandpa left us did I understand what had happened to the two of us. Because Grandma and he had let life pass them by just like we did. They thought they could make up for everything once Grandpa retired.

Next weekend, next summer, next year.

Later.

That's what the two of them focused on, and in doing so they overlooked the fact that this "later" might not come at all in the end.

Grandma's pain over Grandpa's death broke a dam inside me. And behind the dam lurked panic. I didn't want anything but to live instead of just existing. Because that was what the two of us were doing at that point. We were good citizens, working hard and somehow just forgetting what we used to dream of.

We didn't want a dream house. And no sensible jobs where we wouldn't be happy, either. We didn't want debts and we didn't want obligations.

To be free. To see the world. To experience something. That's what we wanted.

I know what you're thinking. That those were just youthful fantasies. That none of it could ever last in reality.

But is that really true? Is something that you never even tried with all your strength already doomed to die just because our society talks us into believing it's impossible? Is it really wrong to want to have everything you need for a happy life?

Each of us should allow ourselves to build a life according to our own dreams. We don't have to do what others do. All that matters to us is being happy. And I know we can be. Together.

Lukas and Marie. Forever. That was what we promised each other, and that's what we both still want. I saw it in your pictures. And I feel it all through my body when I think about the future.

Can you feel it too? When you set your reason aside and forget your upbringing for a moment. When you listen only to yourself and to what your longing is telling you. Can you feel it?

The letters blur before my eyes. I don't want to let that happen, just as little as I want to keep reading. I do it anyway, because the "but" inside me suddenly falls silent all on its own.

A wise man once explained to me that dreams don't come true unless you make them come true. And that's what I'm doing with my dream of photography. I won't let anything stop me, no matter how big the setbacks I have to accept.

There's nothing I wish for more than for you to dream with me. The way we did back then.

We can. And I'm going to prove it to you. In three weeks, on October 21, I'll take flight FZ536. It'll take me via Dubai to India, where I'll capture the beauty of the country with my camera, with the smell of curry in my nose, red dust on my skin, and a feeling of happiness in my chest that effortlessly puts any so-called "good life" behind me.

I have only one request for you: come with me. Let's experience a time together that we'll never forget.

Don't worry, this isn't a decision for eternity. Just for a few weeks. Come with me, and I'll show you the stars. Exactly the ones I kept hidden from you for far too long, because at first I didn't know myself what they should look like or where I could find them.

Just take a look at it, that's all I'm asking of you. Give us a chance to find out whether my world and your world can merge and become a single constellation.

Whatever happens, I love you. Forever.

Yours, Marie

With trembling fingers, I fold the letter and smooth it out. Once more. And then once again.

"She's only dreaming, it's not real." That's what my mind is screaming at me. It also reminds me that I couldn't get on a plane anyway.

But there's also Joe's voice, asking me in its warm tone what I would do if this were the last day of my life. And for the first time I feel the answer glowing deep inside me.

Chapter Thirty-Three

Nervously, my client flails her arms. Although she moves like a startled chicken, her ashy-blond short haircut sits rock solid. Just like the tight-fitting midnight-blue suit that shows off her astonishingly slim figure. I can hardly believe this woman had a baby only a few weeks ago.

"This is the best spot. Grandpa goes here and the stroller there. My husband will stand on the right-hand side," she explains to me at a pace as if she were taking part in a speed-talking contest.

I give her an awkward smile.

Should I tell her that the light here is about as bad as it gets for photos? The faces of the christening party will look partly washed out, partly disappear in the shadow of the chestnut tree. I quickly look around so I can make a counterproposal. Back there at the church entrance would be a good spot. Between the massive stone balustrade guarded by two statues of Mary. The sculptures with their folded hands create a wonderful atmosphere. I could also take great photos of the baby and the godparents there.

"Come on, come on. Everyone line up over here," I suddenly hear my client shout across the entire forecourt of the church.

With a professionally friendly smile on my face, I take a step toward her. "Mrs. Weingartner, what do you think about taking the pictures back there?" I gesture toward the church with my hand. "The sunlight would be much softer and the background very festive."

Her uncomprehending look hits me. "But everything is gray over there," she says contemptuously. "This isn't a funeral, it's a celebration. We want flowers in the picture. And trees."

I know I have to stay professional. She's the client, and her satisfaction matters most. After all, I want her to recommend me. But will she do that if the photos turn out awful thanks to her suggestion?

No, she definitely won't. I have to do my best here. Even if it's only a small photography job, it's important for my reputation. "I understand. Give me a moment and I'll find the perfect spot with flowers for the keepsake photos."

My smile doesn't reach her. "I already said this is the optimal place. We're doing it here," she snaps at me, exasperated, then raises her arm to wave the others over to us. "Come on, hurry up," she yells to her relatives, who actually start moving obediently toward us.

Great. How am I supposed to take nice pictures here? I rack my brains for a solution while my client busily arranges her guests around the chestnut tree. But there isn't one. Even if I took the photos from an unusual angle for group shots, I'd still have the same problem with light and shadow.

The photos are going to look catastrophic.

I'd most like to scream, but I'm not allowed to. Instead, I force myself to smile and take exactly the picture that Mrs.

Weingartner wants so badly. I use different lenses and perspectives to at least get the best out of the situation. I already know the post-processing will be difficult. I'll probably have to get help from my course instructor, Peter. Hopefully he'll have a solution. I cling to that thought, ask the christening party to laugh heartily, and press the shutter.

This was not how I'd imagined life as a photographer. But if I've learned one thing by now, it's that it just isn't easy. Sometimes the clients are nice, sometimes difficult. This is my fifth job; I'm earning barely a hundred euros for an entire afternoon on site and probably several days at home at the computer, trying to turn the pictures into something at least halfway presentable. I don't even want to calculate what that works out to as an hourly wage. I'd much rather mentally stash the money in my India fund, which by now at least holds four hundred and fifty euros. There will hardly be any more expenses before I leave; I don't have to pay rent anymore. My security deposit should also be refunded to me soon. After all, I handed the apartment keys back to the landlord two days ago. With tears in my eyes and a queasy feeling in my stomach.

No, I really can't think about that right now. I shouldn't let myself get distracted; I need to focus entirely on this job here.

That's exactly what I do over the next few minutes, and when the christening party disperses again, I even get the chance to take the kind of pictures that make my heart beat faster after all.

I capture moments.

An older lady holding on to her hat so the wind doesn't blow it away, laughing heartily as she does. The baby's three-year-old brother kicking up the autumn leaves from the ground. And finally I actually manage to get the shots

I'd been so desperate to take earlier: the baby and the godmother in front of the statue at the church entrance.

"Lift the little one up, look at her, kiss her forehead. Do whatever feels natural, and imagine I'm not even here." Those are the instructions I give the woman with the perfectly blow-dried, shoulder-length hair and the expensive gold jewelry. It doesn't take long before I get exactly the picture I'd hoped for. It shows so much more than just a forty-year-old woman with a baby. There's familiarity and happiness, love and security.

Tears well up in the corners of my eyes. Not just because I myself am happy in this moment to be able to take such a photo. But also because it reminds me of what I'm still missing. Lukas.

He must have found my message on his desk on Monday morning. Today is Wednesday and he hasn't been in touch.

What is that supposed to mean?

That question stays with me all morning, but I don't find an answer. As long as I'm accompanying the christening party at their celebration, taking pictures of dancing couples, artfully wrapped presents, and guests laughing warmly, I manage not to fall apart. But when I say goodbye to Mrs. Weingartner, who is now very grateful, and promise her the photos for next week, the uncertainty hits me again with full force.

What else could I do to reach Lukas? If I went to him now and just showed up at his work, how would he react?

He would send me away, for sure. His pictures were clear, he has to work a lot and I'd only be in the way. No, I need a different solution. Lost in thought, I dig my phone out of my bag on the way home and dial Grandma's number.

"He's not getting in touch," I say instead of a greeting, and I can hear myself how dejected I sound. I probably look the same as I walk down the street. With slumped shoulders and a sad expression. And that even though I've just experienced such beautiful moments while taking photos.

In the background I hear the creak of the sofa. "Maybe he really does need more time."

"He already had…"

"No," Grandma interrupts me at once, "not everyone thinks like you. Don't forget that."

Nervously, I gnaw on my lower lip and quicken my pace to get rid of the pent-up energy. "Today is October second. My flight leaves in nineteen days!" Do I sound panicked? Absolutely. "I can't just sit back and watch while time is running out on me."

"Of course not. But ambushing him makes just as little sense. You know him. All you'll do is push him further away from you." The warmth in her words does me good, maybe because it sounds as if at least Grandma is sure that everything will turn out fine in the end.

"So what am I supposed to do? Is there even a way to do this right?" Agitated, I wave my free hand around in the air. The skeptical looks from the teenagers I'm walking past let me know I must look like a crazy person. But I couldn't care less. "Tell me how I can win him back. Please."

For a moment Grandma is silent, and in the same instant it's clear to me that she doesn't know the answer either. "Give yourself a deadline," she then suggests. "If he hasn't been in touch by the day before your flight, you go to him." She sounds uncertain; I can hear it clearly.

"And what if I don't find him? What if he's with Anna?" I hesitate, because I don't even want to say out loud the thought that's now taking shape in my head. What if he sends me away? What if he doesn't want to talk to me? And anyway, can I tell him more than what he already knows from my message?

"We'll worry about that when the time comes." Yeah, sure, it's easy for Grandma to say that. "Chin up. Love finds a way, you know that."

"Mhm," I grunt. I can't manage anything more, because my fear of losing Lukas for good wraps itself around my neck like a noose that tightens with every passing second.

Grandma notices what's going on with me. She clears her throat. "Come over to my place. We'll bake our famous apple strudel and drink hot cocoa."

That sounds tempting. Like a short break full of warmth and coziness. Besides, I want to spend a lot more time with Grandma before I leave for India. I look down at myself. The ruffled blouse and high heels are hardly the right outfit for baking. "I'd love to. I'll just quickly stop by Alex's and change." Even as I say the words, I already feel a little better.

"I'm looking forward to it." Grandma sounds like she'd like nothing better than to pull me into a hug, and I'm sure she'll do just that very soon.

I can't help but smile. "Me too," I say in farewell and end the call.

Right after I press the red button on my phone's display, a symbol at the top edge catches my eye. There's a new message in my inbox.

Is it from Lukas?

Excitement immediately surges through me, my pulse races, my hands turn shaky and damp. Hurriedly I look around for a good place to read the message. Because one thing is clear: I need to be sitting down in case my legs give out on me when I find out what he wants to tell me.

On the opposite side of the street I spot a waist-high wall. It looks uncomfortable, but that doesn't matter. I cross the street as quickly as I can and let myself sink down onto the hard bricks.

Then I take several deep breaths.

The answer to every question I have about my future could be waiting for me in my inbox. Maybe everything will turn out fine. No, everything will definitely turn out fine.

With nervous, fumbling movements I unlock the display and see the message preview.

It's not from Lukas. It's from the scholarship office.

"Dear Ms. Berger, thank you very much for your …" is what it says in the message preview; nothing more is shown.

A completely different kind of panic floods me at once. What if it's an acceptance?

And what if it isn't?

Chapter Thirty-Four

Bernd looks up from his pasta dish and studies me with a skeptical expression. "What's going on with you, anyway?" As if he wanted to keep this conversation in the cafeteria secret from our coworkers, he leans across the gray laminated table toward me.

He might as well have saved himself the trouble. Because I'm not going to answer anyway. It doesn't matter how close the colleagues from accounting are sitting next to us or whether the cafeteria worker wiping down the table opposite hears anything. "Everything's fine," I say, force a smile, and stick my fork into the casserole Anna cooked for my lunch today and neatly packed into a container.

"Oh, come on. You're not even eating the cafeteria slop, and you still look like you've forgotten how being happy works." He shakes his head vehemently, then pushes his half-full plate a bit away from himself with a disgusted wrinkle of his nose. "Is it because of our new super boss?"

The boss's nephew. The one who was absolutely incompetent and still got the job I once thought would save me. Is this about him? At least partly. "Could be." I shrug and stuff a whole load of broccoli into my mouth at once so I don't have to keep talking.

It tastes like bland diet food, which really shouldn't be possible. Anna is a great cook. Her dishes are neither over-seasoned nor overcooked. She doesn't burn anything and doesn't just forget ingredients you simply can't do without. Unlike Marie…

"He won't last much longer, believe me. And once he's gone, we'll have our pleasant old life back." Now he's leaning over to me again. "Because I've heard something," he whispers conspiratorially.

That makes my ears prick up. Whether I want to or not, hope flares up in me at once. If these mindless tasks would finally come to an end and if everything no longer had to be done urgently after lying around for weeks on the junior boss's desk, then at least something could be like it used to be. "That would be great."

"Well, look at that, I do believe I see a little smile." Satisfied, Bernd leans back in his chair and folds his arms across his chest. "Overall you still look pretty miserable."

Listlessly, I poke around in the mix of eggs and vegetables in my container, but my appetite seems to have left me. "I'm tired, that's all."

"Are you sleeping badly?"

Bernd doesn't let it go. Why, anyway? He's not usually this caring. On the contrary, we sometimes do things together after work and help each other out with our tasks. But we're definitely not best friends who pour out their hearts to each other.

"Too many appointments. And too much work." I sound exasperated, and I am. A bit too forcefully, I press the lid onto my lunch container and get ready to stand up. "I should get back to it."

Bernd pushes himself up from his chair as well. Suddenly he's standing right next to me and puts his hand on my upper arm. "Take care of yourself," he says, and he sounds so earnest, as if he were warning me about something he knows I can't see.

He's barely spoken the words when he reaches for the pack of cigarettes in his pants pocket. He's going to have another smoke. Thank God. I couldn't have dealt with him continuing to pester me with his strange behavior anyway.

"See you in a bit." I sound relieved; he must hear it too. The thought of that immediately makes a pang of guilt flare up in me. He just wants to help me, and I treat him like he's an annoying fly.

My guilty conscience joins all the other awful feelings, the ones I don't even know where I feel them. In my head, in my chest, or just everywhere. I've stopped thinking about it, because it doesn't change anything anyway.

Because nothing will change anything.

On the way to the office, I pull Marie's message out of my pocket. I carry it with me all the time and keep reading it over and over. By now I know every word by heart. The text is in my thoughts, no matter what I do. I wish I could answer her, but I just can't. Because I don't know what to say to her. And ever since I found it on my desk two days ago, I haven't been able to sleep.

It's grotesque how I lie awake at night beside Anna, eyes open, filled with desperate restlessness. I hear her even breathing and the contented purring sound she makes when she nestles against me, while my longing for the old Marie threatens to devour me from the inside out. No matter how hard I try, switching it off seems out of the question.

Joe's question won't let me go either. Nor will his advice to ignore the *but.* Still, it appears on its own whenever I try to imagine the life I stopped dreaming about because I know it's impossible.

Then I ask myself whether feelings can ever be forced. And whether I really have to love Anna, or if I'm only imagining exactly that. And what torments me even more is the question Marie doesn't actually ask in her message, but that still dominates everything. It's like an essence of the events of the past few months, condensed and viscous.

What kind of life do I want to live?

I don't know. But when I lie awake at night with nothing but the distant rush of traffic and Anna's breathing in my ears, there's something else. Inside me, the voice of a twelve-year-old version of myself is roaring. He wants his freedom back. He wants to be carefree again, to do only what excites him, and to enjoy life to the fullest. The twenty-seven-year-old version of me doesn't want to allow that. Not at night and certainly not now, when I have to be functioning in my job again in just a few minutes.

All at once my legs feel as heavy as concrete, my head hurts. Still, I drag myself farther down the hallway and enter the office where an overpowering mountain of work is waiting for me.

I let my gaze drift over the folders and on to the flickering screen with its endless-looking rows of numbers. The desk is gray. The swivel chair is gray. The windowsill, the filing cabinets, even the ballpoint pens. Everything is gray.

What I'd like most is to have a beer right now. Or better yet, something stronger. I picture my thoughts gradually losing their significance while I drink, and the pressure on my chest disappearing.

What if I fake a stomachache and sneak off to Joe's? For just a few hours I could forget who and what I am.

My God, what am I thinking? I'm not an alcoholic who's lost control!

I quickly shake the thoughts of an afternoon at Joe's out of my head. They don't belong here; I have to pull myself together and keep going. Because this here is reality, everything else doesn't exist.

Just as I slide onto my desk chair, I feel my phone vibrate in my pocket. I pull it out and find a message from my realtor.

"The documents for reversing the house purchase are final. As announced, realtor fees of 10,000 euros and 25,000 euros as compensation for the seller are due. I still need a few signatures from you. Would the 21st of October work for you? At 2:00 PM?"

The date jumps out at me immediately. It's the day Marie will be flying. And therefore also the day on which I have to make final and irrevocable decisions about my future.

On impulse, I start typing. "Thank you, that works."

I have no idea whether I should really give up the house. I don't know if I want to live there with Anna. Or if I can give Marie and her new way of living a chance. Whether I myself want to keep running in the safe hamster wheel or overcome my fear of flying and open a door that I locked so tightly inside me a long time ago that I don't know if it's even still possible.

I'm completely at a loss. Only one thing is clear to me: by the 21st of October I have to know the answers to all these questions.

Chapter Thirty-Five

Spellbound, I stare at my phone's screen. My fingers don't know what they're supposed to do next. Thousands of thoughts buzz through my head like an entire swarm of bumblebees. There's hope right next to fear. And worry right beside optimism.

The message I'm going to open in a few seconds will decide my future.

It could be pouring with rain, a hurricane could be devastating half of Vienna. The Danube could burst its banks and turn the city into one single raging river. I wouldn't notice. Only my phone and I still exist, now, in this moment when I take one last deep breath.

My breath left my mouth in shaky bursts, my fingers moved nervously to the screen and tapped the message open.

"Dear Ms. Berger, thank you very much for your application," I read again, even though I already knew this part of the text. It was as if my head didn't want to miss a single word. As if my eyes were afraid of overlooking something important.

But they didn't. On the contrary, they grasped at once what the next sentence meant.

"Choosing the winner from over a thousand entries was extraordinarily difficult for us. Unfortunately, we must inform you…"

I didn't get any further. I didn't want to read what it said. Not only because I already knew how this sentence would end anyway, but also because all my muscles suddenly gave way. I couldn't hold the phone any longer; it slipped from my hand. It hit the dark asphalt sidewalk with a loud smack, the screen shattered.

Just like I did.

Something broke inside me, I felt it clearly, and yet I was powerless against it. My dream burst. Like a soap bubble in the wind.

Shouldn't tears already be squeezing from the corners of my eyes? Scalding hot and full of disappointment, leaving me no chance to hold them back? Shouldn't the sun be setting, because there's nothing left in this world for it to shine on?

Yes, maybe that's exactly what should have happened, but it didn't. My eyes stayed dry. The sun beamed down at me without a cloud in sight. And me? All of a sudden I didn't know anything anymore.

Not who I am. And not where I'm supposed to go.

So I'm crouching here, with muscles that won't obey me and an emptiness in my head that keeps me from feeling anything at all.

Seconds. Minutes. Hours.

Life. Love. Dreams.

All of that loses its meaning in the face of this one thing that I feel so clearly.

I risked too much and lost.

I don't have an apartment. No steady job, no money, and no love. And in one blow my dream was just taken from me as well. Along with my belief in myself.

My photos aren't good enough. And maybe they never will be.

By now the wall I'm sitting on is pressing hard into my thighs. It's as if it wants to force me to stand up. But to do what?

I look around and push myself up. Suddenly my body feels tired, and weak. Still, my legs start moving and carry me to the subway station. There they take the U6 toward Floridsdorf.

Of course. They want to go to the water park. Because they believe that only one person can help me now. The stranger who always seems to know what's right and what I need to move forward.

Barely an hour later I enter the park. I hardly notice the crunch of the gravel path under my shoes, just as little as the cool breeze that loosens the brown leaves from the trees. My eyes scan my surroundings in haste, constantly searching for the man with the long blond hair and that special aura that could take away my worries again today.

He's nowhere to be seen. I walk on to the lake, to the exact spot where we so often sat. The place where I thought I could see my future clearly. And even though I already sense from afar that he isn't here, I don't want to give up.

I walk around the lake, looking for him behind every bush and in every cove.

No matter how little I want to accept it, he isn't here. Of

all times, now, in the darkest hour of my life, I'm on my own.

I guess this is it. In this moment I hit the hard ground of reality. From here I won't fall any farther. But I won't fly anymore either. Not with all the broken bones my crash has left behind.

From far away, it seems, I hear a beeping. It's my phone. I pull it out.

"The strudel dough is already ready," I read in a message from Grandma. "When will you be here?"

Despite the heaviness weighing on me, I have to smile. Because I still have my grandma. With her warmth and the sense of security she gives me. Even if my head refuses to cooperate, I can at least feel that I have to go to her. There's nothing I want more than to slice apples with her, to nibble raisins with the smell of cinnamon in my nose, and for a moment forget that the rest of my life lies in pieces.

"On my way," I type and start running. As fast as if I wanted to flee. Maybe even from myself.

Chapter Thirty-Six

Tense, I let my gaze sweep around the room. This office is frighteningly large. And it looks as if nobody works here. The oversized desk with its lacquered wooden surface is empty except for a monitor, a keyboard, and a mouse. There are no files or other documents, I don't even spot a telephone. The desk chair behind the table looks imposing with its high backrest, and the leather upholstery is surely velvety soft. The chair I'm sitting on, by contrast, is hardly padded at all. I'm sure that's on purpose; visitors are meant to feel uncomfortable here.

I certainly do. Even though I've only been waiting here for a few minutes for the managing director of my company, I can hardly stand it anymore.

There's no reason to be nervous. At least that's what I tell myself as I concentrate on keeping my fingers still and the corners of my mouth up. In my head I frantically run through the past few weeks at work. Have I done something wrong? Where did I make a mistake, what wasn't finished fast enough?

The junior boss has definitely ratted me out to his uncle. He's probably even pinned one of his own blunders on me. I was surely summoned here to get a written warning for something I didn't even do.

In the now four years I've worked for this company, I haven't had a single appointment with the boss. I only know from my department head, Marianne, that she has to show up here from time to time. And that she's never experienced anything pleasant here. God, what does the boss want from me? I'd love to jump up so the energy in my legs can discharge. But if the boss walks in and sees me pacing up and down his office like I'm crazy, I've probably already lost.

If I haven't already anyway.

At last the door behind me is flung open. Even though I flinch instinctively, it still feels like a relief. Whatever happens in the next few minutes, at least I'll have it over with soon.

With a friendly smile, I get up and turn around. "Good afternoon," I say and give the boss a polite nod.

He doesn't look particularly happy, and he seems stressed on top of that. He strides hastily across the room and signals with a wave of his hand for me to sit back down. Then he unbuttons his midnight-blue jacket and takes a seat himself. "Mr. Richter, thank you for coming."

Even though he's so small and skinny that he almost disappears into his chair, I mustn't let myself feel safe. It's better to keep quiet and just keep watching him closely.

His gaze drifts to his wristwatch. "I'll keep this brief, we all have a lot to do."

Instinctively, I slide forward on my chair and straighten my back.

For a moment, a deep crease forms between his

eyebrows, the corners of his mouth twitch downward in contempt. "My nephew will be leaving the company."

Finally.

That's the first thing that comes to mind, and although the atmosphere is more than tense right now, relief spreads through me. No more pointless instructions, no forced smile at jokes that are anything but funny. No more unstructured ideas and no more arrogant brush-offs. I have to make an effort to hide my delight, because it's obvious the boss is anything but pleased. He must know that his nephew has failed.

"He has a great opportunity at one of the most prestigious consulting firms in Great Britain. Naturally, he has to seize such a chance." He's lying; I can see it clearly.

"Of course," I say. I play along with his game; anything else would hardly make sense.

Calmly, he folds his hands into a triangle and looks at me intently. "You will take over."

It doesn't sound like a question. More like a statement. "You mean…?"

"Acting head of department. At least until Marianne Eberhart goes on maternity leave. Then of course you'll move up."

Marianne is pregnant? All the loose threads in my head suddenly come together on their own. Of course! She was the one who could still keep the junior boss under control and prevent the worst from happening. If he had taken over after she left, everything would have ended in chaos. The boss had to act, he had no choice.

His expectant gaze meets mine. "Can the company count on you?"

"I… um…" I have no idea what's going on with me right now, but nothing more than this absurd stuttering will come out of my mouth. Because there's something holding me back. A feeling that this is something too big to make a decision about right away.

The boss raises his hand reassuringly. "Of course we'll adjust your salary accordingly. We're willing to negotiate and we know the value of your work."

That's great. Or is it? Isn't this exactly what I'd longed for so desperately just a few months ago, as if my very existence depended on it? Isn't this my chance at that one life I've always wanted to live?

But if that's true, why is every part of me suddenly resisting it? Why do I suddenly hear Joe's voice in my head asking me what I would do if today were my last day.

Would I take the job?

No.

I'd much rather leave something behind for the world. Something that will last longer than this one day I still have.

This realization hits me unprepared, as if a typhoon had formed around me in a matter of seconds, sweeping away everything I thought was important. Only what defines me at my core is still left.

That's not a career.

And it's definitely not money. Not owning a house, and certainly not the sensible, good life I've focused on over the past few years.

"Mr. Richter, what do you say to our offer?" The boss's voice pushes into my ear and pulls me back to reality.

I clear my throat because I don't know the answer to his question. Because what defines me at my core still has no connection to real life. I know that, not just in theory, but also from my own experience.

"I need some time to think it over," I finally force out in a hoarse voice.

Wherever this flash of inspiration came from, I'm glad it just left my mouth. Because one thing is clear: once I've said yes, I can't back out. My sense of duty would never allow that.

The boss's eyebrows immediately draw together. He isn't used to his wishes not being fulfilled instantly. His fists clench, yet he forces a smile onto his face. "All right. Today is October 10th. I'll be back from my business trip in ten days, and then I expect your answer."

I nod with effort. A moment later he shoots up from his desk chair. I know my time here is over, so I follow his lead and walk with him toward the office door.

"Thank you for the conversation," he says in farewell. He barely looks at me; his gaze is practically glued to his wristwatch.

"I should be the one thanking you," I reply politely and make sure I get away from here.

He gave me ten days. That's two hundred and forty hours to make up my mind. I still have more than fourteen thousand minutes left.

But is that enough?

And if it isn't, how many seconds, minutes, or hours would I need to finally know what's right for me?

A solid life as a purchasing manager. With a pretty little house on the outskirts of town and a wife by my side who would simply do anything for me. Or a leap into the unknown. Hand in hand with the person who had never been anything but the love of my life, I could find out what freedom feels like. And whether I'd just been telling myself all these years that dreams have no place in reality.

Chapter Thirty-Seven

With a pitying expression, Alex sets a wineglass down in front of me. I huddle into the cushions of the sofa that has been something like my new home for almost two weeks now.

"Thanks," I murmur and pull the tall-stemmed glass toward me. I don't care that the pale liquid inside takes on a very special color when it moves and that the surface sparkles in the light of the elegant living room lamp. Just like I don't care about anything else.

"Just one sip, then you're going to help me cook." Alex plants her hands on her hips with determination.

She knows perfectly well that I need a distraction. Still, she must also be aware that I'm a terrible cook. "Are you sure that's such a good idea?" I ask, raising my eyebrows.

"You can chop vegetables." She gives me a resolute grin. Then she hooks her arm through mine and drags me into the kitchen.

Once we're there, she shoves four large carrots into my hand. "Slice them thinly, please."

"Yes, chef." I almost manage a smile, but only almost.

Alex isn't impressed. "It's time, Marie. You have to decide. How do you want things to go on for you?" she asks while she rummages in the base cabinet for a pot.

If only I knew. For days I've been pushing that question aside, even though I know I have to face it. Instinctively, I nibble on my lower lip and lift my shoulders in a questioning shrug.

"All right then. First we'll take stock." She looks at me with a grin. "What do we know for sure?"

"Nothing good," is the first thing that comes to mind. And also the only thing. Alex won't let me get away with that; I can see it clearly in her eyes.

"Number one: what do you have?" she continues, unimpressed by my answer. Holding an oversized stainless-steel pot in her hand, she straightens up from her crouch and looks at me expectantly.

"Thanks to you, I have a roof over my head." Does that sound like a question? Maybe. But what else am I supposed to say? There's hardly anything that's going well at the moment.

In response I get an elaborate eye roll and a sigh. "Hard facts, Marie, you know that. So, I'm not asking again. What do you have?"

Thoughtfully, I turn to the carrots, and as I slice one round after another, a few things actually start to add up. "A plane ticket to India. Just under two thousand euros from unemployment benefits, the rent deposit, and the few jobs I've had over the last few weeks. A camera kit." Which only brings me bad luck, I'd love to add, but I don't say the words out loud. I also don't mention the fact that I won't get a cent from the job center as long as I'm abroad. Those things don't belong on the assets side of this inventory.

"You're still missing something. Even if you might not want to hear it, you have a qualification. And you have me. And your grandma," Alex adds, full of motivation, reaches for her wineglass, and takes a sip. "Right, on to inventory part two: What don't you have?"

That's an easy question to answer. "Lukas, financial security, a future as a photographer, or any kind of future at all."

"That's not true." She seems fired up, the way she suddenly grins at me over the rim of her glass. "Think it through again, properly."

What is she trying to hint at?

"Oh come on, don't look at me like that." Rolling her eyes, she grabs her pot and carries it over to the sink to fill it with water. "Have you ever thought that maybe you rushed some things a little? That not everything in life has to work out right away and not every wish is granted on the spot?" For a moment she pauses, then fixes me with her intense gaze. "That sometimes you have to take a step back so you can move forward again?"

I've never seen Alex like this. But wherever these strangely wise words are coming from, they're already gnawing their way through my stomach. I know what she's trying to tell me. But just allowing myself to think it is hard for me.

"Just because you do one thing doesn't mean you absolutely have to give up another for it. You can have both, for as long as it's necessary." She nods so vigorously it's as if she's full of hope the movement will rub off on me.

But it doesn't work. Instead, my eyebrows pull together. "My feet on solid ground and my head up in the clouds at the same time," I murmur thoughtfully. "How is that supposed to work?" Wouldn't I have to be much taller, inside and out, to touch the ground and the sky at the same moment?

"You could even apply for your old job," my best friend suddenly says with a smirk. "Word got out today that your former boss quit."

I immediately stop chopping the carrots. I can hardly believe it actually happened. "Excuse me?"

"After the tenth secretary quit because of him just last week, management simply couldn't sit back and do nothing any longer." With a shrug, Alex puts the pot filled with water on the stove.

Unbelievable. "So there really is such a thing as karma after all." I can't think of anything else to say. I'm shocked and relieved at the same time.

"Oh yes. But now back to you." Her expression turns serious again. "Let's get this straight: you have a future. At any time you can work as a secretary again and give yourself enough financial security to work on your photography career." The way she says it, it sounds simple.

I shake my head vehemently. "Wouldn't that, in truth, put me right back where I started in the spring? That's more than just one step back. A lot more." It would be proof that I'm a failure. And the moment I'd have to admit to myself that Lukas was right. About what he thinks of dreams. About his attitude toward my search and, not least, about his solid views on life itself.

All of this was a huge mistake.

How could I ever have thought that happiness would find me so easily and then even stay with me? How could I have believed I deserved to have it all?

"Damn," I whisper in a choked voice. I can hardly

breathe. My upper body curls in on itself, tears well up inside me. "I was so naive. And stubborn," I force out with effort.

In a flash my best friend is at my side. "You just took a turn a little too quickly, that's all."

"I just wanted to keep from ending up like Grandma. From waking up one day and realizing that life has passed me by. That I won't have any of the things I kept putting off until later anymore." Hot tears push out of my eyes and pour down my cheeks like torrents. I gasp for breath.

Alex steers me toward one of the chairs at the kitchen table. I let myself drop into it and prop my head in my hands because I can't carry it by myself any longer.

"All I ever wanted was a happy life. With Lukas I wanted to enjoy every moment we have together." I hardly dare to say it out loud, but it finally has to happen. "What I got was the exact opposite. And it's my own damn fault."

Alex says nothing, just strokes my back and hands me a tissue.

Through the veil of tears over my eyes I look at her, searching for help. "Do you think Lukas could at least love me again if I went back to working as a secretary?"

She shakes her head almost imperceptibly, her forehead creasing. "No, I don't think so," she replies gently, "I'm convinced he'll always love you exactly the way you are."

"Then why isn't he getting in touch with me?" I sound harsher than I intended, but that doesn't matter anymore. "I've already been waiting ten days for a sign of life. How am I supposed to keep hoping that this miracle will actually happen?"

Even Alex has no answer to that. Instead, she suddenly jumps up as if out of nowhere, runs into the living room, and comes back a few seconds later with my phone. "Call him. Right now."

"As if I hadn't already tried that a hundred times," I mutter like a stubborn toddler. "I don't even get a dial tone." He wants to keep me so far away that he's even blocked my number on his phone. Maybe it was Anna, too, I don't know.

"I don't believe that." I wish I had her certainty. But the way she's looking at me right now, I don't really have any choice but to try again.

Taking a deep breath, I unlock my phone's screen and dial his number. As if I wanted to prove something to Alex, I turn on the speaker.

Silence. A brief click. Then the connection cuts out.

I might well be looking at her defiantly. "See?"

"What if you try calling him at work?" Alex doesn't want to give up.

I quickly shake my head. "First of all, private calls are forbidden there. If I call him, he'll get into trouble as well. And second, he's definitely finished work for ages by now."

Disappointed, I lower my gaze to my phone. How many times have I stared at the stupid thing in the past few weeks and begged it to send me a sign of life from Lukas? But the display has just stayed black the whole time.

Suddenly the phone screen lights up; a new email appears.

I don't dare look at it. Because I'm afraid of being disappointed. Because if it's not from Lukas, I won't know what to do anymore. Because I don't have any strength left in me to keep hoping. And no energy to keep dreaming about our love.

"What's wrong?" I hear Alex ask, as if from far away.

Answering her seems impossible. Instead, I press my lips

together and let out my breath in short bursts. This message just has to be from Lukas. It has to be! Tense, I raise my eyelids, my gaze finds the display.

"Herbert Salcher," it says in bold letters in the sender field.

Immediately I'm disappointed. No, it's more than that. I'm sobered, dejected, and disillusioned. My shoulders slump forward, my nose swells up even more.

Still, I tap out the message and read what this Herbert wants to tell me.

"Good day, Ms. Berger, I've just discovered your photos on the internet. They're unique, I'd like to buy two of them. Please tell me the price for Sill Lake and Rose Garden as a high-gloss version behind acrylic glass."

I read the text again, and then again. A third time I even read it out loud so that Alex also knows what has just turned my life upside down in a matter of seconds.

"He wants to buy your pictures? That's insane!" With a mixture of surprise, joy, and disbelief, she throws her arms in the air. "Marie, do you know what that means?"

Of course I do, and yet I can barely manage to form the words to say it out loud. "Someone is paying for my photos." Not for the boring ones from some family party, but for the pictures I love taking most.

"Someone is paying for your photos," Alex repeats my words, her face beaming as she spreads her arms wide.

Out of nowhere I feel energy flowing through my body again. A fierce feeling of happiness floods me and brings with it something I thought I had already lost.

Hope.

The tears still roll down my cheeks like waterfalls, unchanged, but between the salty, bitter drops for Lukas, sweet pearls of happiness are beginning to mix. "I can do this," I murmur, over and over again. Then I jump up and throw myself into Alex's arms.

She rocks me back and forth. We swing higher and higher until we're dancing with abandon. And while we move in time to a music only the two of us can hear, I can see perfectly clearly what I'm going to do next.

Chapter Thirty-Eight

"First we have to warm up." Full of energy, Anna storms onto the training floor of the gym and weaves her way through the multitude of other fitness fanatics.

Unmotivated, I watch women sweating on bikes and still not getting anywhere. In the back, a group of men are standing next to a rack of dumbbells. They're apparently comparing the size of their upper arms. It smells of sweat, and the bass of the club-like music thumps in my chest.

This isn't my world. Why on earth did I let myself be talked into coming here? Anna said something about it being a counterbalance to office life and chattered on about how important it was to keep your body fit. I didn't want to contradict her, because my energy is needed elsewhere at the moment.

Anna turns to me as she walks and gives me an impatient signal to follow her. "What's keeping you?"

Obediently, I trudge toward her, but she seems unable to bear having to wait for me. I haven't even made it halfway when she's already marching purposefully toward the treadmills. There's something sweet about her when she's this full of anticipation, and it's nice to see how much sport means to her. Still, I don't believe it could ever be that way for me. So as not to disappoint her, I step onto one of the machines anyway and let her show me what to do.

"Just nice and easy at first, like a walk," she says, tapping at the buttons until the belt starts moving under my feet.

Beaming, she hops onto her own machine and sets off at a brisk pace.

It takes less than a minute for me to realize she's eyeing me from the corner of her eye. "You think I didn't notice?"

"What? That I'm not a born athlete?" I try a crooked grin, even though I know perfectly well she's not alluding to my tired legs.

"You're brooding over something, I can see it. It's been like this for a good two weeks now. What's going on?" she asks, fixing me with that drilling look I really don't like on her.

I could never answer that question for her. If she knew that a part of me was practically screaming for Marie's closeness every single day. That I'm too tired to lock this longing away inside me, and that my idea of a good life has suddenly turned into a dark, colorless picture. She would never forgive me. Never.

"Come on, you can tell me anything." There's desperation in her voice. I'm sure Anna also senses how much this new kind of relationship we've been in for two months now has changed both of us. And our friendship along with it.

Even though I'm only strolling along on the treadmill, I notice the heat rising inside me. I should just bring this up. Tell her that I don't know what to do anymore, and confess how afraid I am of losing her as my best friend.

And explain to her what it feels like to know, deep down, that this thing between us isn't true love.

Just thinking about it tears me apart. I can't do it. Not here and not now. "I've been offered a new job and I don't know if I should take it," I say instead, because at least that's one part of the truth I can share with her.

Her tense smile relaxes. "That sounds great." She increases the speed of her treadmill. "What's holding you back?"

Every fiber of my body. That would be the right answer, but it's not something I can confide in Anna. To buy myself some time, I increase my speed too, just to the point where I can still manage to walk. Who knows, maybe it'll even help to wear myself out. "Sure, it would be more money. At the same time, more responsibility. And more work."

"But that's how life works. That's what you call a career, and that's your goal, after all." Anna blows a strand of her dark hair out of her face; by now her cheeks are tinged a delicate pink.

Is it? I don't know. "Career," I repeat, drawing the word out. Inevitably I have to think of Joe and of what his career has brought him.

"I'll iron your shirts too, don't worry," Anna suddenly comments, a broad grin on her face.

That's really not what this is about. Still, I wink at her, because it's the only thing I can think of despite feeling so helpless. "How generous of you."

"The plan is great. We'll move into the house. I'll have your back with everything that comes up, so you can focus on work. We're going to be damn well off, if you ask me." Now Anna fixes me with her gaze. "And we'll have something we can keep building on. We should grow up, you know."

I almost stumble in shock. She doesn't mean kids or a wedding, does she?

Immediately it feels like I can't breathe. And even though I slow down the treadmill, my pulse is racing. I sneak a look at Anna and try to read in her face what's going on inside her.

She's afraid of what I'm going to say next. Just like I am.

"I don't know if I want that," I suddenly blurt out uncontrollably.

In the very next second, Anna's disappointed expression hits me. She looks at me as if she were falling into a bottomless pit. She keeps blinking, but her eyes still fill with tears. The corners of her mouth tremble dangerously; she bites down hard on her lips.

No, I don't want that. I don't want her to feel bad because of me. "This job is going to cost me every last nerve," I say quickly, to soften my careless words from just now. "Long workdays, maybe even on weekends. I'd have to be reachable on vacation too. Then there are the monthly reports to the boss."

"It might be difficult at first." Anna tries to sound encouraging. As if the fast running pace wasn't strenuous enough, she even increases the incline on the treadmill. "I'm sure you'll have the work under control soon so it runs great. I know you. You always have everything under control. That's what defines you."

Is that so? Or has it in truth never been that way? Haven't I just constantly worked on keeping my damned life under control and, in the process, forgotten to just let myself drift for once?

I try to remember when I last experienced a day that was supposed to be like my last one. I have to travel weeks, months, and even years into the past before I find it. Back then in the flower meadow. When Marie and I dreamed together without any ifs or buts. Of a life full of freedom and love. Of that one future we both wanted to live.

It never came. Short trips, sometimes a week of vacation. And in between, what my mother calls real life.

"You think too much." Anna's voice pushes into my thoughts. "It's not a decision for life, after all. Take the job. If you don't like it, you can just look for something else." By now she's breathing heavily, the effort of running is clearly visible on her, while I'm still strolling along on my treadmill as if I were sightseeing here.

I can't shake the feeling that she'd really like to say more. That a "Don't be such a baby" is on the tip of her tongue, or a "Don't you dare get on my nerves." Of course that's nonsense; it's my own thoughts that make me feel these words everywhere inside me. "It's that easy?" I look at her questioningly. Because in my world it's not easy at all. When you decide on something, you have to see it through.

"Sure." She nods with utter conviction, then slows the pace and claps her hands encouragingly. "Once we're warmed up, we'll move on to the machines."

Oh no, please not. The treadmill is bad enough as it is. "I don't think the gym is for me." I lift my shoulders apologetically. "Better I go home than make an even bigger fool of myself here." And as soon as I get there, I'll cross out all the training appointments in my weekly planner again.

As if her legs hadn't just pulled off a monster performance, she jumps off the treadmill. "You are absolutely not going to do that." Her features suddenly turn frighteningly serious.

I also step off my machine and take a step toward her. "This really doesn't suit me," I try to explain once more.

"Not here either." Anna's hand comes to rest on my stomach.

That can't be true. Is she actually afraid I'll get too fat?

Is that why she's been serving me diet meals more and more often lately?

All at once I'm the one who pulls my eyebrows together. "Are you ashamed of me?"

"Of course not." She's lying, I can see it clearly. "It's only for your own good, darling. After all, I want to have you around for a very long time." She grabs my hand and pulls me along behind her with a flourish. "Come on, my muscles are cooling down," she says, heading straight for the area where those strange machines are set up.

What's this supposed to be? She can't just decide for me as if I didn't have a will of my own. I quickly pull away from her. "I'm tired, Anna, please understand that."

With a disappointed expression on her face, she turns to me. "Then we just won't spend any time together. And you'll keep your raccoon belly."

Why does she have to make it so hard for me? Doesn't she notice that I can barely breathe as it is? Whatever's behind this, this isn't the right place to discuss it. She's willing to let me go. I should do it before she changes her mind again.

"See you later."

A pained smile flits across her lips, she comes over to me and presses herself against me. She feels hot and damp, but that's not what bothers me. What I really don't want is this feeling that's spreading inside me right now, making it more than clear that this is wrong.

"Go on, get yourself home, you lazybones." Affectionately she strokes my cheek, then rises up on tiptoe and kisses me.

Automatically, I return her kiss. "See you soon, hotshot."

Half an hour later I'm sitting at Joe's. Because it's the only place I can run to.

"You really ought to do something about it, don't you think?" Joe asks as he pulls me a beer I didn't even order.

I slide onto the barstool that has by now almost become my second home. "I can't get rid of my *but.*"

With a gentle smile he comes over to me. "No one can take that away from you. Not even me."

He knows I'd secretly been hoping for that. That I could just ask him what I should do and he'd know the right answer. "But…" slips out of me involuntarily.

He immediately raises his hand. "No. No buts."

"But I can't get rid of it, no matter how hard I try." Yes, I sound desperate, and he might as well hear it.

Smirking, he sets the beer down in front of me. "There it was again."

Right. And I didn't even notice it myself. Will I ever get rid of it? And if I do, will it still be in time? "In two days Marie is flying to India. She wants me to come with her to show me what she calls her heaven. But even if I forgave her, how could I ever get on a plane when I'm so terrified of those tin cans?"

Questioningly, I look at Joe, but he still keeps quiet. Because he senses that this is far from everything. And he's right about that.

"Anna is putting on the pressure. She wants the house, to get married, and maybe even have kids with me. Then the other day I was offered this job that I used to want so badly. But how could I stay here and not ask myself every single day what could have become of Marie and me?"

It's quite possible that Joe has no idea what just poured

out of my mouth like a waterfall. Still, he nods understandingly. "Crossroads are a good thing." For the life of me I can't understand what's supposed to be good about them. Wrinkling my nose, I take a sip of my beer. "They're opportunities life gives us. And sometimes they practically force us to make decisions." How does he manage to say that and sound so content at the same time? He looks at me expectantly. "What does your heart say?"

He's asked me that question once before. And even back then I didn't know the answer. Today I just shrug again.

Propping himself up on the bar, he leans over toward me. "You do know, you just don't want to admit it."

"No. This idea of another life is like a mirage. If I let go of everything and run toward it blindly, it'll dissolve into thin air before my eyes before I ever get there." The words leave my mouth hard and sharp. Maybe because I'm trying to convince myself. Because tearing down this last wall inside me would mean that nothing would stay the way it is.

Joe pushes himself away from the bar and raises his hands. "It's your decision alone. And your life." With these words he turns to go. "Your only one," he adds before he leaves the bar area to serve the other guests.

My only one, it echoes in my head. And suddenly I no longer know what would be so terrible about at least writing to Marie. I can tell her that I haven't decided yet. So she at least has a sign of life from me. So she knows that I'm thinking of her.

Before a *but* can settle into my head, I pull my phone out of my pocket and look up her contact. Even before I tap it, I grow suspicious.

She's blocked.

Did I set it up like that? I try to remember, but I can't.

Maybe I was drunk, almost lost my resolve, and wanted to protect myself from myself?

Maybe. Probably. There's no other explanation.

Right away it becomes clear to me what that could mean. Did Marie try to reach me? And if so, how often? Possibly just a few days after our breakup. Back then, when I still so badly hoped that everything between us could be fixed if only she would apologize.

However it was and whatever happened, in this moment I lift the block, and it feels as if I'm unlocking a door that until now had been locked without my knowing it. My breathing is heavy, my fingers move nervously.

"Give me more time," I type, because that's what my heart dictates to me. It's only four words, none of them anything special, and the message itself sounds almost matter-of-fact. Still, it means so much to me. And Marie will see that.

Afraid I might change my mind again, I hit send.

Now she knows.

She knows how I'm doing. And probably also that, at this very moment, a feeling of lightness is spreading inside me. Along with the sense that I might actually be able to let go of my well-adjusted life after all.

Chapter Thirty-Nine

I can't manage to just leave it alone. No matter how hard I try to distract myself, my eyes keep drifting to my phone. And right after that, back up again. I look left and right, scan the sliding doors at the entrance, the airport terminal, and the lines of people in front of the check-in counter. Everywhere something moves, I check to see if Lukas is there waiting for me.

But he isn't here. Maybe just not yet.

With effort I fight back my tears and focus again on Grandma, who nods at me with her incomparably warm smile.

"He's not going to show up." I don't want to sound this hopeless, but by now I can't hold it back any longer. Again I look at my phone's display. It is and stays black. "Only two more hours, he should have been here long ago."

"Even if he doesn't come, this doesn't have to be the end." She wants to calm me, takes my hand in hers and squeezes it tightly. How wonderful it would be if I really could look ahead. If I didn't lose my courage and my faith in love.

Still, it doesn't work. On the contrary, I even have to press my lips together to keep them from trembling. "No," I finally say tonelessly. "This is our only chance to find out if the two of us can start a new life together, one that's exactly the way we used to dream it would be."

"You don't know that. Sometimes you have to take a detour. The only thing that matters is that you never lose sight of your goal, and you won't." In Grandma's expression I see nothing but warmth and confidence. She radiates a certainty that shouldn't leave anyone in doubt. And that even though she herself missed her goal with Grandpa. It's impossible for her to be with him again. The two of them had their chance, and they missed it too.

"What is the goal?" I ask in a choked voice, because right now I don't want to imagine any goal where Lukas isn't there waiting for me.

Grandma comes over to me and pulls me into her arms. "To be as happy as possible every single day," she whispers in my ear and hugs me so tightly for a moment that I can hardly breathe. "Even if not everything is perfect and even if you're sometimes sad. As long as you focus on what makes you happy, you're moving toward your goal."

This trip will make me happy. I'll capture India in images so that others can see this country through my eyes. With every breath I'll inhale happiness, with every encounter I'll take another step forward. But will that ever outshine the dark shadow of my lost love?

Grandma pulls away from me. She can definitely read the doubt on my face. "India is full of places that will help you sort out all your unanswered questions. Use the time, look ahead."

How am I ever supposed to tell her that I don't know if I'm really capable of that when she's looking at me the way she is right now? This woman lost the love of her life forever, and yet today she's standing in front of me, radiating zest for life. Who, if not her, is living proof that I can do it too?

"I'm going to miss you so much." Now it's me who pulls her into another hug. I'd rather never let her go again. She's my rock in the surf. The last little bit of home that I'll be leaving behind in just a few minutes.

Gently, she strokes her hand over my back. "We'll write to each other, and we'll do that video thing too. And when you come back, we'll bake apple strudel together."

Will I even come back?

For a brief moment that question flares up inside me. I don't know the answer, but I feel that Grandma and I will be falling into each other's arms again very soon. Because our bond will never weaken. Not after everything we've been through together.

Once more I bury my nose in her silky scarf and inhale her scent. She smells like an entire Christmas bakery today. I'm sure my favorite cookies are hidden in the package she handed me earlier. "I have to go," I murmur, yet I have no intention of moving even a millimeter away from her.

"Off to your adventure." She tries for a casual tone, but I can hear how hard this farewell is for her too. "The plane won't wait for you."

No. It won't. Any more than Lukas will.

I take one last deep breath and let go of Grandma. "See you soon," I force out.

"Enjoy your trip." She smiles, her eyes covered with a watery sheen.

It's time for me to get going. I give her one last nod,

then raise my hand in a wave and turn to leave. "See you soon."

This is hard enough as it is, so it's better to make it quick. I start walking. A few times I turn back to her, wave, and blow her kisses.

She waits until I've disappeared from her line of sight. As soon as I'm alone, I pull my phone out of my pocket. No call, no message. Once again I read the words Lukas sent me two days ago. He wanted to let me know that things between us aren't over. Deep down he still loves me, but his head is warning him not to support my decision to choose photography and a new way of living.

I look around. There's no one over by the standing tables of the small café, and I can't spot Lukas next to the group of teenagers who are all wearing the same sports team jersey, either. He isn't strolling along the tiled corridor between the tourists, and he isn't standing at the glass front watching what's happening out on the runway.

I shouldn't keep waiting for Lukas; I should focus on India and on all the beautiful things that lie ahead of me. With a sigh I let my phone slide back into my jacket pocket and firmly resolve not to take it out again right away.

But suddenly I feel a vibration. A split second later I hear the ringtone as well.

Lukas!

Impulsively, I yank the phone out of my pocket.

It isn't Lukas. The call is from an unknown number. I answer anyway; maybe he's using a different phone. In a shaky voice I say my name.

"Ms. Berger?" I hear a man ask.

That's not Lukas, definitely not. "Yes, this is Marie Berger." The stranger on the other end of the line can surely hear the disappointment in my voice, but I can't hold it back.

"Wonderful. I hope I'm not disturbing you? No? Very good." He sounds as if he's checking the time after every word that leaves his mouth.

What does this strange man want from me? "How can I…?"

I don't get any further; he cuts me off at once. "My name is Heinzinger, I'm calling on behalf of the Beilsteiner agency. We're interested in your work."

Agency? Work? Is he talking about my photos?

My stomach drops at once. I should say something. Maybe. My mind is blank.

"The images from the corporate presentation of Eco-Design appealed to me. In the course of further research, I discovered your pictures on various online platforms. We at the Beilsteiner agency are considering signing you."

I really ought to answer, but I'm at a loss for words. After all, this could just be someone playing a nasty joke on me. One of those pseudo agents who demand a down payment to put me in a portfolio that never finds any buyers anyway. I've already read more than enough about people like that; every photography forum warns about them. Still, it could just as well be true, because I actually used my own pictures for the corporate presentation of Eco-Design. And why shouldn't an agency be interested in eco-friendly furniture and happen to notice me that way?

"Ms. Berger, are you still there?"

I clear my throat. "Yes. Of course. Um…"

Now I hear a warm laugh at the other end of the line. "I seem to have caught you off guard. Take your time, you don't have to answer right away."

"I'll be in India over the next few weeks." Only after I've

spoken the words do I realize that this must sound completely out of context to him. "To take photos," I quickly add so it doesn't sound totally stupid.

"Wonderful. We definitely want to see those pictures. We could meet after you get back."

We could. If this is actually real. "Gladly." It almost sounds as if I've asked a question.

"I'll send you some information about our agency as well as our standard contract by email today. You can look everything over at your leisure, take great photos in India, and get in touch as soon as you're back in Vienna. Then we'll set up an appointment to discuss the details. Does that work for you?" Even though it hardly seems possible, he has sped up his speech even more.

"Very gladly," I just about manage to say. "My email address..."

"...I already have it. The information will be on its way to you in a moment. I wish you a wonderful trip. See you soon."

Without waiting for my reply, he ends the call. Dazed, I let the phone drop to my side.

Was that really a professional agent? Or just a scammer?

I have to find out right away. My fingers are trembling, but I manage to type the agency's name into the browser's search bar. A little later I find the link to a website.

It looks professional. The list of photographers represented by the agency includes some prominent names. I go through every page of the homepage and even find photos of the staff. What was the name of the man who called me again? Hei... something.

There. Heinzinger. That's him.

Can it really be true? Was that just now the moment when my dream of being a photographer became real?

Yes. It's possible. Or even very likely!

I clap a hand over my mouth and have to laugh and cry at the same time. My legs are twitching, they want to dance, and my throat wants to scream with joy. All the fear that I'd gone completely off track on my path falls away from me like a heavy blanket suddenly slipping from my shoulders.

I feel free.

No, I am free. And so damn happy that I can't keep this feeling to myself.

I immediately text my grandma and Alex to tell them what just happened. Then I look for Lukas's number.

I have to call him. Because once he hears about the agency, he'll have no reason to keep doubting. He'll understand that photography can become my profession and isn't just a crazy dream that will leave me disappointed and broke in the end. And once his doubts disappear, only his love for me will be left.

My breathing is heavy, my pulse is racing. Because I know the next few seconds will decide our future together. But I won't let that stop me. Nothing can stop me now; I'm putting all my eggs in one basket.

Bravely, I dial his number.

Chapter Forty

I shouldn't be making calls here in the office, but Anna has called me so many times in the last few minutes that I couldn't ignore it any longer. With my desk chair turned toward the window, I try to brush her off as inconspicuously as possible. Not that I feel good about it, but there's already way too much going on in my head. And further down, there in my chest, there's nothing but anarchy.

"Oh come on, let's do it," Anna urges me yet again. "There's nothing that speaks against it."

Nothing? Or rather everything? I should tell her the truth. That I don't know if the two of us should move. If we should live in the house that was meant for Marie and me. And if we should even be together as a couple at all. "Anna, I…"

"No, I already know what's coming next. You need time. Time, time, time." The words tumble out of her mouth like a waterfall. I can practically see her in front of me, how she lifts her hand and looks at me, worn out. "How much more?"

My gaze drifts to the time display on the computer screen all by itself. Today is October 21, it's 1:30 PM. No matter how much time I still need, I don't have it. In 30 minutes I have my appointment with the realtor.

And in two hours Marie's plane to India will take off.

Damn. I knew this moment would come, and still I didn't do anything about it. I should have made up my mind days ago. Then it wouldn't feel right now as if I were locked in a room full of doors that are all coming at me. They're getting closer and closer. Each of them has something beautiful about it, but also something that scares me.

I have to choose one, otherwise they'll soon crush me. I'll be left without air to breathe, my bones will break, my muscles will be squeezed together.

"Lukas?" I hear Anna ask, exasperated, at the other end of the line. "What do you think, can I cancel the lease for the apartment now? I have to take care of it this week, otherwise we'll have to stay another month." This accusatory tone in her voice is new to me.

Does it really matter? One month more or less, nobody cares about that anyway.

"In that case we can forget about Christmas at the house. And New Year's Eve too."

At once, an image of Anna and me at the house on Christmas Eve appears. She has conjured up an eight-course menu, of which she hardly eats anything herself, and flits cheerfully around the living room to put up the last decorations. In my imagination she's even wearing a red apron and lined Christmas-themed slippers. It smells of cinnamon and candied apples, a fire crackles in the fireplace.

No. That doesn't fit.

"Weren't we going to go to Joe's anyway and really go wild there?" The question leaves my mouth unfiltered.

For a moment Anna is silent, then she clears her throat. "No, we weren't," she says, and I can hear how disappointed she is. "Apart from the fact that you've been drinking too much lately anyway. We should take the next step, we're ready. Back then you didn't hesitate either when..."

She stops abruptly, and I'm sure she's biting her lip right now. Of course, she's alluding to my marriage proposal to Marie. I didn't doubt for a second that I was doing the right thing. I could feel it everywhere inside me and didn't even have to look at Marie.

Today all I feel is my growing panic about not doing right by Anna. And about making the wrong decision. To top it all off, my work phone starts ringing as well.

Stressed, I let my hand slide from the top of my head down to the back of my neck. Anna doesn't say anything else; an uncomfortable silence spreads between us. The landline keeps ringing without stopping. I can't stand it, just like I can't stand anything anymore.

"Listen, I can't stay on the phone any longer. There are other calls coming in, my inbox is overflowing, and I have to catch a supplier in Mumbai before he calls it a day," I finally manage to say after all. Once again, it's work that saves me. It distracts me and gives me something to hold on to. It's my lifeline, even if it's one with a damn prickly surface.

"Fine, we'll talk tonight. The TV stays off, I'll cook for us. And I don't want to hear any more excuses, okay?" Anna sounds contrite, and of course I understand why. If I were in her situation, I'd feel exactly the same.

Would I want to know the whole truth?

"This has to happen now," she presses again, urgently.

"Absolutely. Talk to you later." I don't want to say anything more. I just wait until she's said goodbye too, then take the phone from my ear with a deep breath.

If there's one thing I know for sure, it's that this can't go on like this for much longer.

My gaze wanders to my phone's display; I press the red button to finally end the call. How wonderful it would be if I could do the same with my life. If I could just switch it off or pause it for a moment. For a few seconds in which I'd be free. For a moment in which, without fear and without doubt, I'd feel what's really going on deep inside me.

I should turn back to my work, but a symbol at the top edge of my phone's screen holds me back. Apparently someone tried to reach me while I was on the phone with Anna. The real estate agent, maybe? Or my mother? It might be important, so I check.

Marie.

The call was from her. She's definitely already at the airport. She's probably standing at one of the window fronts, looking up into the gray sky. She's waiting and hoping. There's no sign of her usually radiant smile. Because I'm not with her.

My God, I really shouldn't get ideas like that. It's not good for me, not at all.

Still, I can't let go of the phone, and if I'm honest with myself, I only want one thing: to hear her voice. To find out how she's doing and know what she's thinking.

Calling her should help me with my decision. Maybe we'll only talk briefly and it'll become clear to me that what we had is over. That my head is blocked only by the nebulous ghost of a past that shouldn't be conjured up any longer.

Or I'll hear her voice. And her laughter. In the worst

case, it won't take a second for my neatly constructed safe world to lie in ruins.

I'd have to finally face the all-decisive questions that have been tormenting me for days.

Would I really be capable of giving up control? Could I unfasten my golden ankle shackle, turn down a supposedly good life, get on a plane, and open myself up to a future with Marie?

And if I manage it, what would happen then?

Chapter Forty-One

By now my pulse is normal, just like my breathing. None of my excitement is left. It had to make room for a dark cloud of disappointment that's spreading inside me unstoppably.

Lukas didn't pick up my call.

Because there are no words inside him that he wants to say to me. Because in his world, neither of us exists anymore. Like a photo that has lain in the sun for too long, his memory has already faded. Just a few more months and it will be gone. What we had will cease to exist.

A terrible thought, yet it seems to be true. Dejected, I stroll along the long airport corridor. Even though I should finally accept Lukas's decision, my gaze keeps wandering in all directions, searching for him. Because a part of me can't give up hope that he'll still show up. Because this longing inside me relentlessly wants to believe that he simply didn't hear the phone ring, or maybe even that he deliberately didn't pick up so he could surprise me here.

Maybe he's waiting for me at the gate? With a bouquet of wildflowers in his hand and that smile that makes my knees go weak. Right now he could already be standing between the dark rows of seats, impatiently shifting from one foot to the other. I shouldn't allow it, but this film keeps running in my head without stopping. I see myself walking hopefully through the gate. I spot him at once. We look at each other. There's music, a whole orchestra playing just for us. And a sunbeam shining through the glass front. It illuminates exactly the spot where Lukas is waiting for me.

For a moment the world stands still. There's only the two of us, looking at each other from a few meters away. Despite the distance between us, we read in each other's eyes everything we need to know.

We walk toward each other. Slowly, without looking away. A smile flits across his face. The world in front of my eyes threatens to blur, my legs lose their strength. Unimpressed by this, I keep walking, because there's nothing that could stop me. Even before I reach him, I can smell the scent of his skin. I hear his breathing; it's heavy and uneven.

In a moment I'll be with him. In a moment I'll be allowed to rest my head on his shoulder. In a moment I'll finally arrive for good.

The film in my head feels so real that I have to let out a heavy sigh. I even imagine I can actually feel Lukas's nearness, even though I'm wandering all alone through the airport among thousands of strangers.

It just has to be true. He has to be waiting for me at the gate.

And if he isn't?

Once again the darkness rose up inside me, but as long as the last spark of hope hadn't gone out, I wasn't going to give it any space. With unerring steps I walked toward the gates, and only a few minutes later the sign with the right number appeared in my field of vision. I still had a hundred meters to go.

Fear and hope were locked in a bitter struggle inside me. In a few seconds it would be decided, and only one of them could win.

To pull myself together, I stopped, closed my eyes, and took a deep breath. This was the moment when I forced a promise from myself.

If hope won, everything would be all right. Lukas and I would find our love and ourselves again in India. The two of us would be like a river that, on its way to the horizon, forces its path through every kind of ground.

If fear won, it would be up to me alone how I dealt with it. I could let it crash down on me like a ten-meter wave and disappear beneath it, never to breathe again. Or I could be like a steep cliff where the tide breaks. The rock is stronger than the elements, because it's anchored so firmly in the earth that not even the highest wave can harm it.

What am I? An unstoppable river or the defiant cliff?

It was time to find out. Bravely, I opened my eyes and marched off. I drew closer and closer to the gate, searching more and more frantically for Lukas. I turned the last corner, then I could see the whole area.

He wasn't back there by the workstations. And not up front at the counter either. I carefully scanned every row of seats. I spotted an old man in a checked blazer. A family with twins. A young woman in a tracksuit with a lollipop in her mouth.

There, in the second row, someone was sitting. A man in a dark blue polo shirt. Brown, short-cropped hair. I could only see him from behind, but the broad shoulders looked familiar. Lukas!

For a moment it felt as if my body stopped working. As

if I couldn't smell or hear or feel. I could only still see, and the image of the back of Lukas's head burned itself into my retina.

My legs won't stay still any longer. They carry me toward him, circle around a tour group, and turn into his row of seats. All at once he moves. His upper body leans forward. He pushes himself up from the chair. Stands up.

It's starting. In a few moments, what was just a movie in my head earlier will actually happen. He turns toward me.

Everything happens so slowly, as if time were stretching. Even so, the disillusionment hits me in a flash. This isn't Lukas. The guy is just some stranger. A nobody I've never seen before.

I stop abruptly, the last spark of hope inside me dies out and leaves nothing but an empty shell. My mind tries to grasp what I can already feel everywhere.

Fear has won. Lukas and Marie no longer exist.

Chapter Forty-Two

With all my strength I try to ignore the phone. Still, my gaze jerks to the display, and my mind keeps showing me images of how I pick it up and dial Marie's number. In my imagination I see myself sitting right here at my desk. With a bittersweet smile on my face. I say, "Hello, Sleeping Beauty, how are you?"

I quickly shake my head to make this image disappear. But it doesn't. On the contrary, it even becomes clearer. And while I watch myself lower my lids so no one here can see the watery shine Marie's voice brings to my eyes, I also hear Joe on top of everything. "If you knew today was your last day, what would you do? Where would you want to be and who would be with you?" he asks me, his voice grounded and steady.

I should call her—no, I just have to do it. Because if I don't, won't I regret it for the rest of my life? Won't I ask myself every day what would have happened if I had at least tried?

By now it's 1:45 PM. Seconds rush past me, minutes

vanish into nowhere. I know my time is running out, and I know I have to act. Right now. Even so, I feel paralyzed. My hand reaches for the phone, my finger hovers over the display. A cool breath of wind makes me shiver.

Suddenly I hear a bang. I startle, look around frantically and spot the managing director in the doorway.

With long strides the gaunt man comes toward me. “Mr. Richter, there you are.”

Instinctively I push myself up from my chair. Out of the corner of my eye I see Bernd doing the same. Now we’re both standing here at our desks, backs straight like two schoolboys.

The boss is already reaching me and, although he is gaunt and rather short for a man, there is something intimidating about him. It’s his eyes, as alert as a lion’s on the hunt. Abruptly he turns to Bernd. “We need a few minutes to ourselves.” His hand points at me.

“Of course.” Bernd doesn’t even throw me a furtive glance. He lowers his head and hurries off. I’d probably have done the same in his place, because the less you’re in our managing director’s focus, the better.

Naturally I’m the one the boss is targeting now. I feel as if he’s shining a spotlight directly on me. “You owe me an answer,” he says, and I can clearly hear how he’s trying to sound friendly, even though he’d really rather not talk to me at all.

I clear my throat. “That’s right,” I squeeze out, just to say anything at all.

Impatiently he signals me to go on. His gaze flicks to his wristwatch.

A feeling of helplessness spreads through me in a matter of seconds. Because I don’t know what to say. Because all my decisions are so tightly interwoven that I can't make one without the other.

"So, are you accepting our offer?" From the way he looks at me, I know he thinks I'm an idiot. And maybe I am. "This opportunity is unique. Now or never, Mr. Richter."

Perfect. That was just what I was missing. As if I didn't already feel crushed from all sides, he piles even more on top. Shouldn't something finally happen to me under all this weight? Shouldn't it be clear to me by now which version of my future is the best one?

Nothing of the sort happens. It's as if this barrier inside me were impenetrable. Nothing from the outside or the inside can harm it. And no matter how hard my head weighs the pros and cons of every possible option against each other, I don't get anywhere.

It's 1:50 PM. The realtor is waiting. Marie is waiting. Anna is waiting. The boss is waiting.

What else has to happen for me to finally make a decision?

"I… I need time," I force out, as if I were a cowardly idiot who keeps putting everything off. As if I really still believed that time could help me.

Nothing and no one can help me. That's the truth.

The boss's dumbfounded expression hits me. "You've had enough time. Is this about money? Is that it? You want to negotiate another bonus or a company car?"

He thinks I want money? What the hell am I supposed to do with that? Will it help me live a better life and make the right decisions? Will it make me happy?

No.

Out of nowhere, this realization is suddenly in my head. It's haunting the place up there, trying to find the right spot from which it can show me what it means for me.

If money and security aren't everything, then what are they?

I glance at the time display on my screen once more. It's 1:52 PM. I have to go. Wherever that may be.

"I'm sorry, I have an appointment." Impulsively, I grab my jacket and push the desk chair neatly up to the desk. "You'll have my answer tomorrow."

For a moment I look into a stunned face. His lips move, but not a single word leaves his mouth. He didn't see this coming. No one did, but that doesn't matter.

I lift my shoulders apologetically and start walking. Because time can't be stopped. That's the only thing I know for sure right now. I have to figure out the rest in the next few minutes.

Chapter Forty-Three

Agitated, I pace up and down in front of the glass wall of my gate with the phone in my hand. "He's not coming, I know it," I say to Alex, and it's not the first time.

"Your flight doesn't leave for another hour, that's 60 minutes in which anything can still happen." Alex sounds so committed that I'd love to have her here with me right now. Then she could hug me and smile at me with so much energy from her elfin face that a bit of her courage would rub off on me.

Still, I shake my head firmly. "Nothing's going to happen." I don't even sound disappointed or bitter. Just matter-of-fact. As if all my feelings had left me in an instant. "In sixty minutes I'll be getting on a plane alone."

"That's not how this works, Marie." Her tone is strict. She's probably furrowing her brow in deep lines right now. "Let's talk about something nice. What's the plan for India?"

She already knows that. I've told her about my flight

times and my idea for the route at least a hundred times. "I know exactly what you're trying to do here."

"Irrelevant," Alex shoots back with utter confidence. "Come on, do it, it'll do you good."

Maybe it will. Because India and photography are the only things I can still hold on to. Everything else is lost. Forever.

"So, your flight leaves in an hour. And then…" If she were here, she'd keep poking me in the side until I finally talked.

It's incredibly sweet of her to want to distract me, and for that reason alone I have to smile a little. "I get on the plane and first I fly to Dubai," I begin to say, even though I feel a bit ridiculous doing it. "The layover is going to last forever. I'll be there a full twelve hours, because that was simply the cheapest flight."

"And what are you going to do there?"

I give a tired shrug and let my gaze wander outside to the busy hustle on the tarmac. "No idea. Sleep?"

"Oh, come on, don't make it so hard for me." Her long, drawn-out snort tells me how hard she's trying with me right now.

What kind of friend am I if I don't at least try? "I could wander around the airport and…" Yeah, what could I do? Definitely not go shopping, because I don't have the money for that. Imagine Lukas being with me. That's what I'll probably actually do. But I don't say that, because that's not what Alex wants to hear.

"And…," she prompts from the other end of the line.

Behind the glass front, people are just boarding a small airplane. Most of them are businesspeople; they look like a dark-clad army of soldiers who have forgotten how to smile.

If they could see themselves, would they recognize the same thing I do?

At once I'm seized by the urge to capture their faces in photos. And in the very next moment I know exactly how to answer Alex's question.

"I'm going to look for photo subjects. I'm sure there'll be plenty." I notice warmth spreading through me, all the way up to my cheeks, which are probably carrying a faint smile in spite of everything. "I'll start documenting my journey right there. I'll look into faces that tell stories without words and capture them so the world can find out about them." Just imagining doing exactly that makes me glow. "Who knows what I'll discover there?"

"That's what I wanted to hear." She sounds very pleased with herself, and she has every right to be. "You can already make your first photo book out of that. You can call it Twelve Hours in Dubai or something like that."

There's no need for her enthusiasm to spill over onto me, because I can already feel it deep inside. "Twelve hours can be everything. Or nothing." Even as I speak the words, one thing becomes clear to me.

I alone decide whether the hours of my life are filled with joy or with sorrow. Whether I want to look forward or back, whether I smile or cry.

Even when Lukas isn't with me, I can be strong. And enjoy life.

Maybe it isn't perfect, but almost perfect is sometimes enough.

Once again my eyes fill with tears. "Let's go," I say in a choked voice. "I'm ready."

Chapter Forty-Four

I run. As fast as I can, I leave the company through the glass sliding doors and burst out into the cool autumn day. A gust of wind tears the red leaves from the trees, it smells of exhaust fumes and smoke. Strange that that of all things is what I notice. As if it mattered. As if it could help me see my future more clearly.

Quickly, I turn off toward the tram stop. I rush down the alley, lower my head, and try to form even a single coherent thought.

"What do you want?" I ask myself. "You have to know that!" Despair spreads inside me; again and again I run my hand through my hair and then immediately knead my fingers nervously. "Don't be an idiot, you hear me?!"

What would an idiot do? I don't know. I don't know anything, except that there are only a few more meters between me and the tram stop. And that I'd most like to walk out on myself. As I walk, I pull my weekly planner out of my bag. It's full of appointments and obligations. They give me security, but at the same time they hardly let me breathe. I want out of this compulsion, away from everything that makes me heavy and tired. And more than anything, I don't want to have to decide and constantly feel as if I might be making the biggest mistake of my life.

Far too quickly I reach the stop. I should stop, but I can't manage that either. Like a caged tiger gone wild, I pace up and down. Suddenly, out of all the chaotic thoughts in my head, an idea takes shape.

Fate should decide.

Why not? A decision has to be made, and if I don't make it, someone or something else has to do it for me. All at once it seems quite simple. Only two lines stop at this tram stop. Number 5 turns off at the next corner toward the south, the other, number 2, continues straight ahead. One would take me toward Praterstern. The realtor is waiting for me there, and so is the S7 that goes to the airport.

The other leads to Anna.

5 stands for Marie, letting go, overcoming my fear of flying, and freedom at the cost of uncertainty. 2 stands for Anna, a new job, and security with an unpleasant aftertaste.

"This is insane," I mutter, yet I still can't stop myself from fixing my eyes on the distance where the trams are supposed to come from.

What if the wrong one shows up first? And which one would that even be?

Nervously, I shift my weight from one foot to the other while four completely different versions of my life flit through my head like ghostly faces. Marie and me, failing financially and emotionally, or becoming as happy together as we've never been before. Anna and me, dragging each other into misery, or finding a way to make it work and leading a good life.

The pressure inside me keeps building. I have to distract myself; my gaze darts over the plain façades of the houses, the furrowed asphalt of the sidewalk, and finally to the column plastered with advertisements. Almost in a panic, I study ads for cleaning products, sweets, and events.

Suddenly I freeze.

Can this be real? Are my eyes deceiving me, or even my mind?

I step closer to the advertising column and read again what it says there.

Ulrike Richter. November 1. Live at Jazzland.

Aunt Ulrike is performing at the most famous jazz club in Vienna? That's not possible. Or is it?

Did my mother lie to me? Maybe even on purpose?

Her sister didn't fail in her dreams. On the contrary, she made them come true.

Does that mean that Marie and I will also…

A squeaking sound reaches my ear. I whirl around at once. A tram is approaching from behind the block of houses, and where there were so many questions just a moment ago, suddenly there's only one that matters.

What number will it have?

For a moment I close my eyes. I wish I could send up a quick prayer to wherever, but I can't. Because I don't know what I should wish for.

5 or 2? Marie or Anna?

The tram comes closer; I can hear it in the humming of the power lines. With a loud noise it glides along the tracks, heading straight for me.

My eyes stay closed. Because my own fear is paralyzing me. Because I know this is the moment I've been putting off for weeks.

Dreams can come true, I know that now. But that still doesn't mean it will be that way for Marie and me.

In these seconds my future is being decided. I have to face it.

"Look, you coward," I order myself, as if that would change the fact that my eyelids suddenly feel as heavy as lead.

I press my lips together and take a deep breath. Then I do it. Despite all the resistance inside me, I open my eyes.

My gaze searches for the tram tracks, follows their course to the car and slides up over the driver's cab. To the place where, in green illuminated letters against a dark background, there can be only a single number.

It's the 2.

Fate has decided. Anna is my future.

Chapter Forty-Five

A jolt tears me from my dreams. Groggy from the restless night, I try to open my eyes. The sunlight streaming through the milky windows shines straight into my face, and for a moment I don't know where I am.

"Ladies and gentlemen, we have already begun our descent. Please fasten your seat belts again, fold up the tray table in front of you, and bring your seat back into an upright position. Thank you," I hear a bored voice say over the loudspeakers.

Of course. I'm on the plane. Delhi lies beneath me. Next to me is still the woman with the boyish short haircut and the old-fashioned knitted cardigan.

Lukas isn't with me, and he never will be again. As soon as my feet touch Indian soil, I'm going to look ahead. That's what I promised myself, and that's exactly what I'm going to do.

Not even fifteen minutes later, the plane touches down on the runway with a violent jolt.

"Ladies and gentlemen, welcome to India. Please

remain seated with your seat belts fastened until the aircraft has reached its final parking position and the seat belt signs above you have been switched off." I can barely hear the stewardess's voice, and I only feel the fatigue of the long journey on the fringes of my awareness. Staring outside, I try to catch my first impressions of the country that has always been part of my dreams.

The airport looks like any other. Of course it does; expecting anything else would be crazy. I need to get out of the plane and into the country. That's where I'll find what I'm looking for. Faces that tell stories, colors full of vitality, and natural spectacles whose beauty will captivate me.

The plane has barely come to a stop when I push myself up from my seat. My legs are stiff, even though I walked around a bit during my layover in Dubai. I shake them out, take my backpack from the overhead compartment, and wait patiently in line until the aircraft doors open. A couple standing a few feet in front of me catches my attention.

They can't be older than their early twenties and only have eyes for each other. They're being jostled from all sides, people trying by sheer force to be the first to yank their luggage from the bins above the rows of seats. Yet the two of them seem to be surrounded by an invisible wall, formed by the affection they feel for one another.

A bitter feeling of wistfulness rises in me as I watch the play of their fingers, constantly tangling together in new ways, and follow the dance of their eyes when they look at each other.

They have what I've lost forever.

As if I weren't quite in my right mind, I scan the cabin. There's a part of me that refuses to believe Lukas isn't here with me. That part is crazy enough to hope he's been on the plane the whole time without my noticing. But the line of people in the aisle is nothing more than a collection of unfamiliar faces, loud voices, intense smells, and colorful bags.

So I do the only thing I can. I move along with the crowd, step into the airport, take my backpacker's rucksack from the baggage carousel, and keep walking toward the exit.

The moment the dust-covered sliding doors to the outside open, hot, stuffy air hits me in the face. A biting smell forces me to press my hand over my mouth and nose. Behind me, huge crowds of people, gesticulating wildly and wrapped in colorful cloths, also push toward the exit and practically shove me along with them.

It's all too much for me. I try to break out to the side, but nine hours on the plane and fifteen hours in various airports have left my body tired and weak. So I let myself be carried along until the pressure behind me eases. I'm already sweating so much that beads of perspiration make their way from my forehead down over my cheeks to my chin and then drip farther down. They land on a floor littered with trash and unidentifiable, foul-smelling stains.

I feel disappointment rising up inside me. This wasn't how I'd imagined India. To make matters worse, doubts are now creeping in as well.

Was it right to come here? Is this really my dream country, or was it only that in my imagination?

Exhausted, I look around. Immediately a man rushes toward me. With his worn-out trousers, yellow-brown teeth, and the hair sprouting from his nose and ears, he looks anything but trustworthy.

"Taxi, taxi!" he yells at me and, with frantic hand movements, signals me to come along.

I quickly shake my head. "No. No taxi," I say firmly so

that he, along with his pungent smell, will leave me alone again.

"Taxi," he repeats. "Cheap!" His thumb rubs over his middle and index fingers.

"No, thanks," I repeat, looking him straight in the eyes.

He looks disappointed. With a dismissive wave of his hand, he turns away, and a second later he's already approaching the next potential passenger. For a while I watch him trying in vain to land a fare. His expression grows more and more pleading, his gestures more and more desperate.

I look more closely, and suddenly the stinking, unlikeable man in the worn-out trousers turns into a human being fighting for survival. If he doesn't earn anything today, he might have nothing to eat. Neither will his wife and children.

That could be his reality, and I'm ashamed that I treated him like an annoying fly I just wanted to get rid of.

He'll get his ride as soon as I'm ready to leave the airport. There are still too many impressions raining down on me, and just as I couldn't really see the taxi driver earlier, I'm probably missing other things in this very moment as well.

Calmly, I look around and imagine I'm viewing my surroundings through the camera. Little by little, my state of shock turns into serenity and curiosity. Hidden in the hustle and bustle of the airport, I discover calm and composure in people's faces. The dark eyes around me radiate confidence and gratitude. The cloths embroidered with gold thread and glowing in every color, the women's arms overloaded with sparkling jewelry, and the children's warm, unrestrained laughter, their shiny pitch-black hair, all have something magical about them. Enthralled, I soak up the atmosphere of this so foreign world and let my gaze wander on toward the horizon, where monumental stone structures stand out magnificently in the shimmering haze of the city.

So it's true what they say about India. Either you love it or you hate it. And I can already feel that I'm going to love it.

Even though the air here is anything but good, I take a deep breath. The exhaust fumes scratch at my lungs, but that doesn't bother me. Because in this second I feel as alive as I've always wished to feel. I've arrived, and if there's one thing I know for sure, it's that this is the beginning of a new life.

It can begin. Finally.

With a broad smile on my face and full of confidence in my heart, I look around for the taxi driver from before. He's disappeared. I even turn in a full circle, but I don't spot him. Instead, there's something else that makes me pause. A feeling that my gaze, in searching for him, has passed over something that should have made it stop.

Even though there's no reason for it, this hunch spreads further in my stomach. Curiously, I let my gaze wander back.

There it is, back there.

Right in the middle of the loud throng of people, something happens that draws me in as if by magic. I blink to see more clearly what's going on there. On the border between dream and reality, a tall figure suddenly detaches itself from the crowd.

Can this be real?

Is it really Lukas who's fixing his eyes on me right now and smiling at me in a way he's never done before?

All the bright colors, the babble of voices, the stench and the noise of the city suddenly seem miles away. All I still perceive is that the love of my life is walking toward me. And the fierce pounding in my chest that reaches all the way to my eardrums. I'm unable to move, not a sound leaves my throat.

Lukas is here. With me.

He did it. For *us* he dared to get on a plane. For *us* he flew thousands of kilometers all the way to India.

Only a few centimeters separate us now. We look at each other. No one says anything, and there's no need, because his eyes tell me everything I need to know. He lifts his hand and touches my cheek. Fierce electric shocks discharge in the thin layer that still lies between us, pierce my skin, and in a matter of seconds reach every cell in my body.

The air around us starts to shimmer. No one moves. Time stands still. It's as if the whole world is holding its breath to witness what happens next.

I don't hesitate and I don't doubt. I press myself tightly against him, wrap my arms around his back, and savor the feeling I've missed for far too long.

No matter where we are and no matter what we do, this person is my home, and that's what he'll stay. Forever.

Chapter Forty-Six

I'm here. In the middle of the hectic bustle outside Delhi's airport, with Marie in my arms and the sure feeling that fate would've made the wrong decision for me.

Even though it's hardly possible, I pull Marie even closer to me. "Hello, Sleeping Beauty," I whisper in her ear, and in the same moment I feel her whole body start to tremble.

"You came. You're really here." Absentmindedly she murmurs to herself, as if she can't believe it's real. And maybe she's even right, because I myself am still hypnotized by everything that happened in the last 24 hours.

Exactly 23 hours and ten minutes ago I was still standing on a street in Vienna, unable to make up my mind. But when the number 5 tram turned the corner, it suddenly became crystal clear what I had to do. My heart no longer just whispered, it roared. For Marie. And for a life beyond the limits that, in the end, existed only in my head.

There was only one thing I wanted anymore: to stop clinging to something that never would have made me happy.

When, a few hours later, my feet boarded a plane for the very first time, I didn't shake and I didn't sweat. While the acceleration at takeoff pressed me into my seat, my breathing stayed calm. Together with the plane I lost contact with the ground, climbed higher and higher, up beyond the cloud layer. To the place where I hadn't allowed myself to be for far too long. To the place where the sun shines in any weather.

I push Marie a little away from me so I can look into her eyes. "Show me the stars," I say longingly, because there's nothing I want more than finally to experience it.

A radiance like the light of a thousand suns spreads across her face. She rises onto her tiptoes, I bend down a little toward her. A second later our lips touch, and it feels as if we're sealing a promise to each other that we don't even need to put into words.

Just one life, I suddenly hear Joe's voice in my head, but this time it doesn't sound like a warning. There's no dangerous undertone, only contented warmth. Down to the tips of my little toes I know one thing for sure: Marie and I are starting a new life in this very moment.

It won't just be a good life, and by God it won't be a respectable one.

It will be a fantastic life full of adventure and passion, overflowing with love, freedom, and happiness. We'll be who we always wanted to be.

All this becomes clear to me while we're kissing so intensely, as if we had to make up for all the weeks we were apart.

Only minutes later does Marie finally pull her lips from mine. "Let's not wait any longer," she asks me, almost out of breath. Even though she should be tired after the long trip, she has that unique radiance on her face that I love so much about her.

She doesn't ask why, doesn't want to look back, only wants to look ahead together with me. What happened no longer counts for her, and it shouldn't for me either. Still, there's something I have to do to finally let go of the past. Without hesitating, I rummage my weekly planner out of my backpack.

Surprised, Marie raises her eyebrows. "What's that doing here?"

I can't help but grin at her. Then I open the page with the yearly overview to show her what I wrote there. There's only a single word, written across all the weeks still to come.

"Live," Marie reads aloud, and I see what those few letters do to her.

With a liberated feeling in my chest, I close the weekly planner one last time and step up to a trash can. "We don't need this anymore."

"Definitely not." She shakes her head, her eyes shining.

I loosen my grip, and the weekly planner disappears between empty gum packets and dirty tissues. With it, the last little bit of weight falls from my shoulders. There's just one thing I still have to tell her before we can both make a completely fresh start. "I reversed the house purchase."

Even though I ended up in a different world here, the memory still catches up with me now. Of the moment when I signed the contract. Not a second later I could breathe a little easier. It was the first sign that I was on the right path. And when I told Anna from the airport that the house belonged to the past, I got the second one.

She was furious. More than that, she totally flipped out, even though she didn't even know where I was at that moment or what I was about to do next.

"You did what?" she yelled into the phone again in my memory, upset all over. "What makes you think you can decide that without me?"

Immediately I was overcome by a bad conscience. Was she right? Should I have asked her?

No. It had been my house and mine alone. And it was my money alone that I had lost with it for good.

Before I could say anything, Anna raged on. "What did I ever do to you that you're pushing me away like this, huh? Haven't you got everything from me? Didn't I twist myself into a rubber doll, just so you could…" Her voice broke then.

"So I could what?" I dared to ask, even though I was already getting scared when I thought about what she might answer.

A sound like a wolf growling reached my ear. "Come home, we're not going to discuss this on the phone." I could hear how hard she was trying to pull herself together, when what she really wanted was to scream at me in anger.

Just because of the house? Why did it mean so much to her?

Uncertain, I shifted my weight from one foot to the other. "I can't," I replied truthfully and fixed my gaze on the ticket in my hand. At the office I had called in to ask for leave because of an urgent, non-deferrable family matter. I had already passed security; my flight was leaving in just under an hour.

"Why? Where are you?" Anna's voice grew more and more pressing, her speech more and more frantic. "Come home. Now!"

"No." Even I'm surprised by the vehemence packed into that one word. "Tell me right now. Why are you freaking out like this?"

Anna stays silent. Then I hear her breathing hard.

"Come on, Anna." If the news about the house is already knocking her off balance, how is she going to react when she finds out I'm about to fly to India? Because I can't help but find out whether Marie and I have a future together. I can't put into words how horrible that makes me feel toward Anna. But I can feel it everywhere. "What's going on?" There's a pleading in my voice; she just has to hear it.

"The house was supposed to be our beginning." She sounds indescribably disappointed. "For a life together. With all the bells and whistles."

No, please don't. I try not to let her words get to me, but I still can't manage it. "Try to understand, I…" I don't get any further because I don't know what to say. I feel lost. She's my best friend. She's always been there for me, even at a time when no one else was.

How could I do this to her? How could I get involved in this relationship when I knew what was at stake for her?

"No." There's a hardness in her voice I've never heard before. "You're coming home right now. Then we'll call the realtor and buy the house again. In December we'll move in, just like we planned."

A strange feeling spreads through me. Is she actually trying to decide for me and for our life together? "And you don't care what I have to say about it?" slips out of me before I can stop it.

"For once, you're going to sit still and do as you're told, got it?! For months I've been busting my ass, I've done everything for you. More than you even realize."

A dark suspicion pushes its way in front of the massive mountain of guilt that just a moment ago had still been bearing down on me so overpoweringly.

Something's wrong here. Something's wrong with Anna.

The way she's talking now, she doesn't sound like my best friend at all. "What do you mean by that?"

Again there's nothing but silence, but I can't accept that. "Tell me. Now. What did you do?"

An indignant snort leaves her mouth. "I protected you. From yourself. And from Marie."

From Marie? What is she talking about? Out of nowhere, a terrible suspicion crawls up inside me. "You blocked her number on my phone." The words leave my mouth unfiltered, because suddenly I'm sure that's what must have happened. It wasn't me who did it in a drunken haze, it was Anna who deliberately cut off contact between Marie and me. "What else?" I ask, and there's nothing but coldness in my voice.

"It was all just for you." She sounds subdued, but that doesn't excuse what she did to me.

"What else?" I repeat my question, because now I just want to know. Everything has to come to light.

"You belong to me. Nobody loves you the way I do, and that selfish Marie least of all," Anna snaps back.

A wild rage rises up inside me. "And that's your way of loving me? Manipulating me so I'll stay with you?" Unbelievable is the only word that comes to mind. "What else did you do?"

"It was only for your own good!" she yells at me angrily now. "Talking that stupid cow into it wasn't even hard! She didn't even want to fight for you, you're too good for her."

The two of them must have met or at least talked on the phone. Anna deceived not only me but Marie as well. Like a damn puppeteer, she tried to pull the strings so everything would work out for her.

Why didn't I see that? And how can she behave so completely without character after years of friendship?

"She doesn't deserve you. I, on the other hand, love you unconditionally and would do anything for you."

Anything? Of course, I've figured that much out by now. No effort is too great for her, no act too despicable. "If that's the case, then there's one more thing you can do for me." My words are as cold as a Siberian winter, I'm shaking all over. "Leave me alone."

Without waiting for her answer, I end the call. And at the same time our friendship, which in truth probably never was one. Anna only wanted to be with me. For years she waited for her moment, and when I finally stood in front of her defenseless and in need of help, she took what she believed had always been her due.

Even here, in the heat of India, the memory of the abrupt end of our friendship makes me shudder all over again. On top of that, a terrible sense of guilt grips me. Why on earth did I let myself be comforted after breaking up with Anna?

There aren't supposed to be any more secrets between Marie and me, so she has to know about it. Right now.

"I messed up. Not just in our relationship. Or with the house," I say, looking her straight in the eyes. So she sees how sorry I am. So she knows how deeply I regret what happened. "There's more."

Although, in light of my confession, Marie should at least be furrowing her brow skeptically, she doesn't. "You couldn't help it." The certainty in her voice is overwhelming.

"You know that…" I look at her, searching for help, because just saying it out loud would be torture.

She nods.

That's when it becomes clear to me what must have happened. Much earlier than I did, Marie saw Anna's true colors. She knows everything, yet there's no resentment in her expression.

Marie must see my confusion, but she only smiles. "It's in the past. Now you're here. We're together, and that's all that matters."

How could I do anything but beam at her, just as openly as she's doing right now? And how could I not agree with her? What Anna did to Marie and me is terrible. Even so, Marie won't say a bad word about it.

I lace my fingers with hers and gently stroke her skin with my thumb. I take one last breath, and as I exhale, I finally let go of the pain surrounding Anna's deception.

"We can go," I say, and by that I mean so much more than just our drive into downtown Delhi.

Two hours later we're standing hand in hand in front of the Gurudwara Bangla Sahib. I've read about this Sikh temple many times. The accounts were already impressive, but to experience it now with all my senses is overwhelming.

In the holy pool in front of the temple, children are bathing. The steps leading to the entrance are filled with people in flowing, colorful garments. Some are laughing together, others are silently devout. Just like me. Because this building, with its delicate white façade and golden onion-shaped domes, radiates an incredible energy.

Suddenly I feel Marie slip her hand from mine. She reaches for her camera and starts taking pictures. It's the very first time I've watched her do this, but it takes only a fraction of a second to see how happy what she's doing makes her.

Seeing her like this catapults me into another universe as well. To the place where I haven't allowed myself to be for years. To the place where my own life's dream is waiting for me, which could suddenly become just as real as Marie's.

Because it's no longer about adapting to the rules of reason.

Because I'm allowed to do what fulfills me too.

Out of the corner of my eye I notice Marie pointing the camera at me. It clicks several times, then all I hear is the joyful laughter of the children at the sacred pond and the sounds of the city.

"My prince is dreaming," Marie says suddenly, letting the camera in her hand slowly sink. As if in a trance, she stares at me without a break, a suspicious gleam in her eyes.

She knows it, without my having to say a word.

With a happy smile on her lips she comes over to me and nestles into my arms. "Never stop doing that. Then your dreams will come true as well."

Just a few weeks ago I would've dismissed that as esoteric nonsense, but today I don't want to fight it anymore. Because I see it so clearly in Marie. And because I feel it deep inside myself too.

Marie had it right from the very beginning. We all have only one life. And what better could we do with it than free ourselves from what holds us back so we can find our heaven?

"I need a notepad and a pen." The words leave my mouth of their own accord. As if they were coming straight from a corner of my heart I want to allow myself to enter again. And nothing has ever felt as right as doing exactly that.

Epilogue

Three months later

The spacious room with its high ceilings and white-painted walls is still quiet. I shiver a little. Not because I'm cold, but because waves of anticipation keep running down my spine as I check one last time that everything is the way it should be. I start at the front, by the entrance. The place where, in just a few hours, the visitors to my exhibition will set off on their journey.

To India.

The first pictures show people whose moods, hopes, and dreams I captured at the airport in Dubai. There are dancing children. Their long skirts swirl, they stretch their arms up into the air, and pure life is written across their faces.

The next photo shows a couple saying goodbye to each other. You can feel that they don't want to let go, and yet both know that soon they'll have to. It's a kind of pain that I feel all over again myself every time I look at the photo.

I reach for the frame and straighten it. I do the same with the caption next to it that Lukas wrote. Then I take a step back and check whether everything is perfect.

It is.

A deep feeling of contentment spreads through me and blends with a kind of happiness that I still can't comprehend. Not even now, as I continue wandering along the exhibition. I pass the photos of the taxi driver in Mumbai and the accompanying story about the living conditions of his caste in this land of such stark contrasts. Like all the other texts, Lukas wrote this one too. It's uniquely beautiful and so powerful in its language that it captivates every reader.

Next come photos of India's immense natural scenery. Only a few feet farther on hangs the photo series that means the very most to me. I've given it a special place in this exhibition, and still even that doesn't do it justice.

There she is up ahead.

I walk toward her. As soon as I get there, I fall under the spell of the images. I can't help but smile blissfully.

A minute later I feel Lukas's arms wrap around me from behind. "My Sleeping Beauty is dreaming," he whispers lovingly in my ear.

My eyes fixed on the photo series, I snuggle close against his chest. "Are you dreaming with me?"

He presses his cheek to mine. "Anytime."

He doesn't have to say more, because I know that in our minds we're both going back there together. We're both back in the moment when I took those pictures.

It's our first morning in Munnar, an area in the south of India that couldn't be any greener. The night was short, but we're already awake to watch the sunrise. What unfolds before our eyes carries a magic I could never put into words.

The hills covered in tea plantations are surrounded by mist, so I can only guess what's hidden beneath the cotton-white blanket. The first rays of sun touch our faces, together we breathe in the warm, humid air and listen to the sounds of nature.

Lukas is sitting behind me and gently wrapping his arms around me. I feel his warmth and his breath on my skin. "Should we do it again?" I ask quietly, so as not to break the spell of this moment.

He doesn't answer, but I feel him nod. So I carefully take the camera out of its case. Even before I take the first shots, a feeling of happiness spreads through me that's bigger than anything I've ever experienced. The two of us, Lukas and I, are in India. We're doing what we love and enjoying what we have. We're living through the best time we've ever had together, we're closer to each other and feel our love even more intensely than ever before.

Many weeks have passed since that moment. But when I stand here today in the modern gallery and look at the pictures with Lukas, I feel warm from the inside out. They're a homage to that one special day when we swore to each other in the flower meadow behind the Gloriette at Schönbrunn Palace that what we had would never end.

In the first picture, Lukas's face is bathed in the golden glow of the rising Indian sun. Behind him, lush green stretches out, veined with wisps of mist. The second photo shows the two of us, smiling blissfully into the camera. In the next one, Lukas turns his head toward me. Wherever you are is where I want to be. That was what he whispered in my ear again that morning in India, and anyone can see it in the photo. The fourth picture shows us kissing. And in the last one, there is only the sky and a small piece of the magical backdrop of Munnar.

I lose myself in the pictures, just as I do every time I look at them. Tears of happiness well up in my eyes, and I don't stop them from making their way outside. They caress my cheeks, tickle my neck, and soak into my thick wool scarf.

What Lukas and I have experienced since we found each other again at the airport in Delhi is happiness in its purest form. It is what I dreamed of on the day I quit my job. What I fought for relentlessly, even though so often I no longer knew where I was supposed to find the strength for it.

This is how our life is meant to stay forever.

And if there's one thing I've learned from the events of the past year, it's that absolutely anything is possible. As long as we believe in ourselves and our dreams, we can overcome any obstacle. No matter how often we fall. If we don't give up, one day we'll fly. Maybe even higher than we ever dared to hope.

Afterword

Whenever I write the end of a novel, I'm cheerful and wistful at the same time. After the sad ending in *Promise Me*, I could hardly wait to write a happy ending for Marie and Lukas. The story of these two has been with me for a long time, and now being able to share the second part of the duology with you as well is the fulfillment of my very own dream.

It's important to me to thank the many wonderful people who accompanied me during the creation of this novel. First and foremost, my family. And also the tireless book professionals, beta readers, bloggers, and release helpers, who by now are so numerous that I can no longer name everyone. There are no words that could express how grateful I am.

But most of all I'd like to thank you, dear readers. I'm delighted that you read this book and I hope that, with Marie and Lukas's story, I was able to give you a wonderful time.

With a short review on Amazon or another online shop, you'd be giving me a great deal of support. Just a few words are enough. Thank you in advance!

All the best,

Belinda

More by Belinda Benna

vinci-books.com/AGlimmerOfHope

The man who broke her heart is the one she must save.

Thirteen years after shattering each other, a driven doctor faces her past when Ashton West becomes her patient—and her rival stands between her and her dream job. As his mysterious illness worsens, old wounds resurface, and saving him may cost her everything.

Turn the page for a free preview…

A Glimmer of Hope: Prologue

JUNE

Some truths we suppress for so long that by the time they surface, it's already too late. Others catch up with us precisely when we're least capable of handling them.

Mine is catching up with me now. In this moment, as Ashton teeters on the edge of life.

I press my thumb so hard against the emergency button that it hurts. Then I turn back to Ashton, who lies in the bed before me, his face contorted in pain. His skin is nearly indistinguishable from the white pillow beneath his head.

My gaze flicks again to the greenish-brown discoloration around his navel.

This can't be happening. Another new symptom. And one he hadn't had before, no less.

If that's Cullen's sign…

Oh God.

"Where does it hurt?" I ask him, but all I get in return is a gruff grunt, followed by a piercing scream. At least his hand points to his abdomen.

Okay, the abdomen. As always. He also has a fever—that's obvious. And he's shivering with chills.

"Can you breathe?" With trembling fingers, I reach for my stethoscope.

At that moment, the door bursts open—two nurses and, of all people, Dr. Young herself rush into the room.

My boss is going to think I've lost control of the situation.

And damn it, she's right.

This situation is slipping through my fingers.

Ashton is slipping away from me!

Sometimes a single moment can change everything.

Those were his words—the ones that, just a few days ago, turned the world I thought I knew upside down.

Deep down, I can feel that I'm living through one of those moments right now. Because everything I've ever cared about is shattering in this very instant.

A Glimmer of Hope: Chapter One

JUNE

Two weeks earlier

The shared apartment is a complete battlefield. The pounding bass thunders in my ears, the smell of fresh paint creeps into my nose and mixes with the scent of pizza wafting from the boxes in my hands.

With my foot, I push aside the box with a whisk sticking out of it and close the door behind me.

"Hello?" I walk down the hallway toward the room where the music is blaring—our future living room. There I find Sonora—in a pair of torn overalls, wildly headbanging with her dark corkscrew curls and holding a power drill in her hand. "Hey, Sonora," I shout in vain over the music.

I turn down the volume, my friend lowers the paint roller and spins around. An excited expression flashes across her face. "Finally!"

"Wow, you got so much done." I nod appreciatively as I look around. The dusty pink on the walls is fantastic; it goes perfectly with the cream-colored couch currently hidden under a protective sheet. "The dining table goes here, right?" I point to the open corner where a ladder stands on a paint-splattered box.

"That's right," Sonora confirms. "Olive and Nyla are getting the decorations, Autumn's bringing her TV and a matching shelf."

"It's going to be amazing," I say dreamily. This room will be our cozy retreat. The place where, after long shifts at Halifax Harbor Hospital, we'll kick back and laugh together—hopefully. "When are the others coming?"

Sonora shrugs. "Olive's out shopping. Autumn texted that she got the job and is just signing the contract now. I haven't heard anything from Nyla."

"Then these are just for us for now." I wiggle the pizza boxes in my hands. "Hungry?"

"I hope you planned on two pizzas just for me." She grins.

While Sonora runs to the bathroom to wash her hands, I stack three moving boxes on top of each other and repurpose two more—filled to the brim with Autumn's books—into makeshift stools.

"Spill it. How was it?" my roommate asks a moment later, grabbing a slice of spinach pizza.

"In a word: grotesque." Frightening would probably be more accurate, but grotesque sounds less like I'm a coward. Chewing, she signals for me to go on. I pick an olive off my slice and pop it into my mouth.

"It wasn't a job interview, it was a military inspection. I had to make diagnoses at record speed." Instantly, I picture the tiny hourglass belonging to Dr. Victoria Young, the head of the diagnostics department. I have no idea what would've happened if I hadn't solved her hypothetical case studies before the last grain of sand squeezed through the neck each time. "On top of that, I found out from the other applicants that everyone got different cases." That was completely unfair.

"But you got the job, right?" Sonora wants to know.

With a sigh, I lower my slice of pizza. "Not yet."

"Why not?" She leans toward me, frowning.

"Apparently, the interview was only part one of the application process." I shrug casually. I don't want her thinking I'm rattled—even though I definitely am. "But at least I passed that part."

"I wouldn't have expected anything less from you." She takes a bite of her spinach pizza. "What's part two?" she asks, still chewing.

My stomach turns. I'd love to put my slice of pizza back in the box, but I don't let it show. "Dr. Young called it the practical stress test."

"That sounds unsettling."

You're telling me. "Today, the applicant pool was narrowed down to three doctors. We all signed a contract for a four-week trial period—one of us will stay in the end." That gives me a thirty-three point three, three, three repeating percent chance of getting the job. "Starting tomorrow, we'll see if we crack under pressure or turn into diamonds," as the boss put it with a mischievous grin.

"As if we didn't already have a doctor shortage…"

Maybe so, but it's different here. Dr. Young is the star among diagnosticians—everyone wants to work for her. "She can afford to do things like this."

"Brrr," Sonora said, reaching for the napkins. "Creepy woman."

Tell me about it. "Imagine—she kept calling me Barbie during the interview."

A mischievous grin spread across her face. "Well, looks-wise, she's not exactly wrong."

"Just because I have light blonde hair and blue eyes doesn't make me Barbie." Not even close.

"Add the button nose, your symmetrical face, and those sexy curves," my roommate countered.

Barbie wears a size XS, I'm a medium—but that's not the point. The point is Dr. Young, who will no doubt haunt my dreams tonight with her dark sense of humor.

"Whatever happens tomorrow—even if she calls me Barbie in front of everyone—I can handle it," I say, steering the conversation back to more important matters.

"Well, I'm curious then." Sonora raises an eyebrow. "Have you met the competition yet?"

"Just briefly. At the end of the application marathon, they announced the list of those moving on to the next round. Alongside my name, there were two male names." Ben and Jaxon. "One of them had already left by the time they made the announcement."

"And the other one?" Sonora's tone carries a hint of tabloid intrigue.

"He was the only one besides me who was happy at the end of the day," I reply, sticking my tongue out briefly, fully aware that she was hoping for something entirely different.

Grinning, she crumples up her napkin and tosses it onto the floor, which is covered in painter's tape and newspaper. "Aha."

Not aha.

"Is he hot?" She scoots forward on her box of books and props her chin in her hands. "Come on, June. Under that lab coat, I bet he's hiding a six-pack that could burn your fingers if you even get close."

Now I lean in toward her, locking eyes. "Even if he were the hottest guy in the entire world, I wouldn't be interested."

She pouts in disappointment. "You've always got work on the brain."

"For good reason." Even though it's the last thing I want to think about right now, my thoughts drift to where my problem with men began.

To Ashton. The boy from back then.

And to that warm September day that changed my life forever.

"School is bullshit." My seatmate juts out her lower lip and flips open the math book.

"Well, I'm glad it's finally starting again," I reply, smiling as I glance around the classroom. Sure, vacations are great, but I want to become a doctor, and that means I have to study.

She shakes her head, sizing me up. "There's something wrong with you…"

The door swings open and our teacher, Mr. Simmens, bursts in. I quickly place my hands over my papers, so they don't fly away in the breeze stirred up by his hurried steps.

Suddenly, a heady, earthy scent hits my nose. A split second later, I know exactly where it's coming from.

Leather jacket. Dark hair. Stormy blue-gray eyes.

Wow.

Who's the guy walking behind Mr. Simmens who looks like a rockstar?

I'm pretty sure my mouth is hanging open.

Am I actually drooling?

No idea. But my heart is definitely beating faster.

"This is your new classmate," Mr. Simmens says as I stare at the new guy.

That roguish look. That smile. The way he runs his hand through his hair.

A tingling sensation spreads through my stomach.

"His name is Ashton West, and he just moved here from Toronto."

Ashton West.

What a name. Beautiful.

I rest my chin in my hands and let out a long breath. Maybe Mr. Simmens is still talking, or someone's asking a question. Maybe a bird just landed on the windowsill outside, or the fluorescent light above me is flickering.

Whatever's happening right now is completely irrelevant. All I want is for Ashton West to look at me with those stormy blue-gray eyes.

Stop. No. Get rid of that memory!

Ashton West has no place in my head. That's the only thing I should be thinking about. That, and the fact that there's no room for men in my life anyway.

I turn to Sonora to get back to what really matters. "I want this job. Desperately."

This is going to be a fresh start for me. Not just moving into this apartment. Also the specialist position in the diagnostics department at Halifax Harbor Hospital, which will hopefully be mine soon.

She raises her hands. "Got it. June's heart belongs to her job alone, which she'll one day marry so she can become the best diagnostician in all of Nova Scotia."

I raise my index finger with mock seriousness. "In all of Canada."

A smile plays at the corners of her mouth. "If you say so," she replies with a wink.

No. Not if you say so, but definitely.

But before I can say exactly that, Nyla appears in the doorway. Her doe eyes sparkle, competing with her oversized earrings.

I wave her over. "Where were you?"

"Had to take care of something," she replies vaguely,

letting her gaze drift over the pizzas. Her short, tousled hair looks even wilder than usual. "By the way, there was some mail in the mailbox. It's on the stack of boxes in the hallway."

"Damn," Sonora mutters suddenly.

I turn to her and spot a wild mix of spinach, cheese, and tomato sauce clinging to the tips of her hair.

"It's always the same." With a sigh, she gets up, and Nyla and I nod in agreement. "Be right back," she says, disappearing through the doorway.

High heels clatter in the hallway. That can only mean one thing. Miss Perfect is back.

"Hey, Olive, we're in the living room!" Nyla calls out.

Olive's shoulder-length hair, parted precisely down the middle, is—as usual—perfectly in place when she enters the room. Just like her subtle makeup and her Marlene Dietrich-style trousers. How does she always manage to look like she just stepped out of a glossy fashion magazine?

"I'll get plates and cutlery," she says, her eyes on the pizza boxes.

Nyla and I burst out laughing at the same time.

"You're honestly the only person who doesn't eat takeout pizza with their fingers," Nyla says, shaking her head. Her earrings bounce in rhythm.

Olive casually shrugs, her silky, shiny hair brushing against her cheek. "Order is everything. You'll thank me soon enough when I make sure this apartment doesn't descend into chaos."

She might be right about that. Living together here is bound to be turbulent—after all, we're all starting our jobs at Halifax Harbor Hospital tomorrow. Well, everyone except me. I still have to prove myself before I can get a permanent position.

A cautious "Hello?" drifts toward us from the hallway.

Autumn's here. That makes our five-person apartment complete.

"Hey there!" I call out.

A few seconds later, Autumn joins us, her beloved book bag slung over her shoulder and her usual reserved smile on her lips. Her hair gleams as red as the fall foliage in Nova Scotia.

"Got it!" She holds up her employment contract, prompting the rest of us to cheer and applaud. Her cheeks instantly flush. Her green eyes, nearly hidden by her bangs, widen when she spots the pizza boxes. "Is there a Margherita?"

"What do you think?" As if I'd ever forget… I gesture to her and the others to help themselves.

With both hands on her stomach, Sonora returns as well. Wet strands cling to her mane of hair. "I think I've had enough pizza for today," she groans, joining us.

Autumn settles cross-legged on the not-so-clean floor, Nyla examines the food selection as if she's making a life-or-death decision. Olive pushes aside the transparent plastic cover on the couch and pats down the seat cushion before sitting.

I can't help but grin to myself as I undo my ponytail.

Moving in with the four of them—even though each of us could afford our own place—was the best decision I ever made.

We're all doctors, we all studied together, and for all of us, a new chapter is beginning.

We have so much in common, and yet we're all so different.

"You know what?" I glance around the group.

"Wha?" Autumn asks, her mouth full.

A warm smile spreads across my face. "I think this is going to be amazing."

A Glimmer of Hope: Chapter Two

ASHTON

They say you can't run from your past. Instead, you have to process it.

What a load of bullshit.

If you really want to leave something behind, you need something entirely different: a boat.

I switch off the circular saw, take off my safety goggles, and brush the sawdust from my T-shirt. Silence surrounds me, broken only by the rhythmic sound of the surf in my ears.

Deliberately, I let my hand glide over the grain of the oak wood, its resinous scent having spread through my improvised workshop as I cut it. This piece is perfect.

To be sure, I pull the folding ruler from the side pocket of my work pants and glance at the wall—where I pinned the plans to the wood paneling years ago. On the third one from the left is the component I just cut.

The plank is supposed to be four meters and ten centimeters long. I hope it's long enough to stabilize the sailboat properly, but I don't have more space here in this half-collapsed barn anyway. It just has to be enough.

I measure again—the length checks out.

A plaintive meow reaches my ears, and moments later, I feel warmth against my shin.

I can't help but smile as I look down. "Back in town again, huh? Where have you been all this time?"

The red tabby stray looks up at me and meows again.

"So that's how it is." I stroke his head and take the dry food I always keep stocked for him out of the cupboard. Gently, I let some of it spill onto a clean wooden board.

He dives in immediately. "Not so fast, little guy, it's all for you," I say with a chuckle and watch him eat for a moment before getting back to work.

Time to shape the plank so I can attach it to the side of the bow tomorrow. Using the drawknife, I begin shaving the wood little by little to create the necessary curve. Beads of sweat form on my forehead, my arms ache and feel heavy as lead. Strange how exhausted I already am after barely three hours of work today.

A knock blends with the scraping sound of the drawknife. Seconds later, the door swings open.

My shaggy visitor takes flight with an alarmed hiss.

"Until next time," I murmur, watching him disappear through the widening gap in the door.

The low afternoon sun streaming into the barn from outside blinds me. Still, I can make out who stands in the doorway: Jeremy. Grinning artificially, surrounded by dust motes floating in the sunlight.

My smile vanishes instantly.

I straighten up and wipe the sweat from my forehead. "What do you want?"

"Happy birthday." He spreads his arms and grins stupidly.

This can't be happening.

I step aside and set my drawknife down on the workbench. "You're supposed to be in New York."

"I took some time off." He lowers his arms. "Thought we'd celebrate a little. After all, you don't turn thirty every day."

So that's why he's here? Because he wants to celebrate my damn birthday?

Is he still pretending this is just another day? Or has he really forgotten what we had to do on this exact day fourteen years ago?

With the worst stomach pain I've ever had, I stand in front of the mirror and stare at the black tie in my hand.

I take a deep breath and try again. "The wide end goes over the narrow one," I whisper, crossing the two ends with a clumsy motion, but a second later, the image blurs before my eyes, and once again I can't manage to tie the knot.

"We have to go. Are you ready?" I suddenly hear Father ask behind me, his tone cold.

No, I'm not.

Not for this.

I'll never be ready for this.

"In a minute," I reply anyway. My voice sounds hoarse.

Once again, I grab the two ends of the tie.

Despair grips me again.

Every part of me is trembling.

Father steps up beside me. Our eyes meet in the mirror. "You're sixteen years old. Don't be such a wimp," he mutters and yanks the tie from my hands.

With harsh movements, he ties a knot while I watch in the mirror as fat tears push their way out of the cursed corners of my eyes and drip onto my black blazer.

"Don't you dare start crying now," Father snaps, pulling the tie so tight I lose my breath for a moment. "You have no reason to, understand?"

No reason?

"Mom is dead," I whisper soundlessly.

Just like that.

Dead.

I still can't comprehend it.

My nose is swelling shut, my head feels heavy. And dull. And full.

She'll never hold me in her arms again. She'll never look at me with that understanding gaze again, even when I've acted like a complete idiot. She'll never secretly comfort me again, because she always knew when I needed it—even if I never would've admitted it myself.

I look at Dad pleadingly. "Mom is dead," I repeat.

"And why…?" he begins, but Jeremy cuts him off, appearing behind him in the doorway.

His gaze lands on me, and my brother rolls his eyes toward the ceiling. "Come on, Ashton…" he grumbles, annoyed. Be a man, he adds silently.

I want to. More than anything.

But I can't.

Mom. Is. Dead.

I glance back and forth between the two of them. Like me, they're wearing black suits, but they're not sad.

"Don't you realize where we're about to go?"

"And what we'll have to do there?"

I bite my tongue until it bleeds, but it doesn't stop the tears from falling.

Now Father digs his fingers into my shoulders. His icy stare pierces through me. "Stop crying right now," he hisses at me. His grip tightens. Painfully. "Or you'll have a real reason to cry soon. Got it?"

"Got it," I force out. Then I rush past them and out the door, just to get away from them.

The dreadful feeling that everything good in my life left with Mom stays with me. Just like the grief.

"Ashton?" Jeremy's voice pulls me out of my memory, but not out of the emotions it stirs in me.

Back then, I thought the day of the funeral was the darkest day of my life.

Today I know that, in that moment, I had no idea how dark a day could really be.

After my mom died and everything that followed, I learned to be tough.

And I still am.

"Come on, let's toast to your birthday," I hear my brother say.

"Not in the mood," I reply, because there's no point in explaining why I don't feel like celebrating, and I turn back to the plank. It'll take hours to shape and sand it. Tomorrow I've got a temp job and won't have time for my boat.

Out of the corner of my eye, I see my brother shove his hands into the pockets of his tailored suit. "I've been on the road for five hours and skipped an important hearing to be here today."

"No one asked you to." I reach for the drawknife again and get back to work. Can't he just leave already?

For minutes, he does nothing. He says nothing, doesn't move, doesn't leave my workshop. I ignore him—eventually he'll get the message that this conversation, and his visit, is over.

"What's the point of this boat, anyway?" he suddenly wants to know.

I shoot him a poisonous look. "None of your business."

As if he doesn't get that he's not wanted here, he walks toward me, shaking his head. "Don't be like that—tell me."

I straighten up. My breathing is heavy, hot air trapped beneath my long-sleeved shirt. "It might surprise you, but I want to sail it."

"Sail it where?"

Away. Just away. From him, from this goddamn backwater, from this life.

From the memory.

Deliberately, I turn away. "You'll see soon enough." The tool grows heavier in my hand; my fingers can barely hold it anymore. A split second later, the drawknife slips from my grip and crashes onto the wooden floor.

"What's wrong?" Jeremy is already beside me, studying me intently. He even reaches out, as if to place his hand on my forehead. "Are you sick?"

I pull back before he can touch me. "Don't."

He narrows his eyes, scrutinizing me. "Do you have a fever?"

Bullshit.

"This," I say, pointing to my workshop and the half-finished sailboat I've been building for years, "is hard work. Not something you'd know about, I get it. But here's a little secret: when you do physical labor, you sweat sometimes."

He presses his lips together as if he has to stop himself from telling me what he really thinks of me. But he doesn't have to—I already know.

"Spit it out, Jeremy. Come on, don't be so shy. Tell me what an asshole I am." Then I'll tell him no one asked him to show up here with his damn perfect-world face, and that he should finally get lost.

I notice his nostrils flare. "What did I ever do to you?" he asks, trying to stay in control.

"Get lost," I reply instead of answering.

Screw him—and not just today.

The moment I say the word, my stomach cramps so violently that I lose control of my body for a moment. I double over, unable to stifle a cry. My brother is at my side instantly, offering his arm to support me.

"Hands off," I snap at him and lean against the workbench.

He shakes his head with a mock-concerned expression. "You're sick."

"Just an upset stomach," I mutter, even though the next wave of pain hits me—far too intense for just an upset stomach. It knocks me down onto the sawdust-covered floor of the shed. The fine wood shavings scrape at my lungs.

"I'm calling an ambulance." Jeremy's voice sounds strangely distorted.

I force my eyelids open. "No!" It is supposed to sound forceful, but even I can't hear myself.

Too weak.

I am far too weak.

"Right, Ashton doesn't need any help." He pulls a phone from the breast pocket of his blazer. "Ashton wants to be alone, grumbling at himself and the trees."

That's exactly what he wants.

"But let me tell you something." With a hard expression, he unlocks the screen. "What Ashton wants right now—just to put it in your language—I don't give a damn."

My eyelids grow heavy, and I feel like I am on fire. The center of the flames is my stomach.

Jeremy dials a number and raises the phone to his ear. "We need an ambulance at 27 Church Road, Peggy's

Cove," he say a moment later into the phone. "Follow the narrow path that branches off from the last house for about two miles, then you'll see a trailer and a barn. We're in the barn."

"I don't need a..."

Oh God.

The fire inside me blazes high, and the only thing I can still hear is my own piercing scream.

Grab your copy...

vinci-books.com/AGlimmerOfHope

About the Author

Belinda Benna is an award-winning author whose moving romance novels are filled with emotion, allowing you to lose yourself between the lines and find yourself at the same time.

Experience stories that will make you cry, laugh, and fall in love—each with a message that will stay with you for a long time.

www.ingramcontent.com/pod-product-compliance
Lightning Source LLC
LaVergne TN
LVHW040921110826
845155LV00041B/715